MW00528805

THE HOUSE OF CROSS

BOOKS BY JAMES PATTERSON
FEATURING ALEX CROSS

For a preview of upcoming books and information about the author, visit JamesPatterson.com or find him on Facebook, X, or Instagram.

THE HOUSE OF
CROSS

JAMES
PATTERSON

LITTLE, BROWN AND COMPANY

NEW YORK   BOSTON   LONDON

Little, Brown and Company
Hachette Book Group
1290 Avenue of the Americas, New York, NY 10104
littlebrown.com

First Edition: November 2024

Little, Brown and Company is a division of Hachette Book Group, Inc. The Little, Brown name and logo are trademarks of Hachette Book Group, Inc.

ALEX CROSS is a trademark of JBP Business, LLC.

The publisher is not responsible for websites (or their content) that are not owned by the publisher.

The Hachette Speakers Bureau provides a wide range of authors for speaking events. To find out more, go to hachettespeakersbureau.com or email hachettespeakers@hbgusa.com.

Little, Brown and Company books may be purchased in bulk for business, educational, or promotional use. For information, please contact your local bookseller or the Hachette Book Group Special Markets Department at special.markets@hbgusa.com.

ISBN 9780316402682 (hc) / 9780316580809 (large print) / 9780316582438 (Walmart edition)
LCCN 2024942031

Printing 1, 2024

LSC-H

Printed in the United States of America

THE HOUSE OF CROSS

PROLOGUE

Potomac, Maryland

MARGARET BLEVINS LOVED HER morning runs. They allowed her time alone, which kept her even-keeled in a beyond-hectic life.

That mid-December morning, the fifty-two-year-old mother of three teenagers followed her normal three-and-a-half-mile route as she ran by headlamp light in the predawn, trying to keep her mind free of thoughts, lost in the delicious feeling of her leg and back muscles warming and firing at the fastest pace in weeks.

For a moment, she regretted slipping out to run without informing her security team. But they always slowed her down, were always fussing, and, my God, she'd been running this route for more than fourteen years, a full thirteen and a half years before she became a U.S. Supreme Court justice.

Justice Blevins felt good enough to pick up the pace a little. And for the first time in a long while, she felt loose and good doing it.

Where's this coming from? Blevins wondered as she approached the entrance to a trail through Watts Branch Park off Lloyd

3

Road. She checked her watch and saw she was three minutes ahead of her usual time.

She glanced up at the sky, already lightening, and felt great, at one with the run.

Still, at the trailhead, she slowed and adjusted the beam of her headlamp so she could better see the bridle path that wound off into the trees.

Blevins bounced into the park on the balls of her feet, amazed again at how good she felt, and trotted into the dawn thinking that there was a particular beauty to the woods in winter, especially this piece of woods. It was a mix of pine and oak and birch, her favorite. There was a stand of birch trees down by the creek that ran through the park.

She realized she was a little early and took a loop that added a few minutes to her run. She could see well enough that she shut off the headlamp, casting the woods in grays and shadows at first. But as Blevins's eyes adjusted, the scene grew lighter, filled with deeper contrasts—the tree trunks against the barest skift of snow on the leaves, the barren crowns against a sky turning rose.

As she'd hoped, the first rays of sunshine were hitting those white birches in the creek bottom when she turned off the loop trail. The air was crisp as she puffed her way toward a tight stand of young hemlock trees growing amid the birches and marking the entrance to a little footbridge that spanned the creek and led to a park bench on the far side. She liked to stretch there before she walked home, part of her cooldown routine.

Blevins could see her breath in the chill air and the sparkle of frost on the birches, and she felt as if all were right in the world as she grabbed the handrails and took two steps up onto the footbridge. She heard an odd noise, a soft thud, coming from that tight group of hemlocks and felt like the side of her head had been slapped.

4

She felt it most in her ear, hard and painful. She immediately got dizzy and lost her balance.

For a moment, she thought she was going to black out and go down but she held tight to the footbridge railing and did not. After several seconds, the pain in her ear disappeared, the dizziness faded, and her eyes could focus again.

She got her balance back and was able to walk the rest of the way across the little bridge to the bench, although she felt nauseated from the effort. But then the wave of nausea passed too.

Blevins decided not to stretch and, feeling slightly disoriented, started walking home. She knew the trails by heart but got puzzled at two places where side paths met her route.

Once she had them straightened out, however, she found herself thinking more clearly and wondering what had just happened to her.

Was that really a noise back there? Or did I just suffer some kind of attack like Dad? Transient ischemic attacks, that's what Dad's doctor called them. Is that what just happened to me? Aren't I too young?

By the time she left the woods and reached the cul-de-sac where she lived in a large Colonial home set back from the road, she felt absolutely fine and decided not to tell her husband, Phillip. She had a lot on her plate the next few days and could not afford the time to listen to all the mumbo-jumbo from the doctors and undergo all the tests they'd want to do.

I'm fine, she told herself as she went through the door. *Margaret Blevins is just fine.*

5

CHAPTER

1

Independence Mountains, Northern Nevada

COMING DOWN THE ALPINE road in a wheelchair-adapted van with Massachusetts handicap plates, Malcomb felt groggy, still heavy-headed from the drugs, but also anxious and sweaty.

He glanced in his rearview and caught a glimpse of big sections of the dirt road winding along the rim of a canyon that fell away to his left.

Not back there yet, Malcomb thought hazily. *But he's coming for you. Expect nothing less now.*

He was afraid then and checked the van's large operating screen. He saw on the active navigator that he was on a U.S. Forest Service road, heading north and downhill toward a flat ribbon of highway far in the distance. He glanced right at the little metal wallet and the iPhone on the passenger seat and cursed when he saw no bars on the screen.

Then he checked the gas gauge and was shocked to see he had

less than a quarter tank. *That son of a bitch! He wants to limit how far I can go. But screw him. I can make that highway wherever I am. I know I can.*

The road got very steep and twisty just ahead. Unsure of the controls, Malcomb squeezed the handbrake on the steering wheel, glanced in the rearview again, and headed into the first curve. Still nothing behind him.

He made it down through back-to-back S-curves just as snowflakes began to fall from the leaden sky. He hit a short straight, squeezed the gas control, and didn't look at the rearview again until he had to use the brakes to enter another corkscrew.

This time he caught a glimpse of them exiting the upper part of the S, a half mile back.

The blue Tahoe, he thought, trying to breathe, trying to stay calm, trying to tell himself he could make it to the highway.

But with only a quarter of a tank? And what happens after I get there? Will I have cell service? Will anyone believe the story I have to tell?

Malcomb heard a thumping sound. He looked in the rearview and almost lost it. *They've got the helicopter!*

He looked at the cell phone screen again, saw one bar.

"Tor message, Siri," he said. "Voice."

"Tor activated," Siri said. "Recipient?"

"Cross," he said, glancing again in the rearview but not seeing the chopper. "Alex Cross."

"Start message on the beep."

"Dr. Cross," Malcomb said as he reached the third and final series of S-curves. "There's a good chance I will not survive. There are things I want to tell you so that you may bring to justice those responsible for my death. First, you know me as—"

The thumping came again, louder this time. Panicked, he accelerated into the first turn of the last S. He came around the apex of the turn, and to his shock the Bell Jet Ranger helicopter rose up out of the depths of the canyon to his left.

The blue and white chopper hovered in the falling snow. The man in the copilot's seat wore headphones and sunglasses, but he was without a doubt Malcomb's double.

Then the tail of the bird drifted. There was a man in a harness tethered to the interior roof hanging out the side, one foot on the strut, shouldering a military-style rifle.

Malcomb did the only thing he could think of and squeezed the gas control. The van went shooting out of the first curve in that final S and grazed the canyon wall with the passenger-side door, sending a shower of sparks into the falling snow.

He glanced at the sideview, saw the helicopter turning to follow him. He shouted, "They're coming for me, Cross. You know my brother, but—"

The helicopter roared up behind him as he reached the last tight turn in the road. He ducked a little, looked in the sideview, and saw the bird coming fast, the gunman hanging out of it.

As he came out of the turn, he saw the road ahead was blocked by a big dump truck with a snowplow. Without thinking, he slammed on the brakes and tugged hard left on the wheel.

The van smashed into the guardrail going fifty-plus. The bumper caught the rail and hung up on it, causing the rear of the van to catapult up and over.

Malcomb screamed and caught an upside-down image of the bumper tearing free of the rail. The helicopter came into view as the van fell. It caromed off the side of the cliff, plunged another two hundred feet, and hit a pile of rocks.

The gas tank exploded. The wreckage began to burn.

Back up on the cliff, a woman wearing a tan sheriff's uniform and a heavy coat came out from behind the snowplow; she was followed by an older guy in coveralls. They went to the edge and looked down at the van burning, sending black smoke up through the snow.

"Didn't expect that," the plow driver said. "But it'll work."

The deputy nodded, picked up her radio, clicked the mic button, and looked up at the helicopter swinging away.

"That went easier than we thought, sir," she said. "And the new snow won't hurt our cause none."

CHAPTER

2

Washington, DC

AT SIX P.M. ON a mid-December day, Emma Franklin hurried out of the elevator and down a long hall in the basement of the Prettyman U.S. Court House. The tall forty-six-year-old carried a purse and a leather briefcase and wore a long gray puffy coat over her navy-blue pantsuit.

Franklin pushed through the door into the annex garage and was relieved to see her ride waiting. The driver, a tall redhead in her late thirties, jumped out of the Cadillac town car.

"Good evening, Judge Franklin," she said, coming around to open the rear passenger door.

Franklin smiled. "How are you, Agnes?"

"Outstanding, ma'am. And you?"

"Just peachy," the judge said. She climbed in and put her attaché case and purse on the seat beside her.

Agnes closed the door, got in the driver's seat, and turned on the car. "I don't hear that expression—'just peachy'—too often."

Franklin laughed. "It was something my grandmother used to say."

Agnes put the car in gear and drove to the exit. "She lived in Georgia, ma'am?"

"Valdosta," Franklin said. "Pretty place."

"Had to be warmer than here," the driver said, pulling by the guard shack and out onto C Street. Snow had begun to fall.

"I heard it's going to be sixteen degrees tonight," the judge said, and involuntarily shuddered. "Older I get, the more I can't stand the cold."

"I hear you," Agnes said. She took a right on Third Street and headed south. "Days like today, I'm thinking Miami."

"I'll be there for Christmas."

"Lucky you."

"My brother bought a place and invited my sisters and their families and me."

"That's nice for you. First year after and all."

Franklin smiled sadly and nodded. "How's the divorce going, Agnes?"

"I keep telling myself I can see the finish line."

Judge Franklin looked out the window at the Christmas displays, her mind flickering with memories of the prior December, walking at night in Alexandria, admiring the lights with her late husband, Paul. *What a difference a year makes.*

"What do you think of Sue Winter's pick for attorney general?" Agnes asked.

Franklin turned, happy for the distraction and change of subject. "She made a solid choice in Malone. Impeccable record when he was U.S. attorney in Phoenix."

"I was surprised she didn't pick a woman," Agnes said.

The judge shrugged. "Sue's from Arizona and worked with Malone. And State and Defense have already gone to women."

"I say load the entire cabinet with women. The more the merrier."

Franklin chuckled. "I like the way you think."

As they crossed the Fourteenth Street Bridge, the driver asked, "Are you going to the inauguration?"

"Absolutely. Wouldn't miss it."

"What about the inaugural balls?"

Franklin looked out the window at the inky darkness of the river. "I haven't decided if I'm ready for that yet."

"Understandable, ma'am."

The judge nodded and looked at her left hand, wondering when the time would be right to take off her wedding band. It had been almost nine months now.

They drove on in silence.

Ten minutes later, Agnes turned onto Franklin's quiet street in Alexandria.

In the headlights' glare, through the snowflakes, she saw a powerfully built, short-haired blond woman running down the sidewalk in a warm-up suit with a reflective vest, a neck gaiter, a fleece headband low over orange-lens safety glasses to block the snow, and one of those hydration backpacks. As they passed her, Franklin saw she wore a headlamp as well.

Agnes pulled into the drive of Franklin's bungalow. "Home again, home again."

Franklin looked at her dark house, said, "Jiggety-jig."

Agnes left the headlights on, came around the back of the car, and opened the door. "Same time in the morning, Judge?"

"Fifteen minutes earlier, please," Franklin said, climbing out with her briefcase and purse.

"Judge Franklin!"

Both the judge and the driver turned to see the blond runner on the sidewalk just a few yards away, her headlamp aimed down and between them. She was squared off in a horse stance, gripping a pistol with a suppressor with both hands. She said something, though Franklin did not catch the words.

"Why are—" Franklin managed before the woman shot her twice, once between the eyes, once over her right eyebrow.

Agnes spun, tried to run. The woman shot her twice between the shoulder blades, then bent over and retrieved the knapsack and the four shell casings from the sidewalk. She stuffed the casings and the gun in the little pack, zipped it up, put it on. She pushed hard against the left side of her neck, felt it crack, and jogged away.

CHAPTER

3

I WAS HOME, FINISHING the dishes, when Ned Mahoney called.

Mahoney was the supervising special agent in charge of an elite FBI unit that worked high-profile investigations. I was a consultant to that unit, focusing on criminal psychology.

"What's up?" I asked.

"We're not going to Boston in the morning, Alex."

"C'mon." I groaned. "This is the third time we've postponed going up there."

"Yeah, well, we've caught a major one. Judge Emma Franklin, only Black woman on the DC Court of Appeals, and her driver were gunned down in Franklin's driveway in Alexandria about an hour ago. The acting director wants us on it pronto."

Aaron Gleason, the prior FBI director, had died of a massive stroke two days after the election. The lame-duck president had named Marcia Hamilton, a former U.S. attorney for Chicago, as acting director until the incoming president took office.

"Jesus. Text me the address. I'm on my way."

I hung up and turned around to see my wife, Bree, standing there with her arms crossed and a scowl on her face. "On your way where? And you'd better say Boston."

I held up both palms. "This is out of my control."

"This is the third time we've put it off!"

"A District Court of Appeals judge, Emma Franklin, was just gunned down in her driveway and the FBI director wants us there," I said.

Bree softened. "Franklin? Didn't her husband die recently in a plane he was piloting?"

I nodded. "Got into wind shear and went down in the Chesapeake last spring."

"This is going to set the city even more on edge than it already is with the inauguration coming up."

Before I could reply, my phone buzzed, alerting me to the text.

"Go," Bree said. "Maybe we'll get to Boston before the inauguration."

"We can only hope," I said, giving her a kiss. "Don't wait up."

"Maybe," she said, and kissed me back.

I left the kitchen and went through the dining room and down the hall, past the front room where Nana Mama, my ninety-something grandmother, was on the couch watching a documentary on rock and roll drummers. My daughter, Jannie, eighteen, a freshman at Howard University, was home after finals and sitting on the couch with her laptop. Ali, my youngest, was on the floor studying a math textbook.

Nana Mama looked over and saw me. "You ever watch this? I

guess I never knew how influential Ringo was to generations of drummers."

"Sounds like a good one, but duty calls," I said.

My grandmother frowned. "I thought you were going to Boston in the morning."

"Not anymore," I said.

"Bundle up, Dad," Jannie said. "Gonna be freezing tonight."

"I heard that," I said. I went to the front hall closet and took out a down jacket, a hat, gloves, and my credentials, then retrieved my pistol in its holster from the lockbox there.

Twenty minutes later, I pulled up and parked by an Alexandria police cruiser. A length of yellow tape had been stretched across the road to seal off the crime scene. Despite the cold, there were neighbors out on their porches up and down the street.

Ned Mahoney, a fireplug of a man in his late forties wearing an FBI windbreaker over a heavy jacket, was on the sidewalk in front of the bungalow looking at the bodies. Judge Franklin was on her back, slack-jawed, one bullet hole between her open eyes, another above her right eyebrow. Her briefcase and purse lay beside her.

The driver, who had been identified as thirty-seven-year-old Agnes Pearson of Bowie, Maryland, was sprawled facedown on the driveway, two bullet holes through the back of her black wool overcoat.

The car was still running.

"Pretty sharp shooting even at close range," Mahoney said.

"Double tapper," I said. "Casings?"

Mahoney shook his head. "Looks total pro to me."

"Me too," I said. "Who found her?"

"Cop said the lady across the street saw them lying here when she took her dog for a walk. I haven't talked to her yet."

I looked over and saw an older woman dressed for a blizzard sitting on her front porch and smoking a cigarette, a small dog in her lap.

After a criminalist arrived and photographed the scene, we shut the town car off, put on gloves, and went through the judge's purse. We found her wallet, credit cards, two hundred in cash, her cell phone, and the keys to her house.

The briefcase was unlocked. In it was a laptop, legal briefs relating to a case she was hearing, and four tickets to a Miami Heat home game against the LA Lakers on December 23.

"I think we can safely assume they weren't killed as part of a robbery," Mahoney said. "I'm going to go through the car."

"I'll talk to the lady with the dog."

The little black-and-brown shorthair dachshund wore a Christmas sweater and was snuggled in the lap of the smoker. He growled when he saw me approach.

"Hush now, Bernie," the woman said.

"I'm Alex Cross," I said. "I work with the FBI."

"Eileen Dawson," she said, then coughed. "And I know exactly where I'd start if I were investigating this."

"Where's that?"

"George Washington University Law School," she said. "Professor Willa Whelan. She hated Emma's guts, made all sorts of threats against her at a fundraiser at the Hilton not two weeks ago."

"How do you know that?"

"I was an eyewitness."

4

THE ALARM ON MY phone went off at eight thirty the next morning. I'd gotten home around two. I forced myself out of bed and into the shower.

I was in the bathroom shaving when Bree came in, carrying coffee and the *Washington Post* and looking as frustrated as I'd ever seen her.

"I can't believe it," she said. "I knew we should have gone to Boston two weeks ago when we had momentum."

"What's going on?"

"He's dead."

"Who's dead?"

"Malcomb."

"C'mon!"

She showed me the headline on the front page of the paper's business section:

Reclusive Billionaire Dies in Nevada Accident

Beneath it was a picture of Ryan Malcomb, dead at the age of forty-eight. He'd founded Paladin, a data-mining company based in suburban Boston that did contract work for federal security and law enforcement agencies, including the NSA, the CIA, and the FBI.

I flashed on Malcomb, whom I'd met on several occasions, seeing him in his wheelchair explaining how his remarkable proprietary algorithms were able to sort through stupefyingly large amounts of raw data and home in on specific subjects.

"Read it to me," I said, rinsing my face.

Malcomb, the story said, had been on a sabbatical of sorts for the prior two months and had crashed his van on a remote mountain road during a snowstorm.

A graduate of MIT, Malcomb had been stricken with muscular dystrophy as a teenager, which put him in a wheelchair much of the time. He had been traveling alone around the West in a van adapted for his use, looking for ranch land to buy, and had apparently lost control of the vehicle in the remote Independence Mountains, northwest of Elko, Nevada.

Elko County sheriff's investigators said Malcomb had skidded on a notoriously bad turn and hit the guardrail; the vehicle flipped into a canyon and caught fire.

" 'The van's VIN and the handicap plates identified the vehicle as Malcomb's, and the billionaire's Massachusetts driver's license survived the fire in a metal wallet,' " Bree read. " 'The Elko medical examiner will take DNA samples of the remains found and seek dental records to confirm the identity of the billionaire, as the crash victim's body was burned beyond recognition.'

" 'According to an Elko real estate agent, who asked not to be named because of a nondisclosure agreement with Malcomb, the day before, the entrepreneur had visited a ranch at the top of the same canyon he died in.' "

I shut off the water. "What's the company saying?"

Bree read, " 'Steven Vance, the CEO of Paladin, said he and the rest of the company's four hundred employees were in shock. He added that Ryan was their visionary and that without him, there would've been no Paladin.' " Bree stopped, turned the page. "Vance also said, 'This loss is enormous. He is irreplaceable.' "

She tossed the paper onto the counter. "So that's the end of the story. M is dead. He got away with all of it."

"We still can't say Malcomb was M," I said.

"Of course he was. Who else could have run something like Maestro? Like Sampson always said, it had to be someone who had access to all sorts of law enforcement and national security files. No one had more access than Malcomb."

John Sampson, my best friend and former partner when I worked full-time at DC Metro, had taken his young daughter, Willow, to Disney World for the week. And it was true that John had been the first to suggest that Maestro must have access to top secret files. That had led to our early suspicions about the vigilante group, which was headed by a mysterious character who called himself M.

At times, M had helped us, sending us leads on various investigations. At other times, he had hindered and taunted us. And he had tried to have me and Sampson killed when we were on a wilderness rafting trip in Montana.

In the wake of that trip, Bree, who used to be DC Metro's chief of detectives, had become obsessed with finding M and taking down Maestro.

"There's more evidence right in that article that Malcomb was M," she said. "He started his sabbatical two months ago, which was about the time I began suspecting him."

That was also true. Prior to that rafting trip, M and Maestro had been involved in the killing of U.S. drug agents and the leaders of a Mexican drug cartel that had corrupted them. More recently Maestro had been behind the murders of several pedophiles and a famous fashion designer who had been involved in human trafficking. Evidence we'd gathered during those investigations had led Bree to the conclusion that M was Ryan Malcomb.

"The FBI still has to look into him," Bree said. "We need to know for certain that he was M. Or I do, anyway."

"Good luck," I said, heading to the closet. "I don't think Ned's going to get a whole lot of traction with that idea now that Malcomb is dead and a federal judge has been murdered in a professional hit. I mean, with the inauguration coming up, this murder puts us all in the hot seat."

CHAPTER

5

AS I'D PREDICTED, AS soon as Mahoney learned that Ryan Malcomb was dead, he decided to hold off on a deep dive into the late billionaire and his company.

"I spoke with Director Hamilton earlier," Ned told me in the car after he picked me up at home. "Franklin's case is our top priority."

"Agreed," I said. "Hard to believe Malcomb's dead, though."

"Yeah. What's a guy in a wheelchair doing up on a mountain road alone in a snowstorm, even if he's driving a handicap van?"

"The *Post* article said he was interested in buying property up there," I said. "The Independence Mountain range is mostly U.S. Forest Service land, but evidently there's a big landlocked place up there he wanted."

"All the billionaires are buying up big ranches out west. I read a piece about it in the *Wall Street Journal*. They're all looking for hard assets."

"Good to know for when I make a billion. Where are we going, by the way?"

"DC Metro headquarters. I contacted them first thing. They're pulling together footage of Franklin's car between the courthouse and her home."

"How do they know the route?"

"Pearson, the driver, was running Waze on her phone, which was still active and linked by a USB cable to the car's onboard computer when we arrived on the scene. We know exactly how they went to Alexandria."

Quinn Davis, a Metro PD sergeant who specialized in video surveillance, met us in the lobby, and took us to a control room where a team of eight people were monitoring cameras all over the nation's capital.

"We've got your car all the way into Alexandria," Davis said. "No CCTV cameras in the judge's neighborhood, though."

"We'll take what we can get," Mahoney said.

Davis called up the footage. We watched the Cadillac sedan leave the courthouse parking annex, take a right on C Street, then another right onto Third. South of Pennsylvania Avenue, Third was blocked off for construction, and Pearson started driving side roads, angling west toward Fourteenth Street and the bridge to Northern Virginia.

When the town car was crossing Seventh on Madison Drive, Mahoney said, "Stop. Back it up. There."

Davis froze the footage on the town car as it sat at the traffic light. You could see Agnes Pearson clearly in the streetlamp glow.

"See the gray Dodge Durango, three cars back?" Mahoney

said. "It's been following her three cars back and turn for turn the entire time."

"Good catch," Davis said, typing. "Let's slightly expand the time frame to include our Dodge Durango."

A few minutes later, she stopped typing, and the footage of the Cadillac town car continued along with the Durango, which stayed three or four cars back on Fourteenth Street, across the bridge, and down the George Washington Memorial Parkway to Alexandria. But when Pearson left the parkway at West Abingdon Drive, the gray Dodge SUV drove on.

"We lose the town car just ahead here," Davis said, and froze the picture.

I looked at the time stamp on the video and did the math in my head.

"We lost them at six twenty-two p.m.," I said. "It could not have taken more than three minutes for them to reach Franklin's house. Can we get cell transmissions around this time? See if there was a call from that Dodge to the killer?"

"Maybe," Mahoney said. "I'll try." His cell phone buzzed with a text. He looked at it, said, "Well, this is good."

"What's that?"

"Alexandria police canvassed the neighborhood first thing this morning. They got footage from several doorbell cameras. They've got the shooter."

"That definitely helps," I said.

"Have them send it here," Davis said, and gave him her secure email address.

"Meanwhile, can you reverse the footage?" I asked. "See if we can get a good look at the Durango's license plate?"

While Mahoney contacted the Alexandria police, Davis rolled the footage we had backward. We quickly determined by the black lettering on a reflective white background that the plate was from Maryland. But the plate lights were dim at best. All we could make out was *9-UU*.

Before Davis could check the Maryland DMV, the video from the Alexandria police came in. She loaded it and hit Play, and we were suddenly looking out at Judge Franklin's street from a house on the corner.

At 6:24:50 p.m., a blond woman wearing a reflective vest, headlamp, neck gaiter, safety glasses, and a small hydration pack ran by. Seconds later, at 6:24:58, the Cadillac rolled past the camera.

The footage cut to a second doorbell camera, more wide-angled than the first, positioned cattycorner to and west of Franklin's house. At 6:25:10, the Cadillac pulled into the drive at the far right of the frame. Pearson exited the car and went around the back to open Franklin's door. At 6:25:16, as Pearson passed the trunk, the runner appeared and cut diagonally across the street.

"Pack is off and in her left hand," I said.

When she hit the sidewalk, Mahoney said, "She's got a gun."

We saw the whole thing. The killer dropped the pack beside her on the sidewalk and adopted a classic combat-shooting stance, both hands on the suppressed pistol, squared off to the target and slightly crouched. She said something that caused the judge and her driver to turn, shot Franklin twice in the face and Pearson twice in the back as she tried to escape.

Then she calmly picked up the pack and her spent shells, put the gun with the shells in the pack, and put the pack back on. With her left hand, she pushed against her neck as if to crack it and jogged off at 6:25:28.

The footage ended.

"We don't know where she came from or went afterward?" I asked.

"That's all they've sent us so far," Mahoney said.

"It's phenomenal. Just wish we could see her face without the glasses, headband, and neck gaiter. Do me a favor, Sergeant Davis?"

"Sure, Dr. Cross, anything."

"Google 'Professor Willa Whelan, George Washington University Law School.'"

Davis did and up popped a picture of a pretty blond woman in her forties, very fit, who was lecturing a group of students in an amphitheater. Below was a link to a faculty bio. The sergeant clicked on it and I read that, like Emma Franklin, Whelan had attended Harvard Law School; they had been in the same class. After graduation, Whelan had done a clerkship with a judge in the Tenth Circuit Court of Appeals, worked ten years as an assistant U.S. attorney in Little Rock, then joined the faculty of GW.

I read all the way to the bottom and smiled at the last line, which I read to the others: "'And in her free time, Professor Whelan enjoys running and competitive shooting.'"

CHAPTER

6

BREE SAT ALONE IN the kitchen, staring at her laptop, reading more coverage of Ryan Malcomb's death, which was not as extensive as she would have expected, given that his personal wealth was in excess of four billion dollars.

She kept picking up the remote control and changing the channel on the small TV in the kitchen from one financial-news network to another. All of them were giving Malcomb's death airtime, and the reports all told the same story: a brilliant young man with physical challenges who had managed to build a powerful, ultra-secretive tech company, only to die looking for a ranch in the American West.

Bree knew Mahoney thought getting involved in Malcomb's death would be a waste of time. But she couldn't shake the feeling that they did not have the entire story.

After leaving DC Metro, Bree had been almost immediately hired by the Bluestone Group, an international investigative and security firm based in Arlington, Virginia. She no longer had the apparatus and clout of law enforcement behind her, but the move had given her the freedom to pursue leads wherever they took her.

She searched for real estate agents in Elko, Nevada, and took out her phone. On the second ring of Bree's first call, a woman picked up. "High Desert Realty," she said in a nasal voice. "Regina Everly speaking."

"Hi, Regina. I'm Bree Stone with the Bluestone Group here in Washington, DC. We have been hired to independently look into the death of Ryan Malcomb and I am trying to find the real estate agent who signed the nondisclosure agreement with him."

There was a long pause before Everly answered. In a much quieter voice, she said, "You did not hear this from me, but that would be CeCe Butler over at Nevada Ranch and Land Company."

"Regina, if I'm ever looking for real estate in Elko, you'll be the first person I call."

"Why, thank you, Ms. Stone," she said, and hung up.

Bree found the number for the Nevada Ranch and Land Company, called, and asked for CeCe Butler. Bree was told Butler wasn't in at the moment, so she left a vague message asking her to call back.

She figured it was probably common knowledge in Elko that Butler was the real estate agent who had helped Malcomb, which meant reporters knew. Bree feared the woman might not return the call, but to her surprise, twenty minutes later, she did.

"This is CeCe Butler," she said. "You're not a reporter, are you?"

"No, ma'am," Bree said. "I work for a private investigative firm out of Washington, DC. We look into stuff all over the world for our clients."

"Who hired you to look into Malcomb's death?"

"That, I am not at liberty to say," Bree said, knowing she was walking a fine line between truth and fiction.

"Uh-huh," Butler said. "I suppose the nondisclosure agreement I signed doesn't matter anymore, but I don't know what I can tell you that I haven't told the police already. He contacted me about a month ago. We went back and forth on a couple of ranches, big, big properties. But he liked the look of the Double T Ranch in the Independence Mountains, so we arranged to go see it."

Bree said, "You drove up in his van?"

"No. We flew there from Elko in a helicopter he rented and piloted."

"I didn't know he was a helicopter pilot."

"Had trouble getting in and out of it, but he was excellent once he was seated."

Bree asked the woman what Malcomb had thought of the ranch. Butler said they'd flown all over it, and he'd loved certain aspects, like the high alpine meadows and timber. "But he was concerned it had been overgrazed," Butler added.

"By the current owners? Who are they?" Bree said.

"A big beef conglomerate, own cattle ranches all over the world."

"Why were they selling?"

"Who knows?" Butler said. "They probably couldn't use it as a write-down anymore. That's what usually happens. People come in, hold the land for ten, fifteen years, run cattle hard, take all the depreciation they can, then sell at a profit to wannabe gentlemen ranchers like Malcomb."

"He went back up in his van," Bree said. "Why?"

"Honestly, I have no idea," Butler said. "He sure did not tell me he was going up there alone. I would have told him it was a bad idea in a vehicle like his with tough weather on the horizon. Patty Rogers said it was because he was from back east. You know, oblivious to the dangers out here."

"Who's Patty Rogers?"

"Elko County sheriff's deputy. She was first on the scene."

Bree thanked the real estate agent and hung up. She called the Elko sheriff's office and asked for Deputy Rogers.

A few minutes later, a woman with a hoarse voice said, "This is Patty Rogers. How can I help you?"

Bree identified herself as the former DC chief of detectives, named her current employer, and again implied that Bluestone had been hired to look into Ryan Malcomb's death.

"There's nothing to look into," the deputy said firmly. "He was an inexperienced driver on a road that is difficult on the best of days. There was two inches of wet snow on the ground, and black ice from a freeze-thaw we had about a week ago. It's a tragedy, but he was in over his head and he paid for it."

"I heard he was up there the day before in a helicopter that he flew himself."

"True. With Mr. Malcomb's physical issues and the kind of terrain involved, it's not surprising that he wanted to view the site from the air. He would have been unable to see large pieces of the ranch otherwise because there was deep snow on the ground at higher elevations."

"How long after the car crash was he down in the canyon before he was found?"

"Not long at all," Rogers replied. "A guy from our county roads department was driving a dump truck and backhoe up

31

there to put in a culvert, and he spotted the smoke. He radioed it in. I responded. End of story. Now I need to go. I have to be on patrol in five."

"You've been so helpful, Deputy Rogers," Bree said. "Two more questions?"

She sighed. "Go on."

"Is there a ranch manager?"

"They're between managers, evidently. A caretaker lives up there during the winter, but he was visiting his ailing mother in Denver."

"And, last question, who are the ranch owners? I heard it's a beef conglomerate."

"Correct. O Casado Cattle Company. They're out of Brazil. They've owned the ranch a little over ten years."

Something about that struck Bree as odd, but she couldn't figure out what. "You've been very helpful."

"My pleasure. Can I ask who your clients are?"

Bree felt she had to give the woman something, so she said the first thing that came to mind. "Insurance company."

"Makes sense," the deputy said. "Good to know. Have a nice day, Ms. Stone."

"You too, Deputy Rogers."

They hung up. Bree went over her notes of the conversation, beginning to end, and kept coming back to the ranch owners.

O Casado. A Brazilian beef conglomerate.

She couldn't shake the sense that there was something important there, and then she saw it. With her pen, she circled the words *Brazilian beef* and added three exclamation points.

CHAPTER

7

A RAW WIND WAS blowing when Ned Mahoney and I reached the George Washington University Law School at Twentieth and H Streets in Northwest DC.

A security guard told us we would find Professor Willa Whelan's office on the third floor, rear of the building. When we reached her door, we saw a sign reading WRITING! DO NOT DISTURB!

I knocked anyway. Inside, we heard her shout, "Are you illiterate or an imbecile?"

"Just the FBI, Professor Whelan," Mahoney said, causing a passing group of students to turn their heads.

We heard a chair push back and the door opened a crack, revealing a thin woman with short blond hair and a suspicious look on her face. She was in her forties and wearing a running outfit that looked a whole lot like the killer's.

"Credentials?" Professor Whelan said.

Mahoney showed her his FBI ID and badge. I showed her my identification as a consultant to the Bureau.

"How does that work?" she asked, opening the door a little wider. We saw a cluttered office with stacks of books and files everywhere. "Consultant to the Bureau?"

"It works well, actually," Mahoney said. "Dr. Cross used to be with us full-time in the Behavioral Science Unit."

"A profiler?" she asked, sounding impressed.

"Among other things," I replied. "Can we come in?"

"For?"

"We'd like to talk about the late Emma Franklin."

The law professor's face lost color. "Yes, I heard this morning. It's...unthinkable that she's gone. Emma was a rare talent."

We stood there in silence until she opened the door all the way. "One of you will have to stand," she said. "This is where I write and there's not much room."

"Standing is fine," I said and stepped inside.

Professor Whelan went around the back of her desk, jiggled the mouse on her computer, and closed a text file she was working on. Mahoney took the overstuffed chair. I stood with my back to a wall of law books.

"How can I help, Mr. Mahoney?" she said finally, turning to face Ned.

"We heard you had a long-standing beef with Judge Franklin, possibly going back to your Harvard days," Mahoney said.

Whelan laughed caustically. "And, what, you think because Emma and I never got along, I was involved in her death? C'mon."

I said, "Out of curiosity, what was the problem between you two?"

The professor squirmed a little.

"The truth will set you free," Mahoney said.

Whelan sighed. "I'd call it more a rivalry than a problem. At Harvard, we both wanted to make *Law Review,* and we did. Emma became the editor, then a Supreme Court justice's clerk. Because of my associate editor status and, frankly, the way she treated me on the *Review,* I didn't even get an interview to clerk for a justice."

I said, "But you clerked for a Tenth Circuit Court of Appeals judge."

"I did," she said. "And worked ten years as an assistant U.S. attorney, so again the idea that I was involved in Emma's death is, well, preposterous."

"Probably," Mahoney said. "But as a former federal prosecutor, you know how the FBI works. We have to ask you certain questions."

"Asked and answered," Whelan said.

"Not quite," I said. "We were told about an altercation you had with Judge Franklin two weeks ago at a fundraiser at the Hilton."

She scowled. "Altercation? I've never been in an altercation in my life. Who said something like that?"

I said, "A witness puts you in a corridor off a banquet hall at the Hilton with Judge Franklin. You were described as drunk, confrontational, and belligerent."

"That's not—"

Mahoney cut her off. "You evidently insinuated that Judge Franklin had attained her lofty status in life because of her skin color."

The professor glanced at me. I said nothing, just stared at her.

"I don't think that at all, I really don't," she said, looking a little trapped.

"But you said it," Mahoney said.

Whelan chewed the air a little, looking off into the distance as if disgusted by something. "I really don't know what I said to Emma that night. I…I don't drink at home, but I get extreme social anxiety in crowds, and I always drink too much. Honestly, the only thing I remember is seeing Emma and wanting to offer my condolences about her husband's death. What happened, what I said after that, is…unclear to me."

"Our witness says that as the judge was walking away after your racist comments, she told you to get help," I said. "And then you evidently yelled at her that you would ruin her someday, take her down."

There was suddenly something very sad about the professor. "I don't remember."

Mahoney said, "You're a runner, aren't you?"

8

PROFESSOR WHELAN PERKED UP at the question.

"I love to run," she said. "Keeps me sane and it's another reason I don't drink at home or alone, or even in small groups. I like getting up early and running, or sometimes I run after work, to manage stress."

I said, "It's the social gatherings that are the trouble."

"The big social gatherings, yes. There were at least two hundred people in the room that night."

"So you don't go to big sporting events?"

"Never. Complete trigger."

Mahoney said, "Speaking of triggers — we read that you are a competition shooter in your spare time."

She shrugged. "My late husband got me involved. It's fun. A way to blow off steam on the weekends."

"You good?"

"Not bad," she said. "I don't practice enough to be good."

I said, "You said you run in the evenings sometimes."

"I will this evening. The mornings have been too cold, even for me."

"Wear a headlamp?"

"I do. And a reflective vest."

Mahoney said, "Hat? Gloves?"

She squinted at him. "Gloves, yes. Hat, no. I wear a headband that keeps my ears warm and my head less steamy."

I said, "Neck gaiter?"

"If it's cold enough, yes."

"Wear it up over your mouth?"

"If it's cold enough," she repeated. "What does what I wear to run have to do with your investigation?"

Mahoney glanced at me. I nodded. He reached into his suit coat and drew out a still from the doorbell-cam video footage showing the killer running past the house on the corner.

"That you, Professor Whelan?" Mahoney asked, handing her the picture.

Whelan took it, studied it.

"Could be," she said, her eyebrows rising. "I mean, that is usually how I dress running at night this time of year, except for… where was it taken? Arlington?"

"Alexandria," I said. "Just down the street from Judge Franklin's home, not far from your place in Arlington. Two, three miles, depending on the route."

"Really?" Whelan said, frowning and looking at the picture again. "I mean, maybe. I run different routes and take side streets at times. When did you say this was taken?"

Mahoney pointed at the time stamp in the corner that said

6:24:50 p.m. "That was yesterday. Just before Judge Franklin was shot."

She tensed and sat forward, wary, but then made a sweeping gesture over the still shot. "It's not me. In fact, it's impossible. Not only do I wear bright yellow safety glasses, not orange, when I run in the evening, but I was home at that time, preparing one of those organic-food-in-a-box deals. I just got the subscription. It's a pain in the ass, to be honest. Too much chopping for my taste."

"Can anybody corroborate that, Professor?" I asked.

"Well, I don't live with anyone, if that's what you mean," Whelan said.

"Neighbors see you?"

"I have no idea," she said. "I pulled into the garage and used the remote to shut the door behind me."

"Stayed in all night."

"Yes."

"No running?"

"It was my rest day."

I said, "Did you talk to anyone on the phone? Text anyone? Answer any emails?"

She thought about that, then shook her head. "Nope. I just ate my stir-fried organic ground pork, kale, peppers, cabbage, and a bunch of hot spices and watched three episodes of that *Mrs. Maisel* show. She makes me laugh."

"I like that one too," Mahoney said. He got up out of the chair and dug out another still from a different doorbell camera.

In the still, the killer was running across the street toward Pearson, the driver, who was going around the back of the Cadillac to open Judge Franklin's door.

"Notice the pack in your left hand," I said when Mahoney set the picture in front of Whelan. "Notice the suppressed pistol in your right."

"No," she said, a slight waver in her voice. "That is not me. It is someone dressed like me. But I don't wear that color safety glasses in the evening. I'm telling you, I am unequivocally being set up here."

"If you are being framed, they're doing a hell of a job so far," Mahoney said.

I nodded. "You might want to think about shopping for a lawyer. Preferably one with experience in federal homicide cases."

Whelan looked shaken. "Are you saying I'm under arrest for Emma's murder?"

"Not yet, Professor," Mahoney said, and we left.

CHAPTER

9

THREE HOURS LATER, I was in suburban Bowie, Maryland, riffling through the mailbox in front of a slate-blue, split-level ranch. Mahoney was trying to see into the attached garage, looking for a gray Dodge Durango.

"Not here," Mahoney said, walking back to me.

I shut the box. "Everything here is addressed to Agnes Pearson or AP Limo. Nothing for Aldo in the last two days."

After leaving Professor Whelan, we'd filed for warrants to search her home and office. While waiting for the warrants to be signed by a federal judge, I called an old friend in the Maryland state police and asked her to run a search in their DMV files for a gray Dodge Durango with 9-UU in the plate number.

She eventually got a hit: a 2015 silver Dodge Durango with Maryland license plate 309-UU. The registered owner was Aldo

Pearson, husband of the deceased driver of the late Judge Emma Franklin.

The registration of the Dodge SUV and the address on Pearson's driver's license was this house. We found out he had a rap sheet—several arrests for dealing small amounts of illegal steroids. His license photo showed a man with a shaved head, a neck like a tree trunk, and bad skin.

This was why we'd been going through his mailbox and looking in his garage. Maybe we didn't understand the dynamics of the murder. Maybe Judge Franklin was not the primary target and her driver, Agnes Pearson, was.

Since we were dealing with a murder victim's house, we felt we had ample cause to enter, so we did, using a crowbar to jimmy open the rear door. We put on protective gloves and boots and went inside. The place was spotless but badly in need of updating. The counters and appliances looked fifty years old.

We walked through a living area with a huge TV screen, a couch, and a couple of chairs; there were a few pictures on the walls, mostly of Agnes Pearson with a Belgian Malinois in various settings.

"Let's try the bedrooms first," I said, glancing down the stairs to the front door and the lower floor.

We went through a guest room, a sewing room, and a master bedroom, all of them revealing very little about the owners' personalities. Then we noticed that one side of the closet in the master was empty.

"I think they split up," I said. "Aldo moved out."

"Which makes it more disturbing that he was trailing her until moments before she died," Mahoney said, and gestured to a home office off the master. "I'll look here."

"I'll start with the lower floor," I said. I went back to the stairs, which descended to a landing at the front door and then dropped again into a furnished basement with another bedroom on the left and a second living area on the right.

There was a closed door ahead where the hall doglegged left. As I stepped into that dogleg, I picked up motion to my left.

Twisting, I saw a very big guy — like, pro-football-big — charging at me. He growled some guttural curse I did not understand and threw a haymaker that caught me on the right cheek.

I was slammed back against the wall and fell to the floor, dazed, seeing things in wavy triplicate.

He stepped over me, his ham-like fist cocked back, and said, "That will teach you not to go messing with what's Aldo P.'s. You got me, mo-fo?"

CHAPTER

10

STILL DAZED, I SAW Mahoney step into the hall, gun drawn.

"FBI, Pearson!" he shouted. "Hands in the air!"

For a moment, the big man looked like he was about to hit me again anyway, but then he raised his hands. "FBI? What's this all about? Where the hell's your warrant?"

"We don't need one," Mahoney said.

"The hell you don't. I know my rights."

My head was clearing. "This is a double-homicide investigation, Mr. Pearson."

"What?" he said, a little less sure of himself. "Who got killed?"

"You haven't been watching the news?" Mahoney said.

"Never. Screws up your mind."

I said, "I'm sorry to say that your wife and her client, Judge Franklin, were murdered last night. Shot down in the judge's driveway."

Pearson stood there, blinking, his face twitching. He whispered hoarsely, "Aggie? Dead?"

Mahoney said, "I'm afraid so, sir."

The man's bear-paw-like hands began to tremble. The shaking traveled to his shoulders and stomach; his knees buckled and he sank down against the wall and started sobbing.

After a while, in my line of work, you learn to recognize manufactured displays of grief, but if this was an act, it was worldclass. The cries came from deep in the big man's chest, the unmistakable sound of a heart shattering.

"Noooo, Aggie," he moaned. "Not after everything. Not now."

I stood up slowly, feeling my cheek already swelling from the punch. I went and got ice from the freezer and put it on my face while Pearson's crying slowed. He wiped at his nose and face with the sleeve of his shirt.

"Why? Why would anyone want to shoot Agnes?"

"We were hoping you could tell us," Mahoney said. He took out his cell phone and showed Pearson the video of the gray Dodge Durango following his wife's Cadillac town car.

Pearson stared at the video. "That's not me."

"It's your SUV," I said. "We got a partial plate, and this is the only silver or gray Dodge Durango in the state of Maryland that matches it."

"I don't care," he said. "That's not me. When was this?"

"Last night, as your wife drove Judge Franklin home."

"What time?"

"There's a running stamp on the video," Ned said. "As you drove onto the Fourteenth Street Bridge, it was six thirteen p.m. We lost you at six twenty-two, near the exit to Judge Franklin's home."

Pearson's lower lip trembled as he shook his head. "Honest to

God, I was nowhere near Alexandria. I live about six miles from here in a place I rent above my friend's garage. I was there studying. I'm an EMT and I'm trying to get my nursing degree."

"Can anyone put you there?"

He shook his head. "My friend's on vacation."

"And your Dodge Durango?"

"It was parked in my driveway all night. Look, I didn't kill my wife. We had an agreement. No killing each other."

I said, "Run that by me again."

"Back when we got married, like fourteen years ago, the two of us, we watched a lot of those true-crime shows," Pearson said, wiping at a tear. "You know, they're always about husbands and wives killing each other. We'd always say, 'Why didn't they just get divorced if they didn't love each other anymore?' So we promised that if one of us wanted out, no killing, just ask for a divorce, which is what I did."

Ned said, "You were getting divorced?"

"Amicably," he said firmly. "We'd just outgrown each other is all."

I said, "We're not going to find records of domestic violence between you two?"

His expression hardened. "Once. Three years ago. I was drunk and on the juice. The incident was enough to get me off steroids and into AA, and I still go. I've been sober in every way ever since."

"If you were separated, why did you come in here?" Mahoney asked.

"We co-own the house," he said. "I come over when I'm off duty and not in class to work on some upgrades. We were getting ready to sell it, use the money to start new lives for ourselves."

CHAPTER

11

WE PRESSED PEARSON ON his alibi. He insisted he'd been in his room studying. He remembered he'd been online with his laptop several times, submitting assignments for various courses.

"There will be records of that, right?" Pearson said. "I mean, the IP address of my computer and the school's computer and the time and all that."

"There should be," Mahoney agreed. "And your Wi-Fi router history."

"Okay," he said. "My laptop's in my rig."

"The Durango?"

He nodded. We went outside with him and saw what looked to be the same silver-gray Dodge Durango that had followed Agnes Pearson and Judge Franklin.

Pearson's laptop was in the front seat. Mahoney took it and bagged it. "We're going to need this for a day or two," he said.

Pearson squinted. "I guess I can borrow one from school."

"And your cell phone."

"C'mon, man." He groaned. "I've got my life on that thing."

Mahoney said, "And the keys to the Durango."

"What the—" Pearson said. "What am I going to do, walk to school? I swear to you, I had nothing to do with Agnes's death."

I'd been circling the Durango during the conversation and I noticed something odd at the front end my second time around.

"Mr. Mahoney," I said, stepping away. "Can I have a word?"

"Don't touch the vehicle in any way," Mahoney told Pearson.

Pearson held up his hands and moved back.

"What's up?" Ned said when we'd walked a good ten yards away.

"Show me the still of the partial plate." Mahoney called it up. I looked at it. "No registration sticker."

"Because they put them on the rear plate in Maryland."

I gestured over at the Durango and the front plate with the registration sticker.

Mahoney walked back to Pearson. "Maryland law says your registration sticker goes on the rear plate."

"I always put it there," Pearson said, frowning as he came around the front of the SUV. "That's not right. That has never been that way."

We looked at the screws that held the plates on the bracket but could not tell if they'd been tampered with recently.

"Crime lab will tell us," Mahoney said. "So what's your relationship with Willa Whelan?"

His left eye crinkled. "Who?"

"She's a law professor at GW," I said.

"Never heard of her."

"We won't find her on any of your devices?"

"To my knowledge, that's correct," he said evenly. "Now, can I at least use my phone to call an Uber home? I mean, I'm cooperating. I'm not under arrest, am I?"

"Not today," I said. "But don't go leaving town on us."

"I told you, I'm in school," Pearson said, and got a sad look on his face. "And now I guess I've got to start planning Agnes's funeral."

After allowing him to hail an Uber, we bagged his phone and called for FBI criminalists to come take possession of it, the laptop, and the Durango. In our minds, we still had not cleared Pearson when his ride came and picked him up.

Nor had we excluded Professor Willa Whelan.

Mahoney dropped me off shortly after dark in front of my home on Fifth Street in Southeast DC. The cold wind blew leaves off the front lawn as I hurried up the stairs and into the house, which smelled incredible.

"What are you cooking?" I called into the front room where Nana was watching the evening news.

"Short ribs," Nana Mama called back. "Been braising them for hours."

I hung up my coat, put my weapon in the lockbox, and peeked around the corner into the front room. My grandmother was alone. "Where is everyone?"

"Jannie's at a friend's house, Ali's in the kitchen working on a science project, and Bree is upstairs getting showered and changed."

"I'll do that too. When's dinner?"

"Forty minutes."

"Perfect," I said, and went and kissed her on the cheek.

"What's that for?"

"You just being you," I said. I winked at her, winced.

She adjusted her glasses. "What happened to your face?"

"A very big guy hit me," I said. "But I'm fine."

"You don't look fine."

"Thanks," I said, and climbed upstairs.

I found Bree dressing in her walk-in closet.

"Oooh," she said when she saw me. "Who hit you?"

"A suspect who may or may not be a suspect," I said, and gave her a short rundown of my day before getting into the shower. "And you?"

She described her calls to the real estate agent and the sheriff's deputy in Elko, Nevada.

"Sounds open-and-shut from what the deputy told you," I said.

"As far as she's concerned, it's a closed case," Bree said, frowning. "But why would he go back up that mountain alone? In a handicap van without snow tires?"

Standing under the hot water, I said, "How much were they selling the ranch for?"

"Sixty-three million for twenty-seven thousand acres."

"Well, that kind of money would warrant a second visit in my book."

"But why alone? I mean, he couldn't get around very far, I'd imagine."

"Maybe that was the point," I said. "He got up there, it started to snow, and he realized that he wasn't going to get far in his wheelchair."

Bree remained skeptical. "I still don't get why he wouldn't just use the helicopter to go back up in there again. He was a pilot. Oh, it snowed in the mountains—maybe the poor visibility made him take the van?"

"Makes sense. Was there anyone up there at the time he died?"

She shook her head. "There's a winter caretaker, but he was in Denver with a sick mother."

"Absentee owners?"

"A Brazilian cattle company, O Casado." She perked up. "Which is familiar, isn't it?"

"How's that?"

"Remember that ranch in Colorado where the Alejandro cartel slaughtered all those Maestro operators?"

In the shower, I cocked my head. "That's right. It was owned by some Brazilian cattle company, but it wasn't O Casado."

"Still, we've got two different ranches owned by Brazilians coming up in the same web of evidence that surrounds M."

"That's a pretty broad web, but it does seem an odd coincidence."

A knock came at the door, and Ali called from the other side, "Nana Mama says dinner's almost ready, and John and Willow just got here. Wait until you see all the loot she scored in Disney World!"

CHAPTER

12

Potomac, Maryland

MARGARET BLEVINS WOKE UP a minute before her alarm was set to go off.

Ordinarily, the justice came wide awake after a good sleep, ready for her morning run or her weight routine in the basement gym. But as she reached over to turn off the alarm on her phone, she felt kind of foggy-headed. Which was odd, because she hadn't stayed up late or had any alcohol the evening before.

Yawning, she sat up and almost immediately felt dizzy. The sensation lasted a few seconds before clearing enough for her to stand and walk to the bathroom, thinking she needed a morning off from exercise.

Blevins sighed at her sleep-mussed hair in the mirror and turned on the shower. Her head and neck began to throb dully when she climbed in.

But she didn't feel feverish. No body aches. And she hadn't lost her sense of smell, so it probably wasn't COVID.

Then she got dizzy again and sat on the shelf in the shower. Phillip, her tall, older husband, came in a few minutes later, scratching his belly.

He saw her there, looking dazed. "You okay, Maggie?"

"No, actually," she said. "I feel kind of out of it, and I can't afford to be today."

"Final oral arguments of the year," Phillip said.

"Why are you up?"

"I promised to get the kids off to school so you could go in early, remember?"

Blevins closed her eyes and nodded. Why hadn't she remembered that? They'd talked about it last night before they turned off the lights.

"You look like you could use a double espresso," Phillip said.

She opened her eyes. "A quad, and I don't know why. I didn't wake up once last night."

"You didn't have any wine either."

"Exactly," she said.

After dressing, applying her makeup, and checking the itinerary her senior law clerk had emailed late last night, Blevins felt a little better. She hurried downstairs to the kitchen and made herself a double–double espresso. After drinking a few sips, she noticed the fog beginning to lift.

Well, that was more like it. Probably something in last night's takeout dinner hadn't agreed with her.

She would not allow herself to think about that little attack she'd had in the woods the day before yesterday. *This morning's fog had nothing to do with that.*

Blevins retrieved the newspaper from the front porch and drank more of the espresso while reading the news stories about the death of Judge Emma Franklin, whom she knew more as an acquaintance than as a friend.

Phillip, a patent attorney, walked into the kitchen dressed for work and saw what she was reading. "That was horrible," he said.

"A tragedy," Blevins said. "Emma had a first-rate legal mind. Kids up yet?"

"Just rousted them," he said. "You have time for breakfast?"

"I'll have it in chambers," she said. She finished the espresso, put the cup in the dishwasher, and went over to kiss and hug her beloved husband. "I adore you. Tell the kids I love them."

"First thing," he said. When she turned to leave, he said, "Be brilliant."

"Always," Blevins said, waving as she left the kitchen. She retrieved her briefcase from her office and went to the front hall closet for her overcoat and umbrella. It was drizzling and cold outside, another good reason not to run.

She'd no sooner gotten the coat on than a horn honked in the driveway. "See you around seven!" she called.

"Bye, my love!" Phillip called back.

Blevins felt warmed inside as she walked out the door and opened the umbrella. They'd been married almost twenty years, and Phillip still said silly romantic things like that. *How lucky am I?* she thought.

Despite the rawness of the day, that made Blevins smile. She hurried to a black Chevy Suburban and when she opened the back door, she found her clerk, Natalie Martin, sitting on the opposite side and U.S. Supreme Court Police officer Jim Frazier at the wheel. Martin said, "Good morning, Justice Blevins!"

"How are you this fine morning, Justice Blevins?" Officer Frazier asked.

"Hello to all and trying not to get soaked," she said, handing her briefcase to Martin and setting her umbrella on the floor. "Get the heat blasting in here, Jim," she said, shivering.

Frazier did, then put the car in reverse.

Her clerk said, "Did you have time to check your itinerary, Justice Blevins?"

"Last night," Blevins said. "One thing: I'll be eating breakfast in chambers."

"Already arranged," her clerk said. "Breakfast burrito, extra salsa, large OJ, double espresso."

"Cancel the espresso," she said. "I've already had four and don't want to hear oral arguments with my knees jiggling about."

"No, ma'am," Martin said, and laughed. "I put the latest for your review there in your door pocket."

Blevins got out her reading glasses and opened the first file. The case and appeal involved state and federal statutes relating to interstate transport of organic fruits and vegetables.

Ordinarily, the young Supreme Court justice was an extremely quick study, but as she scanned the first page, she had some trouble following it. She read the page again but couldn't get the gist of the argument.

Blevins had been known as one of the sharpest legal minds in the country even before being named to the high court, but now she was having difficulty focusing.

What is going on? Should I see a doctor?

"Justice?" her clerk said. "Did you hear what I said?"

"About what, Nat?" she asked, a little confused.

"Justice Mayweather," Martin said. "His cancer may be back."

CHAPTER

13

IN SOUTHEAST DC, I was finishing my scrambled eggs, reading the *Washington Post* online, and drinking unusually great coffee. Ali had left for school, Bree was sitting across from me studying her laptop, and Nana Mama was upstairs changing.

I took another sip of coffee and raised my cup. "What coffee is this? It's amazing."

John Sampson walked into the kitchen. Before Bree could answer my question, he said, "I'll bet it's Blue Mountain coffee. I got it from a friend who just came back from Jamaica and I gave some to Nana last night."

"Phenomenal taste," I said. "So smooth."

"The way life should be," Sampson said, and looked at Bree. "Already at it on Malcomb?"

She nodded but did not look up.

"Anything?"

"A little."

"Show me."

John, my oldest friend, had become obsessed with identifying M even earlier than Bree because the alleged head of Maestro had taunted him in the wake of his wife's sudden and tragic death, saying that Billie hadn't died of complications of Lyme disease, as John had been told, that she had been murdered.

Sampson was forced to exhume Billie's body to be sure. It was one of the crueler things M had done and he'd made Sampson a hardened enemy even before his men tried to hunt us down in Montana.

The evening before, as we were eating Nana Mama's braised short ribs, we'd heard all about Sampson and Willow's trip to Disney World, which included a "chance meeting" with a woman named Rebecca Cantrell.

"She's nice," Willow said. "I like her. A lot."

We all grinned because John and Rebecca, who was the U.S. attorney for Northern Virginia, had been seeing each other quietly. The Disney trip had been set up so Willow could meet and get comfortable with Rebecca before she was told about the relationship. Willow had been very close to her mother, and they thought neutral ground would be a better place for Sampson's daughter to get to know her father's new love interest without the words *girlfriend* and *boyfriend* being thrown around.

After dinner Willow went into the other room with Ali and Jannie, and Bree told John about the death of Ryan Malcomb. Shocked, he pumped her for details and agreed there was something off about the entire thing.

"Why would he drive a handicap van with no snow tires up a canyon like that?"

"Exactly one of my points," Bree said. "Here, look at this."

She turned her laptop toward him and showed him the Google Earth image of the area: a large block of alpine terrain with snow high on the peaks. "This is the Double T Ranch, the one Malcomb was interested in buying."

"Lot of trees, lot of grassy areas," I said. "Beautiful terrain."

"What's the name of the Brazilian company that owns it again?" Sampson asked.

"O Casado Cattle Company," Bree said, "based in Belo Horizonte, Brazil."

"Google that," I said.

She searched for the company but got only results regarding the ranch in Nevada. Sampson suggested translating the words *cattle company* into Portuguese and searching for that.

O Casado popped up with a Belo Horizonte street address and little else.

"No website?" I said.

"Not according to Google," Bree said.

My cell phone buzzed with a text from Ned Mahoney: I'm picking you up in five. Big break in the Judge Franklin case!

"Gotta go," I told Bree and Sampson.

I took my coat from the front closet as my wife called to me, "What's the name of the Brazilian company that owned the Circle M Ranch in Colorado?"

"Haven't looked yet!" I bellowed back, taking my service weapon from the lockbox.

"It's okay, Alex," Sampson called. "I know it."

In the kitchen, Bree frowned. "You do?"

Sampson nodded. "Circle M was owned by Melhor Ranch and Cattle Company, Belo Horizonte, Brazil."

She used Google Translate and soon had a listing up on the screen similar to the one for O Casado. "Again, all we have is a street address."

"Type it in," John said, coming around to see her screen. "Then the other one. Let's see them on a map."

Bree called up Google Maps and soon had the two addresses on the screen, each marked by a glowing yellow pin.

"They're on the same block," she said.

Sampson nodded. "Right around the corner from each other."

"It's the same operation, different doors."

"Or they're just shell companies, designed to hide the identity of the real owners."

"Like I said, the same operation. We just need to prove it, find the common denominator."

Sampson started studying all the recent news about Malcomb's data-mining firm, Paladin, and Bree searched for ownership records of the cattle companies in Brazil and their ranches in the United States.

Twenty minutes later, John said, "*Wall Street Journal* says that since Paladin is held privately and Malcomb was one of the primary stockholders, we won't know for months how big a blow his death is to the value of the company, though all of the analysts contacted believe it will be significant."

Bree looked up. "Malcomb was the brains. How do they continue to innovate without him?"

"That's the big question," John said. "Anything at your end of the table?"

"I found the Double T Ranch in public property listings filed in Reno," she said, returning her attention to the screen. "Says here the agent of record at the sale nine years ago was a Reno attorney named Glenn Star."

"Give him a call."

Bree ran a search on him and sighed. "He's dead."

"How long ago?"

"Wait a second—it says here his body was found in a fleabag motel in Lockwood, Nevada; he was naked, and he'd been shot in the head. His wallet and car keys were gone."

"So some traveling hooker rolled him," Sampson said.

"Or her pimp," Bree said, nodding.

On a whim, she went to Colorado property records and found the ranch outside Durango where there'd been a firefight between the Alejandro cartel and Maestro operators. It took her a while, but she located the ranch sale documents on file in La Plata County.

Similar to the transfer in ownership in Nevada, the shell company in Brazil had been represented by an agent, in this case Delores Raye, an attorney in Durango.

She googled the lawyer and whistled.

"What do you got?" Sampson asked.

"The attorney representing the Melhor Ranch and Cattle Company in the purchase of the Circle M was kidnapped, raped, and murdered fourteen months after the deal closed."

CHAPTER

14

Baltimore, Maryland

TWO HOURS AFTER NED texted me, we met with an FBI agent working organized crime. Adriana Lopes, a handsome woman in her early thirties, climbed into the back seat of our car, which was parked by a strip mall. Lopes was dressed for the street: jeans, hoodie, and a bandanna around her hair. A bunch of bangles clinked on her wrists.

Mahoney introduced us. Lopes said she'd been working undercover for the past thirteen months, slowly infiltrating the Haitian arm of a loose federation of organized crime families in Baltimore.

"Narcotics?" I asked.

"That's the Venezuelans, and the DEA is on them," she said. "I'm working the traditional Haitian stuff: smuggling, stealing, girls, betting, loan-sharking."

I asked, "You speak French?"

"And Haitian patois."

"My wife does too. Learned it from her mother."

She smiled. "My mother and grandfather taught me. Which is why I heard what I heard. Le Couteau and the others know I speak French, but I haven't let on how well I understand the street language."

"And Judge Franklin's name came up in that language?" Mahoney asked.

"Not Franklin's name. The name of her driver. Agnes Pearson."

Lopes explained that the day before, she was at work as a barista in a bakery and coffee shop that served as an informal meeting place for the loosely connected gangs. There were two Russians, three Haitians, and two Hispanic gangbangers in the shop.

The truly dangerous guy was the smallest: a Haitian, Jean-Jean Papillon, otherwise known as Le Couteau, or "the Knife," a weapon with which he was said to be expert. Papillon grew up an orphan in Port-au-Prince. Legend had it that at the age of thirteen, he became an assassin for gang bosses who ruled the slums.

Lopes said, "He applied for asylum here after that big earthquake in Haiti ten or so years ago."

"And now?" I asked.

"He owns and operates the bakery, which I've learned is a center of gambling, loan-sharking, and money laundering."

Lopes said there had been an intense private meeting at the bakery the prior afternoon. Afterward, she overheard Papillon telling someone in patois that one of the Russians, Boris Kroll, had informed him they had a problem.

It turned out Agnes Pearson owed Kroll and the Knife a hundred and forty thousand dollars, money she'd borrowed to buy the Cadillac town car and cover other expenses because her credit was shot. To make things worse, Pearson also owed them thirty grand in gambling debts. She liked to bet on football games.

Mahoney said, "One hundred and seventy K. Even in this day and age, it's got to be a hit to them."

"And they're not happy about it," Lopes said.

"Is there any way the debt and the murder are linked?" I asked.

"I don't know. Maybe she wasn't making her payments?"

Mahoney said, "Let's ask."

Lopes got a little antsy. "With all due respect, sir, if you press him, he's going to figure you've got wiretaps on him or suspect that I told you."

"Not necessarily," I said. "We can say Papillon's name and number were on Agnes Pearson's phone along with an informal accounting of her debts to him. And we noticed she was taking regular withdrawals of four to five thousand dollars in cash from her accounts."

Her eyebrows rose. "That could work."

"You have an address for the bakery?" Mahoney asked.

"I do," she said. "But give me an hour to get there and settle into my job before you come in and fire questions at him."

"We can do that. Can you text us and tell us if he's there?" I asked.

"Will do, Dr. Cross," she said, but she hesitated before climbing out.

"Problem, Ms. Lopes?" Mahoney said.

"I've put a lot into this," Lopes said. "I hope you know what you're doing."

CHAPTER

15

JEAN-JEAN PAPILLON'S HIBISCUS BAKERY and Café operated out of an old storefront in West Baltimore under a hand-painted sign featuring the Haitian national flower superimposed on a silhouette of the island nation. The big glass windows had been painted over with a mural of tropical life, making it impossible to see inside.

As we approached the closed front door, we heard quickstep Haitian kompa music thumping from the interior. As I grabbed the door handle, Mahoney's phone buzzed with a text from Ms. Lopes: Knife here. So are—that was all. Ned hesitated at the incomplete message, then nodded to me. I pulled open the door and immediately smelled beignets, croissants, and a dozen other baked delicacies.

There was a short entry hall about eight feet long. The kompa dance song was ending. We could hear men talking on the other side of the half wall.

Mahoney's phone buzzed again as I rounded the corner and took in the room in a sweeping glance: A long glass case inside of which confections were laid out on plates and in tiers. Baguettes stood crowded in two wicker baskets. A young woman was loading fresh baked goods into another case.

At the café area to my right, seven men sat at a long table; three were white, two Black, and two Latino. All of them were staring at me and, behind me, Ned as if we were sewer creatures that had suddenly appeared among them.

Mahoney, as usual, was fearless. "FBI," he said, holding up his identification. He pushed back his suit coat with his other hand and rested it on his service weapon.

Before he could tell them who we were there to see, one of the Hispanic guys yanked out a pistol from under the table.

"Gun!" I shouted.

The man shot wildly. The round went between us, shattered one of the glass cases. The girl behind the counter screamed.

I drew my pistol as the other men at the table dived for cover. I fired one round at the gunman, grazing his left shoulder, and Mahoney put two rounds in his chest. He dropped the pistol and collapsed backward.

"Who's next?" Mahoney roared, swinging his pistol around at the remaining six men, who were scattered on the floor. "Who wants it next?"

"On your bellies, hands behind your heads!" I shouted over the ringing in my ears. "All of you! Now!"

One by one, the men rolled onto their bellies. One by one, our guns aimed at the backs of their necks, Ned and I frisked them for weapons.

"You won't find any, my friends," Jean-Jean Papillon said in a thick French accent. He was a wiry guy in his late forties, blue

65

T-shirt, colorful crochet net pulled down over his hair. "It's against the rules."

"Your pal didn't get the message," Mahoney said, putting zip cuffs on him.

The other Hispanic guy seemed shaken. "I told Luis, but he wouldn't listen. He had four felony warrants out on him and said he wasn't going back to prison, so the gun went with him. I had nothing to do with it."

"We had nothing to do with this, my friends," Le Couteau said. "It's against the rules."

"Of what?" Mahoney said, checking one of the white guys for weapons and finding none.

"This is meeting," the big guy said in a heavy Russian accent. "This Alcoholics Anonymous meeting."

"What?" I said, skeptical.

"Once a week, we are here," the Knife insisted. "I have three years of sobriety."

"Six," grunted the Russian.

The other four men on their bellies each announced how many years they'd been sober. Mahoney and I looked at each other.

Were we being conned? Was AA a cover for a criminal meeting?

Sirens wailed and neared. Mahoney went outside with his badge and explained the situation to the patrolmen while I guarded the six men and the corpse.

I realized the girl behind the counter had fled. And where was Lopes? If she was keeping her cover, she probably ran at the shot too.

Mahoney came back with more zip ties and started binding the last few men. "I've got them calling in a criminalist team from FBI Baltimore. We'll be under review."

"Par for the course," I said. "Meantime, we've got a Mr. Knife on the floor."

"We do," he said. He went over, hoisted Papillon to his feet, led him to another table, and sat him down.

"I have nothing to say," Le Couteau told him. "You can talk to my lawyer. I had nothing to do with this insane Luis."

"Let's say we believe that," I said. "What about Agnes Pearson?"

He looked at us warily, said nothing.

"Your name appears on her cell phone and her computer in a file where she keeps accounts of the debts that she owes you."

The Knife snorted. "This woman owes me nothing."

"She owed someone one hundred and seventy grand, and the only notation on the account is Butterfly, your last name in English," Mahoney said, stretching the bluff.

"This is an oddity," Papillon said. "She owes me nothing."

"But you knew her," I said.

"I knew her husband through AA and met her twice."

"She's dead. Someone shot her to death along with a federal judge."

"Hmm," Le Couteau said. "Do you see the illogic of what you are asking?"

"Illogic?"

"You try to say she owes me money, then you imply I shot her. Why would someone shoot her if she owes the money and makes all the payments? No smart man would do this."

16

YOU COULDN'T ARGUE WITH the logic or the fact that Papillon was very sharp. His English was good enough that he had all but copped to loaning Pearson the money without coming right out and saying it.

And his reasoning was spot-on. Why would anyone who was owed a lot of money kill the person consistently making payments on the debt?

"It would be like a bank manager deciding to kill a mortgage holder," Mahoney said after we'd both sat for interviews with the supervising special agent in charge of the Bureau's Baltimore office.

It turned out that twenty-nine-year-old Luis Hernandez, the deceased, had already done five years of hard time in a federal lockup for trying to rob an armory while he was still in the U.S.

Navy. According to the multiple warrants out against him, he was also a wife-beater who ran a protection racket for a local gang.

"We went in to talk," I said in my interview. "Mr. Mahoney clearly identified himself and displayed his credentials plainly. Hernandez just didn't want to go back to jail. Without a doubt, it was a righteous shoot."

It did not matter that Papillon and the other five men in the café at the time of the shooting were all known members of organized crime groups. None were armed, and the AA affiliation was real. The meeting was even listed on the local AA website.

It was after dark when we finally finished our statements and started the drive home. Nearing Bowie, Maryland, I realized something. "Aldo Pearson never mentioned his estranged wife's debt."

"No, he didn't," Mahoney said, taking the exit. "But to hear him tell it, they were in the process of dividing assets. He had to have known about it."

"Exactly," I said.

We drove to the address Aldo Pearson had given us. As he'd described, he lived in a small apartment above the garage of a sprawling ranch house about six miles from the home he'd once shared with Agnes.

The big ranch was on a heavily treed lot set well back from the road, ensuring privacy. As we climbed the stairs to the garage apartment, we heard rock music playing—Pearl Jam.

We knocked on the door. There was no answer, so we knocked louder.

"Supervising special agent Mahoney, FBI, Pearson," he yelled.

Still no answer. He tried the doorknob, which turned. Ned pushed the door open, hand on his pistol, took a look, and froze. "Jesus."

I stepped in behind him and saw what had stopped him.

Aldo Pearson must have put up a hell of a fight. The place was destroyed: Furniture turned over. Television with a big hole in the screen. Glass coffee table shattered. Cupboards in the kitchen open, the contents smashed on the floor. The sofa cushions slashed and flung aside.

Pearson was bare-chested and strapped to a ladderback chair. He had been tortured and then strangled with wire. His bug eyes stared at us.

"We're backing out of here," Mahoney said. "We're still under review."

"I agree," I said. We did, and he pulled the door shut.

We called in the Montgomery County sheriff's department and the Maryland state police, told them what we knew, and left the scene to their detectives around eight o'clock that evening with the understanding that we would brief them the following day on our interactions with the murdered husband of the murdered driver of the murdered federal judge.

Mahoney finally dropped me off around eight thirty that night. I felt wrung out. I wished him well, exited the car, and saw a wreath on the front door.

It surprised me until I realized it was December 20, only five more days until Christmas and I hadn't even started to look for presents. In the house, I heard Burl Ives singing "A Holly Jolly Christmas."

Then other voices started singing it too. I looked into the front room and saw my entire family, including my older son, Damon, back from college for the holidays, sitting around watching *Rudolph the Red-Nosed Reindeer* and singing along with Burl. Sampson was there too, singing along with his daughter, Willow, on his lap.

Despite the strange and deadly day that I'd had, I got tears in my eyes, more proof I was getting weirdly sentimental as the years passed. I joined in on the last chorus, holding Bree's hand, then greeted everyone and hugged Damon.

"You tower over me now," I said.

"Coach said I grew another inch," Damon said, grinning. "I'm officially on the roster as six foot six and a half inches. Two hundred seventeen."

Jannie said, "I don't know how he runs being that heavy."

Damon said, "I'm just up and down the court hustling—I'm not a world-class four-hundred runner."

"I'm not world-class yet," she said.

"I don't know what else you'd call yourself. Anyway, big as I am, I know I'm never going to the NBA, and I'm cool with that."

"Never say never," Nana Mama said.

I learned that there'd been a gas leak at Sampson's house, so they were staying with us for the next few days while it was being fixed. Willow would sleep in Jannie's room, John down on the sofa.

"Nana Mama?" Willow said. "Can I get one more Christmas cookie before we finish *Rudolph*?"

"It is the Christmas season," my grandmother said. "Go on. But only one."

Willow let out a whoop, launched herself off Sampson's lap, and took off toward the kitchen with all of us laughing.

"She run around like that at Disney World?" Bree asked.

"Constantly," he said. "Every time she saw a character, she'd go straight over to get her picture taken."

"Miracle you didn't lose her. Wasn't the park packed?"

"Near capacity. But I always knew where she was."

"How's that?"

Sampson got up and picked up Willow's pack, the one he'd

had made for her after a terrorist threat in DC; it had special Kevlar inserts that might deflect a bullet or bomb fragment. He unzipped a side pocket and got out what looked like a small, pink car-ignition fob.

He showed it to us. "A company called Jiobit makes it."

Ali said, "It's a tracking device."

"A fairly amazing one," John said. "It talks to an app on my phone."

"What's its range?"

"It will talk to any satellite on earth. Has a three-week charge. She doesn't even know it's there and that pack never left her back unless I was holding it."

"What if she lost the pack?"

"She knows better, and anyway we have two tags."

Willow returned, munching on a cookie. "What's next?"

"Bed," Sampson said firmly.

His little girl looked ready to argue, then nodded. "I'm tired."

I went in the kitchen and found some leftover fried pork chops with onion-and-sriracha applesauce, a concoction of Nana Mama's that deserved a place in the recipe hall of fame. Bree followed me in.

"I'm beat," she said, and yawned. "How'd your day go?"

When I told her, she got angry. "You didn't think to call and tell me you'd been in a shooting with Haitian gangsters? When I have history with guys like that?"

"I apologize. But they were totally different guys. From Baltimore. And we were fine. It just got crazy there for a minute."

She came over and hugged me tight. "In the future, promise you'll call me if you're involved in a shooting."

"I hope there isn't another shooting in my future, but I promise. And how was your day?"

Bree described finding out that two real estate attorneys were murdered after representing the cattle companies in the purchase of large ranches in Colorado and Nevada.

"That's no coincidence, especially when the two companies are around the corner from each other in Brazil," I said.

"That's our thinking," Bree said. "John and me. But we can't seem to find anything about them other than the addresses in Brazil."

I thought about that as I chewed the first delicious bite of my dinner, a little sweet, a lot spicy. I groaned a little.

"It's my favorite of her creations too," Bree said. "Any advice on where to go next?"

"I'll talk to Ned tomorrow, see if we can contact our counterparts down in Brazil and have them take a look into the mysterious cattle companies of Belo Horizonte."

CHAPTER

17

MAHONEY PICKED ME UP the following morning, and I told him what Bree and Sampson had discovered about the Brazilian cattle companies. He thought the link to Ryan Malcomb was more than a little tenuous, but in the end, he agreed to contact the Brazilian national police.

"After we execute a warrant on Professor Whelan's home in Bethesda," he said.

"What took so long?"

"We lost one judge to recusal because she knows Whelan personally. The second judge sat on it but ultimately found the testimony of the old lady across from Judge Franklin's house compelling enough to give us a look around the place."

"I get the feeling the professor is not going to be happy to see us."

"Maybe we'll get lucky and she'll be in her office or teaching."

We weren't lucky. Willa Whelan was at home, and when she answered the door to her modest house at the edge of a creek, she took one look at the booties on our shoes and the warrant and let loose with a barrage of insults and curses. Mahoney had to threaten her with obstruction if she did not let us in.

The law professor's lips curled bitterly, but at last she stepped aside, and we entered. As I passed her, I could not help thinking that in my experience, most people who unleash a tirade like that are doing so out of fear.

As we began the search, I believed Willa Whelan had something to hide.

At first, my suspicions ran to undeclared income. For a law professor who had been an assistant U.S. attorney in Arkansas, she had a home that was borderline lavish. It was relatively small and the outside was plain, but the interior held Persian rugs, limited-edition sculptures, original oil paintings by well-known artists, and a state-of-the-art entertainment center. The kitchen appliances were all from Scandinavia; the counters were beautiful green granite; the fixtures were copper, unique, and gleaming.

By the time we turned toward the bedrooms, I believed that the professor had either inherited a pile of cash or was a tax cheat. The sudden appearance of all the finer things in life, the things you can buy when you have a lot of cash lying around, is often an indication that someone is trying to avoid the IRS.

Whelan's spare bedroom was set up for guests and decorated out of Laura Ashley and Pottery Barn. The primary suite was huge, its hardwood floors covered with more Persian rugs.

Then we found embarrassing intimate tools and lubricants in a drawer in the bathroom. For the next half an hour or so, I figured that must have been the source of her fear and I was glad she hadn't been in the room when we made that discovery.

We looked in every cranny upstairs and found nothing to link Whelan to Emma Franklin's death. We did, however, find a gun safe in her basement.

The professor opened it unhappily. It held three different nine-millimeter match-style shooting pistols with brightly colored handles, one green, one blue, and one red.

None of them looked remotely like the suppressed pistol carried by the judge's assassin.

"Are we going to find more weapons in the house, Professor?" Mahoney said.

"No," she said. "I sold all my late husband's. They were too big for my hands."

I said, "If you don't mind me asking, how did he die?"

She gazed at me. "An industrial accident. Tim was a drilling engineer."

"Big insurance payout?"

Whelan appeared insulted. "I sued his company for gross negligence and won."

That explained the house, the lifestyle. I shut the safe.

As Mahoney was leaving the basement, I realized I had not seen any kind of office space in the house. "You don't work at home?" I asked her.

"Rarely," she said immediately, as if she'd been waiting for the question. "And if I do, it's usually upstairs at the kitchen table with my laptop."

I smiled. But then the law professor's eyes flickered toward the far wall of the basement, which was covered in barnboard and adorned with sporting items hanging on hooks: tennis rackets, bike helmets, and the like.

I acted as if I hadn't seen the tell and followed Mahoney back upstairs.

"I suppose you'll want to see the garage and the shed out back," she said, sounding relieved.

"I'll take the garage," Ned said.

"The shed's mine," I said, and left the house by the kitchen door.

There was a small garden shed in one corner of the backyard, but instead of going to it, I walked around the house, looking at the foundation and the well windows. I was able to see into the basement on the back and both sides, but at the base of the front of the house, toward where I believed the barnboard was positioned, two well windows were covered with blackout curtains.

I found Mahoney in the garage. "Nothing," he said.

"Let's take another look below," I said, and we went inside.

When I opened the basement door, Whelan came over. "There's nothing down there. You've seen it. I told you."

"You did, and you're lying," I said, going down the stairs.

She and Mahoney followed me as I went to that wall covered in barnboard. I scanned it, searching for a seam. I looked back at the professor. "You going to show me how it opens, or do I call in an FBI team with chain saws?"

Whelan glared at me for a long moment, then walked to the left side of the barnboard and pressed a hidden button. A door-size piece of the wall clicked and sagged open.

I went in and found a narrow office with a desk and computer at one end and pegboards on the walls. The two pegboards closest to the desk on both sides were covered in clippings about Judge Emma Franklin, both before and after her death.

Mahoney looked back at Whelan, who was standing there with crossed arms, slinging hatred at us with her eyes and posture.

"Uh-oh," Ned said.

CHAPTER

18

San Francisco, California

JUDGE BITGARAM PAK WAS a big man by anyone's standard, well over six feet and built like the former wrestler he'd been at Stanford, long-armed, lean, and hard despite his fifty-three years.

Judge Pak's father had wrestled for South Korea in the Olympics before immigrating to the United States. U-Jinn Pak taught his son everything he knew about grappling and he attended every one of his matches and every one of his graduations.

The old man had finally passed the previous week, and he was on Judge Pak's mind as he left the James R. Browning U.S. Courthouse around nine fifteen that evening.

A chill drizzle fell. It was three days before Christmas Eve, and Pak had meant to leave work earlier to get some shopping done for Allie, his new girlfriend. But time seemed to slip away while he was writing an opinion for the majority on the Ninth Circuit Court of Appeals.

Pak knew he could easily call an Uber, but he had a warm raincoat and an umbrella, and his shoes were Gore-Tex-lined. Further, he was hung up on a certain part of the opinion he was writing and had a looming deadline, and in these situations, Judge Pak found that by walking, he could get out of his head and let his subconscious work.

He glanced at his watch. If he hurried, he could make last call at his favorite ramen joint on the near side of Hayes Valley, not far from where he lived.

Pak had owned his home for decades, since long, long before Hayes Valley became the trendiest neighborhood in the City by the Bay. As he walked toward Market Street, he noted the homeless encampments that seemed to appear out of nowhere every day.

Judge Pak felt compassion for these people. At one point in his father's life, shortly after arriving in the United States, he'd been homeless and hungry. Judge Pak's dad had spoken of that time as the great humiliation of his life.

So the judge cared. He really did. But his compassion was reaching its limit. He had to avoid needles on the sidewalk, and drug dealers were openly selling fentanyl and meth as he passed the public library.

He felt little or no fear at the situation. His sheer size and bearing were usually enough to keep street folks from coming at him.

But something had happened recently. He felt a tipping point had been passed. In his view, the number of homeless and drug-addicted people roaming the streets of San Francisco had grown almost exponentially. So had the number of empty storefronts, many of them boarded over. It saddened and angered him at the same time.

The rain picked up. He had to lower his umbrella against the sudden wind.

Crossing Van Ness Avenue, Judge Pak saw yet another encampment behind the seven spreading jacaranda trees on the lawn at the southeast corner of the opera house. Tarps. Tents. Smoke from a campfire, which was totally illegal.

He did not notice the hippie chick in the filthy long skirt, Ugg boots, locs, and a dark rain jacket slip out of the encampment, pull up her hood, and follow him.

Judge Pak walked along the side of the opera house thinking about Allie, his new free-spirited girlfriend.

He took a left on Franklin Street and headed south past the darkened symphony hall. In his mind, he heard Allie telling him to focus on what was right with life, not what was wrong.

That took all of the judge's concentration. He remained unaware of the hippie chick shortening the gap between them on the otherwise deserted sidewalk, her footfalls muffled by the rain pattering against his umbrella.

From the pocket of her jacket, she eased out a nine-inch double-bladed combat knife. She closed the last few feet and began telling him who she was and why his game was up.

The judge tried to spin around to see her. But it was too late.

With surgical precision and raw power, the hippie chick drove the razor-sharp knife through Pak's raincoat, through his suit coat, shirt, and undershirt, through his skin, and deep into his right kidney. She twisted the blade.

The judge squealed like a pig and continued to shudder after she pulled the blade out. But then she stabbed his left kidney and twisted again.

Pak locked up, paralyzed, not breathing, making no sound, impaled on the blade, his nervous system in complete shock. She yanked her weapon free and walked off, leaving the judge sprawled on the sidewalk, seconds from death.

CHAPTER

19

NED MAHONEY WAS NOTIFIED of the murder shortly after midnight, East Coast time. He called me. Leaving thoughts of Professor Whelan's obsession with the late Judge Franklin behind for the moment, we were on an FBI jet at six.

That was what happened when two judges in the U.S. Court of Appeals system were murdered in cold blood within days of each other. According to Mahoney, our case had gone from a top priority of the Bureau to number one with a bullet.

Mahoney was feeling the heat, fielding calls from Director Hamilton and her deputies for our whole trip across the country. I drank coffee and read everything I could find about the late judge.

When Ned at last hung up, he rubbed his forehead and said, "Any parallels to the Franklin case?"

"Quite a few, actually," I said. "They knew each other when

she clerked for Justice Rolling and Pak clerked for Justice Mayweather."

"Huh," Mahoney said. "I heard Mayweather's cancer has come back."

I made a note of that, then gave him the other similarities in the two dead judges' backgrounds. They were both ethnic minorities: Pak was the son of South Korean immigrants, and Franklin was the great-granddaughter of sharecroppers in Georgia.

Both had lost spouses. Pak's wife, Leigh, had passed three years ago after a long bout with breast cancer. Franklin's husband had died in a plane crash the previous spring.

"They also both had impressive careers early," I went on. "Pak was editor of the *Law Review* at Boalt Hall. Franklin ran it at Harvard."

"And both clerked for Supreme Court justices and at the same time," Mahoney said, rubbing his chin.

"Decades ago."

"Still."

"Any controversial cases Pak was working on?"

"There were a dozen big cases brought before the Ninth in the past year, but I'm not enough of a legal mind to know which ones we need to be looking at."

We landed around eight a.m. local time and were met by San Francisco FBI supervising special agent Claudia Hinkley, a tall redhead who'd played volleyball for USC. As we drove to the scene, she brought us up to date.

"A food delivery driver spotted Pak's body on the sidewalk in front of the symphony hall around ten minutes to ten last night," she said. "Took an hour for San Francisco's homicide unit to respond and identify him."

THE HOUSE OF CROSS

"You're kidding me," I said.

"They didn't know who he was until they got there," Hinkley said. "But SF homicide? Not exactly a stellar bunch."

Mahoney nodded. "Less than fifty percent homicide solve rate."

"Kind of a disgrace," Hinkley agreed. "But at least the two detectives called to the scene were savvy enough to contact us when they realized it was Pak."

"Cause? Time of death?" I asked.

"The ME says stab wounds to both kidneys around nine forty."

"And no one saw him get stabbed? The streets should have been crowded."

"The concert hall was closed. It was pouring rain. Cold. He got unlucky."

"We know why he was out walking in the rain?"

"Rather than calling for a ride? I don't know. He lived in Hayes Valley, which is four or five blocks from here."

"CCTV?"

"Thankfully, yes. We've got Bell and Ponce, the local homicide team, gathering it for us, trying to backtrack Pak between the courthouse and here."

We arrived at the scene at a little past nine in the morning. The wind was raw coming off the ocean. The sky overhead was gray and spitting chill rain as we showed our identification and crossed through police lines.

Judge Pak's body had been removed already, a pity because I found it helpful to see the victim in situ. But Hinkley had access to crime scene photographs taken overnight. She sent us copies.

I studied them on my phone. The judge had fallen on a San Francisco 49ers umbrella. He was on his right side, head facing south, right arm extended back and fingers slashed, as if he'd tried to grab the knife that killed him.

"The stabber came up behind him," I said, backing up a little. "Probably right here?"

Hinkley pointed at a security camera mounted on the far corner of the symphony hall. "That should give us something."

CHAPTER

20

WE COULDN'T FIND ANYONE who could help us with the security footage right away, so Mahoney and I studied a map on his iPad, trying to figure out Judge Pak's likely route from the federal courthouse.

We decided that because of the rain, Pak had probably taken the most direct route, which meant walking toward Market Street to Grove. While Hinkley managed a team of FBI agents who'd just arrived on the scene, we walked back along the south side of Grove, opposite the opera house.

While the homeless problem in the Washington, DC, area was growing, it was eclipsed by the situation in San Francisco. We dodged human feces, tents, and discarded hypodermic needles as we neared Van Ness.

Mahoney's conservative suit and demeanor screamed law enforcement, and most of the homeless people gave us a wide berth. But then a young filthy couple with blankets around their shoulders stepped in our way.

"We need money, man," the guy said. "Give us five."

"Ten," the girl said, sniffing. "You got bucks. We can tell. It's inequity, man."

Ned flipped his FBI badge at them. "Sorry about the inequity."

The guy swore and stepped back.

I said, "But maybe you can help us." I turned to the girl. "What's your name?"

"Alice, but we don't do narc here," she said. "Especially with the feds."

"What narc?" I said. I held out Mahoney's iPad. "We just need to know if you saw this guy last night."

"Nah," she said, not bothering to look. She pulled her blanket tighter around her shoulders. "It was raining hard last night. I was in our tent."

"Look anyway."

Alice rolled her eyes, stepped forward, and glanced at a photograph of Bitgaram Pak in his robes. She cocked her head to one side and studied him thoughtfully for a few seconds.

"What happened?" she asked.

"Someone put a knife in his back."

"Clark?" Alice said to her partner. "Check this out. I think it's the ramen guy."

"Ramen guy, yeah," Clark said, but didn't move.

"What do you mean, ramen guy?" Mahoney asked.

Alice said, "He eats all the time at the ramen place south of the symphony hall on Franklin. There's a grate there we sleep on when it gets cold. He used to give us something when he left the place, money or leftovers. Good guy."

I said, "But you didn't see him last night?"

"Like I said, it was raining buckets."

Clark was standing a few feet away, staring at the ground.

I took a chance, said, "But you saw him, didn't you, Clark?"

"What? Nah."

"You never left the tent?"

He shook his head slightly.

Alice looked at Clark. "You did, twice, to piss."

His hold on his blanket tightened. "Jesus, Alice. I don't want to be involved."

"So you did see him," Mahoney said. "Where and when?"

Clark seemed ready to punch something or run, but then he gave up. "He walked by on the other side of the street, past those tents over there by the opera house."

"How'd you know it was him?"

"He carries a Forty-Niners umbrella. He's a big fan."

Alice nodded. "Clark is too. They used to talk football every once in a while."

"Notice anything odd about him?"

"Nah," he said. "But a white chick with locs came out of the tents there and followed him."

"She followed him?"

"That's what it looked like to me. Wasn't anyone else walking in a monsoon. She stayed right behind him about thirty yards until I lost sight of them."

"Describe her."

He shrugged. "Like I said, white. Had on a peasant skirt and them Ugg boots. A dark hooded raincoat too, but you could see locs sticking out."

Mahoney called Hinkley. "We're looking for a Caucasian

female with locs, peasant skirt, Ugg boots, and a dark hooded raincoat."

"Come back soon," she said. "The symphony hall security chief will be here in fifteen minutes, and the local homicide detectives have pulled other recordings."

CHAPTER

21

Washington, DC

NANA MAMA WAS FEELING tired and went upstairs to lie down after breakfast. Bree was working on her laptop in the kitchen when Sampson came by after dropping Willow at school.

"How many more days off do you have?" she asked.

"Through New Year's," Sampson said. "I accrued a ton of comp time the past year. They told me to burn a bunch or lose it."

"Give me a hand with something?"

"Ryan Malcomb?"

"Who else?" she said. She showed him how little was publicly known about Malcomb's life before he founded Paladin. "Attended the University School in Hunting Valley, Ohio, graduating with high honors and winning the math prize. Then MIT. Shortly after graduating, again with high honors, he founded a private company, Algo Corporation."

"It was also a data-mining thing?" Sampson asked.

"Yes. Malcomb brought on that CEO you and Alex met in Massachusetts."

"Steven Vance."

"Five years later, under Vance, they rebranded Algo as Paladin with very little fanfare. But that was always Malcomb's modus operandi—publicity shy in the extreme, and yet his company explodes, lands some of the biggest government contracts within six years. Had all sorts of offers from people wanting to buy, but he kept it closely held."

John thought about that. "Didn't the aunt fund the first company?"

"Theresa May Alcott and her late husband did," she said. "They were billionaires and his guardians."

"The Alcott soap fortune."

"That's right."

"Where were Malcomb's real parents?"

"Dead," she said. "Murdered, I believe, though I don't know the details."

"Believe?"

Bree shifted in her seat. "Remember when I went out to see Theresa May Alcott in Ohio after that fashion designer was murdered in New York?"

"Vaguely."

"She mentioned her sister and husband had been murdered during a home invasion somewhere out west," Bree said. "She adopted her sister's twins, Ryan and Sean. But afterward, I remembered Alex saying that the first time you visited Paladin, you were told that his mother had just had a fall in her house in Palo Alto."

"Maybe she was referring to Alcott," Sampson said. "Do a search and see if you can find anything about the home invasion."

She did, using the last name Malcomb, and got stories about Ryan's recent death in Nevada.

"Some of these reference Theresa May Alcott, but there's nothing about a murder three or four decades ago," she said, scanning the results.

"Well, his mother was Alcott's sister, right? Do we know their maiden surname?"

"May," Bree said, and typed in *couple murdered May*.

"That's only going to get you murders in the month of May," Sampson said. "Add the name of a western state to limit it."

Bree added *Nevada* and got a long list of stories about various homicides of couples over the years in May in Las Vegas and Reno. She tried *Utah, Colorado, Wyoming,* and *Montana,* with similar results.

"Idaho?" Sampson said.

"Why not?" Bree said and ran another search.

The first story up had been filed three years before in the Boise *Idaho Statesman.* The headline read "Wheeler Murders Still Unsolved 35 Years Later."

Bree clicked it, scanned the first few paragraphs, and said, "This has to be her."

Sampson said, "It is her. Patricia May Wheeler."

CHAPTER

22

THEY FOUND MORE THAN fifteen articles about the case, but the retrospective piece in the Boise newspaper was the longest and most comprehensive.

The gist was that an unknown knife-wielding assailant had murdered Patricia and Norman Wheeler in their summer cabin on Alice Lake near Sun Valley, Idaho, early in the morning of July 14. The Wheelers were found in adjacent bedrooms.

"'Both Patricia, thirty-six, and Norman, thirty-nine, were stabbed in the heart as they slept in adjoining rooms,'" Bree read. "'Their nine-year-old sons, Ryan and Sean, were sleeping in their favorite place, a bedroom in the boathouse down by the lake. When their parents did not come down with breakfast to be eaten on the dock, a Wheeler tradition, the boys went back to the house, discovered the bodies, and frantically called 911.'"

Sampson said, "That would mess a kid up."

Much of the rest of the story was based on interviews with former detectives from the Blaine County sheriff's department and the Idaho state police. The weapon was never found, but forensics determined that the knife used on the Wheelers was a ten-inch fillet knife, something the couple did not own.

There was no unaccounted-for DNA in the cabin or anywhere else on the property, including the boathouse. They had no enemies that anyone knew of. And there was no apparent motive.

Norman Wheeler had been a successful bond trader in San Francisco. An audit of Norman's accounts showed zero signs of malfeasance. Patricia was known for her volunteer work. Both husband and wife were highly regarded in California and in the little lake community they'd come to know and love. Patricia had rehabbed the cabin they'd bought as a getaway, made it their own.

They did not keep cash on hand. Patricia's jewelry was untouched.

There was no indication either of them had ever had an extra-marital affair.

The story also detailed various initial suspects in the case who had ultimately been cleared, including the boys.

"'Sheriff's detectives quickly took Ryan and Sean off their list. The boys were devastated by the loss and the boathouse had an alarm system that showed them inside the entire night,'" Bree read. "'By all accounts, the Wheelers were a loving couple who lavished attention on their sons, who were later adopted by a relative back east. Sheriff's detectives have been working the case on and off for three and a half decades. They still have no solid suspects or motive.'"

Bree looked up at Sampson. "What do you think?"

"For some reason, the kids' last name was changed from Wheeler to Malcomb," John said. "If they were adopted by the Alcotts, why didn't they change the last name to Alcott or May?"

"Good point," Bree said, noting it on a pad.

"Let's talk to the lead detective there, the one with the Idaho police," John said. "Finley Oakes."

Sampson called the Bureau and was told Oakes had long ago retired and now lived in Bonners Ferry in northern Idaho. They found him on a Google search and called him.

"Finn Oakes," he said. "Who's this?"

John put the call on speaker and identified himself and then Bree. When they told him they were running down some loose ends that had made them interested in the old Wheeler case, the former detective said he remembered it all like yesterday.

"Rural Idaho, you just don't see that kind of thing," Oakes said. "Double homicide like that. No DNA. No weapon. No motive. No likely suspects."

"We understand the sons were hysterical," Bree said.

"Pitiful state," Oakes said. "Those kids adored their parents. Ryan sobbed for days. Sean went catatonic but refused to leave his brother's side. Maybe I would have done the same thing if those rumors were true, that they'd been adopted twice."

"What?" Sampson and Bree said.

"Yeah, Patricia couldn't have kids. The Wheelers adopted Ryan and Sean when they were infants. Private, black-market kind of thing. We didn't find that out until years later."

CHAPTER

23

San Francisco, California

WE CROSSED GROVE STREET and talked with people living in the small tent city at the corner of the opera house. They all said last night it had been raining so hard, they were hunkered down in their shelters, and they saw no one who matched the description, though one woman offered that the locs-peasant-skirt-and-Uggs look was common locally.

The two young San Francisco PD detectives, Audrey Bell and Jorge Ponce, had better luck looking through footage from a CCTV camera at Van Ness and Grove; it backed up Clark's version of events the night before. They met us in the symphony hall lobby, and we watched the footage on Ned's iPad.

The feed was grainy due to the low light and the downpour, but we could clearly see Judge Pak with his 49ers umbrella walking past the tent encampment and being followed down the street by a Caucasian female with a mop of long locs. She moved with her head down, as if she were aware of the cameras and didn't want people to get a good look at her face.

Leo Carson, the security chief at the symphony hall, finally showed up at eleven, irritated that he'd been called in on his first day off in a month.

"You got a time frame?" he asked testily.

Hinkley said, "Lose the attitude and rewind us to nine thirty-five last night."

Carson did and we watched an empty, rain-splattered sidewalk until Judge Pak appeared walking down Franklin Street, his back and the top of his umbrella to the camera as he ambled toward his favorite ramen shop. The woman appeared a few seconds later. With her back to the camera, she pulled her hood over her locs, eased something from her sleeve, and stalked in fast behind Pak.

The attack was brutal, precise, swift. The first thrust of the knife—which looked like a KA-BAR straightedge, the kind used by Marines—went through his raincoat and suit coat and deep into his right kidney, a devastating wound. She removed the knife, stuck it in his other kidney, and twisted the blade.

Pak went rigid, up on his toes; she yanked the knife free, and the air and life went right out of him. She strolled off, stuck the blade back in her sleeve, and then pushed against the left side of her neck.

"She's a pro," Mahoney said.

I nodded. "She knows damaging the kidney causes immediate systemic shock."

Hinkley nodded. "Also, see how much smaller she is than Pak? She needed to target him there or risk him fighting."

Mahoney looked at the homicide detectives. "Can you follow her on CCTV? Figure out where she went and see if we get a better look at her?"

Ponce nodded.

Bell said, "We'll get it all if we can."

After the detectives left, Hinkley checked her watch. "I have to vanish here for a couple of hours. Parent-teacher conference for my son, who is having challenges."

"Go," Mahoney said. "You have a home address for Pak?"

"Coming at you," she said, typing a text on her phone. "And I had Bell and Ponce seal the place early this morning. You'll get first look." She handed us a set of keys that she said were taken off Pak's body.

It turned out that the judge's house was one of the famous Painted Ladies Victorian homes on Alamo Square, a short walk from the symphony hall. As promised, police tape sealed the front door.

Ned and I put on booties, gloves, and hairnets, broke the seals, and used Pak's keys to get inside. The home decor was modern and precisely arranged.

There were hardly any pictures on the walls but plenty of places where there were hooks or nails hanging. We later found a crate in the basement filled with framed photographs of Pak with his late wife, Leigh.

The kitchen and bathrooms smelled of bleach. The rugs were all freshly vacuumed. Someone had scrubbed the house before the seal was put in place.

Pak's home office was to the left of the front hall opposite a living room. The office, like the rest of the house, was fastidiously maintained. It featured a parquet floor and a beautiful standing screen with a carved wood frame and stretched cloth painted with landscapes of mountainous South Korea.

The closet door was locked. So were the desk drawers and various cabinets.

Mahoney found a key to the closet on Pak's ring. He opened it, revealing supplies and a wall safe with a digital keypad. Another key unlocked the cabinets and drawers, which were filled with files on hundreds of legal cases.

"We have a lot of work ahead of us," Mahoney said.

"Let's take a look around upstairs, figure out how best to tackle it all," I said.

"More agents."

"That too."

Mahoney stepped into the carpeted front hall. I was right behind him.

Someone jiggled the front door, which was not fifteen feet from us. Ned held out his hand and I stopped, hearing little ticks and taps at the door handle.

Mahoney mouthed, *Someone is picking it!*

He gestured me back into the office, drew his pistol, and eased into the closet, leaving it open a crack. I slid behind the big screen and drew my own weapon.

We didn't have to wait long.

CHAPTER

24

THE FRONT DOOR OPENED and shut with a soft click. For almost a minute, there was no other noise, as if the intruder were listening as intently as we were.

Finally, I heard a few careful footfalls on the carpet in the hallway. Another long pause, then the prowler moved more confidently.

Built in three tall sections, the screen I hid behind had delicate hinges joining the outer two panels to the middle. Between the hinges there were thin gaps I peered through.

I didn't see the burglar I'd expected. The man who appeared in the doorway of Judge Pak's office was a small, muscular Latino in his late thirties. He was wearing a five-thousand-dollar pale gray Italian suit and sporting a puffed-up bleached-blond pompadour that looked varnished in place. Latex gloves covered his hands, and he carried a gym bag emblazoned with the logo for something called Orangetheory Fitness.

I thought he would head for the wall safe in the closet, in which case he was in for a major surprise. But he had another target.

He walked to a small round table next to a bloodred-leather chair in front of blackout drapes. He drew out a phone and snapped a close-up picture of the table legs, then lifted the table and carefully set it aside.

He got down on his knees and pushed at the baseboard; a piece of the parquet floor rose up with an audible click. With a letter opener from the desk, he pried up the square, then set it on the table.

After taking a look around, he turned on his phone's flashlight app, shone it into the hole, and reached down with his right arm up to his elbow. I heard five beeps followed by a thunk.

He reached farther in and came out with a six-inch stack of Benjamins, the crisp hundred-dollar bills still in bank wrappers. He put them in the gym bag and began scooping out more.

Mahoney had had enough. He pushed open the closet door, gun up, and aimed at the back of the guy's head. "Freeze!" he thundered. "FBI!"

The guy startled and jerked forward, pushing his arm deeper into the hole and smashing his head into the wainscoting behind the drapes. He collapsed, groaning.

"Don't move a muscle," Mahoney said, pulling a zip tie from his pocket. He straddled the man, grabbed his left wrist, put the zip around it, and went for the right.

The guy screamed, "No, no! My fucking shoulder! It's dislocated!"

"I don't care," Mahoney said, finishing the job. He hauled the man up and into the leather chair.

"Oh, man, my head and neck are killing me," he said, rolling his head around gingerly, his pompadour crushed. "I think I compressed a disk. And I got a concussion. You are going to hear about this in court, FBI whoever you are."

"Supervising special agent Edward Mahoney," Ned said, flashing his ID. As I stepped from behind the screen, he said, "This is Dr. Cross. He works for us as a consultant in criminal behavior. And you are?"

"Sheldon Alvarez, attorney," he said, staring at me slightly cross-eyed and nodding slowly. "Cross. I've seen you before."

"Oh, yeah, where was that?" I asked, thinking I would have remembered the pompadour.

His eyes cleared a little. "At Quantico. I heard you lecture when I did a six-week course for people working for various U.S. attorneys around the country."

Mahoney said, "You're with the U.S. attorney here in San Francisco, Sheldon?"

"Oh, no," he said. "I quit that five years ago. You can't live here on that kind of bread. I am a wrongful-death litigator."

I took out my phone to check on Sheldon Alvarez, wrongful-death litigator, as Mahoney said, "Care to explain why you broke a federal crime scene seal, snuck in here, and started looting the judge's stash?"

He frowned, winced, said, "What looting? The seal was broken. I thought it was another dodge from Bitty, so I came inside."

"You picked the front lock."

Alvarez rolled his eyes, winced again, and said, "Bitty forced that issue."

I looked up from my phone. "Bitty?"

"Bitgaram Pak."

"And how did he force what issue?"

"He changed the locks on me. Said he was walking the straight and narrow." Something seemed to sag in him then. "My head really does hurt."

"We'll get it looked at after you answer my questions," Mahoney said.

Alvarez shut his eyes for a moment, and his head lolled slightly. It made me think he might indeed have a mild concussion.

"Wait a second," he said, opening his eyes sleepily. "What's this all about? Where's Bitty?"

"Don't you read the papers, Counselor?" I asked.

"I've been up at a friend's cabin, nursing my wounds and plotting my revenge after finding the doors locked. What is this then? The gambling? Finally?"

Mahoney said, "Judge Pak is dead, Mr. Alvarez. He was stabbed to death last night in front of the symphony hall."

He didn't seem to understand, because he just looked back and forth from Ned to me for several moments before shaking his head. "He can't be dead."

"He is, though, I'm sorry," Mahoney said. "His body's at the morgue, awaiting autopsy."

That cut through the fog, and Alvarez broke down sobbing.

CHAPTER

25

BREE TRIED TO ABSORB what the retired Idaho police detective had just said about the Wheeler twins being adopted twice, at least once on the black market.

Sampson said, "Mr. Oakes? How did you find that out? About there being a black-market deal?"

"Came in as a tip, I don't know, fifteen, twenty years afterward?" he said. "Near the end of my days on the job. Not much on specifics, other than Patricia could not conceive, they were having trouble adopting in California, and she decided to become an Idaho resident and try. But just as she started that whole riga-marole, she got word about twin boys being born. She heard about it through some lawyer here in Idaho."

Bree said, "And, what, she bought them?"

"The way the tipster had it, she got around all the years of bureaucracy with a quick signing of a check. I followed the lead a bit but could never prove it. And I really couldn't figure out what bearing it had on the case, so I let it drop."

"Did the boys know they were adopted?"

"Hundred percent no. They were told they were born at the cabin on Alice Lake. That's what the birth records show too."

After they thanked Oakes, Bree and Sampson hung up, not knowing what to think of the unproven tip about the origins of Ryan Malcomb.

"Let's let that sit for now," Sampson said. "Pick up the timeline with Ryan and Sean Wheeler being adopted by their mother's richer sister."

Bree tapped a pen on the table. "She raised them, I guess. She didn't talk much about Sean. It was always Ryan."

"What happened to Sean?"

Her eyebrows rose. "You know, I honestly have no idea. We talked about Ryan."

She googled *Sean Wheeler, Idaho,* and got nothing but the mention in the Boise article about his parents' murder. She tried the name in Cleveland and then in Jackson Hole. Same result.

Bree tried *Sean Malcomb* in those areas, with little luck, then *Sean Wheeler* and *Sean Malcomb* with *Theresa May Alcott.* Again nothing.

"This is bizarre," Bree said. "I know she or someone else — her lawyer, maybe — told me she brought both boys to Cleveland to live with her. But you know, come to think of it, that time I was in her office, I don't remember seeing pictures of anyone but Ryan. Or at least I think they were all Ryan."

Sampson said, "Well, sure, if they were identical twins, how would you know? I guess the only person who can answer these questions is Mrs. Alcott." He got up and poured himself more coffee.

"She struck me as the kind of person who would not like answering a lot of questions about Ryan Malcomb, but I think I have to try," Bree said. "The problem is, where is she mourning her loss? Millionaires' Row outside Cleveland? Or the ranch in Jackson Hole?"

Sampson shrugged. "You got me. Where's the funeral being held?"

"I haven't seen mention of one yet."

"Could be they're keeping it all low-key," Sampson said.

"I think we can assume that, given the way he and his aunt both…"

"What?"

"Maybe I haven't been looking at this correctly," Bree said, typing on her laptop.

Instead of searching for *Ryan Malcomb funeral,* she assembled a list of all the funeral homes in Jackson Hole and in the greater Cleveland area. Reasoning that this close to Christmas, Theresa May Alcott would be in snowy Wyoming, Bree went on the website for every funeral home in the Jackson Hole area; she looked at the obituaries and the death and service notices as far away as Driggs, Idaho.

She saw no one close to Malcomb in age or gender listed. She started to search around Cleveland, beginning with the two mortuaries closest to Hunting Valley.

The first one was another strikeout. She opened the Carruthers Brothers Funeral Home website, thinking that her clever idea might be a bust. But then she opened the death and service notices, scanned down the list, and smiled.

"Got him."

"Really?" Sampson said.

"Ryan Wheeler, forty-eight, private services, December twenty-third, one p.m."

"That's tomorrow afternoon. Interesting she used the Wheeler name."

"Uh-huh," Bree said, jiggling her knee. "We need to go."

"Private services."

Bree shrugged. "Doesn't mean we can't stand outside and wait for his aunt to come out."

Sampson knitted his brow. "I can't see how the chief is going to pay for me to fly to Cleveland on short notice, and after Disney World, there's not a lot of kale in the old Crock-Pot."

Bree laughed. "I've never heard it put that way."

"Gets the point across," John said, grinning.

She paused, then nodded. "I still have a little kale in the old Crock-Pot from my last bonus. I'm going."

CHAPTER

26

SAMPSON HAD TO LEAVE for a dentist appointment. Bree booked herself on a flight at eight forty-five the following morning out of Reagan National. She'd be off the plane at ten fifteen, plenty of time to get to Hunting Valley and the Carruthers Brothers Funeral Home before services for Ryan Malcomb began.

And she'd be back home for all of Christmas Eve.

Nana Mama came downstairs later complaining of a head cold. Bree defrosted a bag of Nana's chicken soup and served it to her on a tray while she watched one of the Madea movies with a blanket across her lap.

Nana laughed and blew her nose. "I've seen these so many times, I almost know the lines by heart, and they still make me laugh."

"Me too," Bree said. "You good?"

"I am, thank you."

Bree blew a kiss at Nana Mama and went back to the kitchen table, where she set Ryan Malcomb aside for the time being and wrote several reports for work. Around four she went out for a run despite the dank cold. Ali came home as she was finishing, with Jannie and Damon coming in soon after. They were all hungry.

"Nana Mama's under the weather," Bree said. "We'll get rib delivery from Dawson's."

That cheered everyone up, including Nana, who requested spicy rib tips, her favorite, a big order of fries, and a cherry Coke.

"That's a lot for you, Nana," Jannie said.

"Feed a cold," Alex's grandmother replied.

Bree put in the order and was upstairs picking out an outfit to wear to Ryan Malcomb's funeral when her cell rang. It was Alex.

"Hey, you," he said.

"Hey, you, back," Bree said, sitting on their bed and kicking off her shoes. "I didn't expect to hear from you for a while."

"Just checked in at our hotel. I'm going to take a shower and then we'll head back out."

"I'm going to Cleveland in the morning," she said, and explained.

Alex paused before saying, "I know you got in to see her last time by just showing up. But going to the funeral?"

"I don't know another way to get her to talk to me."

"I'm not telling you not to do it. Just be careful where you tread. She might have taken you barging in last time in stride. But her adopted son wasn't dead then. And that is an awful rich woman you're going to go poke with a stick."

"I hear you. I do. Tell me about San Francisco."

Alex told her about the hippie chick with the combat knife

and being inside the judge's house when Sheldon Alvarez picked the lock and raided Pak's safe.

"And who was this guy?"

"If he's to be believed, he was Pak's spurned former live-in lover."

"Wait—I thought Pak was married to a woman."

"Alvarez claims the wife was good with it. Evidently Pak told her when they met that he was bisexual. When she found out about the affair, she invited Alvarez to move in."

"That's pretty West Coast."

"My thoughts exactly."

He said that Alvarez described the Paks' relationship as open and working until Leigh was diagnosed with breast cancer. The judge withdrew from his relationship with Alvarez and focused exclusively on his wife.

"And then there was his gambling," Alex said. "Evidently, Pak's secret vice was sports betting, and Alvarez financed it."

Bree said, "Did the judge get in over his head?"

"Multiple times, according to Alvarez. And it got worse during Leigh's illness. He said Pak owed him close to a hundred thousand dollars after her death and kept putting off payment, even when Alvarez knew the judge had hit it big on the Super Bowl."

"The cash in the safe," Bree said.

"Correct. Alvarez said he'd had no idea Pak was dead and had no idea who would want to kill him."

"He could have hired the killer."

"Maybe. But he claimed he loved Pak even after everything the judge did, including shutting him out of his life and taking up with a new, younger woman."

"You talk to the new, younger woman yet?"

"That's on deck," Alex said, and yawned.

"Do you believe Alvarez's story?"

"Enough to check out the rest. He says he has other polyamorous friends that he and the Paks socialized with and they'll back up his story."

"San Francisco's a different kind of place. Even for appellate court judges."

"Evidently," Alex said and chuckled. "Anyway, I've got to take a shower."

"Go," Bree said. "I'll call you on my way out of Cleveland."

"I hope to be on my own plane coming home for Christmas Eve."

"You better be or you'll never hear the end of it from Nana Mama and the kids."

CHAPTER

27

Hunting Valley, Ohio

THE FOLLOWING DAY BREE Stone sat outside the funeral home in the small SUV she'd rented at the airport. She had the engine running, the defroster blasting, and the wipers slapping against a sleet-and-snow mix coming off Lake Erie that had rendered midmorning on December 23 truly miserable in the greater Cleveland area.

The first cars were starting to arrive for Ryan Malcomb's private memorial. A black Mercedes town car went around to the rear of the funeral home.

A big Polynesian man in a dark suit exited the driver's side and retrieved an umbrella from the trunk. Bree recognized him from her earlier visit to Hunting Valley. His name was Arthur, and he was apparently Theresa May Alcott's driver, gardener, and bodyguard. Arthur opened an umbrella and the right rear door and helped out the heir to a soap fortune. Tall, rail-thin, and dressed in a black pantsuit, high heels, and a hat with a dark lace veil, Mrs. Alcott said something to Arthur, and they moved quickly inside.

Bree waited until fifteen more cars had arrived and she'd watched many well-heeled mourners disappear inside, including one she knew immediately: Steven Vance, the CEO of Paladin.

Bree buttoned up her overcoat and retrieved her umbrella, at which point her phone buzzed, alerting her to a new email. She ignored it and put the phone on Do Not Disturb. She got out, opened her umbrella, and shivered at the dank cold as she hurried to the funeral home, trying to avoid the puddles of slush forming. She dropped her umbrella on the porch and went inside.

An older man built like a question mark stood in the lobby. He looked at her with well-rehearsed concern. "Family?"

"Friend," she said.

He stood aside and gestured toward a set of double doors. Bree entered and was glad to find herself at the rear of a chapel where roughly forty mourners sat. There was a green marble urn on a table up front next to a large, close-up photograph of Ryan Malcomb.

She slid into one of the empty pews at the back and then over to the far side, ignoring the few glances she got from other attendees.

I'm the only Black woman in the place. How did I think I was going to pull this off?

She had no time to fret. A silver-haired minister wearing a white collar went to the lectern. He spoke briefly, said Ryan was "an inspiration," then called up Steve Vance. He talked about Malcomb's mind, his humor despite his disease, and what the loss of his corporate vision meant to Paladin. He also talked about Malcomb's outlook near what turned out to be the end of his life.

Vance said Ryan had been figuring out "his next adventure" when he went out west looking for a ranch. "I've never been there, but the ranch he was visiting when he passed sounded like exactly what he was searching for. I hope the prospect of owning it made him very happy as he drove down that mountain road for the last time."

Theresa May Alcott got up before Vance could introduce her. The billionaire's hands, in black gloves, trembled as she went to the lectern with a few pieces of paper.

Mrs. Alcott tried to speak but trembled more. She put her fist to her lips.

"Sorry," she said at last. "This is going to be hard."

After taking a deep breath, the billionaire referred in vague terms to the tragedy that had brought Ryan to live with her. She talked about his grief over the loss of his parents and the resiliency he'd showed throughout his life. She talked about his restless mind and his belief that technology could better lives. She never once mentioned his twin brother, Sean.

"They say the greatest pain is the loss of a child," Mrs. Alcott said, choking and then looking out at the mourners. "I can tell you, it's true."

She returned stoically to her seat.

Bree shifted in the pew, wondering if she'd made a mistake coming here, if she'd made a colossal blunder in thinking Malcomb was M, the brains behind the vigilante group Maestro. She decided that she should slip out.

The minister stood up again and said there would be a luncheon at a local country club and then asked those assembled to stand and recite the Lord's Prayer in Malcomb's memory. Bree started sliding toward the other end of her pew.

She was halfway there when the mourners said, "Amen." She

was at the end of the pew when Malcomb's aunt got up and walked down the aisle on Arthur's massive arm.

The billionaire's veiled face pivoted as she nodded to various grievers, touching a few on the forearms as she came closer and closer. She paused to stare in puzzlement at Bree for a moment, then she nodded to her and left the chapel.

Bree waited until the last mourner had left before exiting. She hoped Alcott would have departed for the country club, but no such luck.

Arthur was waiting for her in the lobby. "Mrs. Alcott would like a word, please."

In her mind, Bree heard Alex warning her about coming to the funeral uninvited. She closed her eyes a moment and then followed the big Polynesian into a small room, where the heir to the Alcott soap fortune sat alone, veil off, looking imperious.

"Why are you here, Chief Stone?" she demanded.

"Paying my respects."

"I didn't know you knew Ryan."

"We never met, but my husband knew him, used Paladin's services. He thought I should be here to represent all the law enforcement officers his algorithms helped in the past few years."

Alcott wasn't buying it. "And how did you know this service was for my nephew?"

"An article I read in the *Idaho Statesman* about his parents' murders," Bree said. "Your sister's maiden name was May. Her married name was Wheeler. I figured it out."

"Hmm," Mrs. Alcott said. "And you came all the way here."

"Actually, I was in Cleveland on business."

"With?"

"A private client," Bree said. "I'm not at liberty to say."

Mrs. Alcott gazed at Bree for several long moments, her face unreadable. "I don't believe you. What do you wish to know about my nephew?"

Bree cleared her throat. "Why didn't he keep the last name Wheeler? Why change it to Malcomb and not Alcott?"

The billionaire shrugged. "He was told in his late teens that he was not my sister's biological son, that he had been adopted from someone named Malcomb. For whatever reason, Ryan decided to use Malcomb as his last name before he went to MIT. So he'd have a completely new start where no one would know he came from a rich family, he said."

"He ever try to see if it was true? Try to track his real parents down?"

"I honestly have no idea," she said, looking annoyed. "He was a grown man. He didn't tell me everything. Anything else, Chief Stone?"

Bree figured she had nothing to lose, so she hit Alcott with a question she knew was bound to elicit a heated response. "There are some people out in Elko I've spoken to who aren't sure it was your nephew in the van. What with all the burning."

The billionaire's nostrils flared. "Some people in Elko?"

Bree said nothing. Mrs. Alcott looked more than a little disgusted. She gestured to her phone. "Arthur set a Google Alert that notifies me anytime something is published or released about Ryan's case."

Bree tried not to react, as she had done the same thing. "Okay?"

"While we were waiting for the service to begin, I got an alert," she said. "The Elko County medical examiner released the results of the DNA tests they did, confirming that it was indeed my nephew's body in that van."

Remembering the alert that she'd ignored before coming into the funeral home, Bree wanted to shrink off somewhere and hide.

"Please leave, Ms. Stone," Alcott said. "You have no more business here."

"Just one more question. Whatever happened to Sean? Ryan's twin brother."

At that, the billionaire's stoicism cracked, and Bree saw deep and genuine pain flood through. "Sean had a long history of mental illness. He blamed me, my husband, and his brother for it. When Sean was eighteen, he took his inheritance, told us he never wanted to see us again, and left."

"No contact since then?"

"We tried several times in the first year, but after that, he was in the wind as far as we were concerned."

"So you've really lost two children."

Tears formed in Mrs. Alcott's eyes and dripped down her cheeks as she nodded.

"I'm sorry," Bree said as she got to her feet. "I truly am sorry for your losses."

28

WHEN I FINALLY WOKE up, I had no idea where I was at first.

Then I heard a creak on the staircase outside my bedroom, realized I was home, and looked blearily at the clock.

I groaned. Nine a.m.

Bree wasn't in our bed, and the blackout curtains had been drawn to let me sleep.

I was about to go back to that when music started playing downstairs—Mariah Carey wailing about Christmas.

I came wide awake. It was Christmas Eve morning. I knew what that meant in the Cross household and refused to miss it.

Although Mahoney and I had landed at two a.m., I forced myself up and into the shower and let the hot water beat on my neck while the events of the prior day played in my head.

Judge Pak's girlfriend, Allie Winters, had been devastated by the news of his death. Winters, a successful artist, believed that the judge was planning to propose to her. She confirmed that he'd led a polyamorous life with his late wife but said he was done with that.

"Too much drama," she'd said. "He was ready for a conventional existence."

Pak's girlfriend also said that she'd had suspicions about his gambling problems, although she knew nothing concrete.

Then the San Francisco homicide department that had been disparaged the day before came up big. Detectives Bell and Ponce and an excellent IT officer named Sally Gable managed to trace the hippie assassin for fifteen blocks; they saw her enter an alley between row houses, and she did not come out, so they theorized she might be holed up in one of the buildings.

Mahoney, the detectives, and I walked through the alley and looked in trash bins. A soaking-wet wig of locs was buried under garbage in one. The peasant skirt and hooded raincoat were in another.

"Is there a camera at the other end of this alley?" Mahoney asked as we bagged the evidence for DNA analysis.

"I'll find out," Bell said, and called their IT wizard. After a minute, she nodded. "There is. Sally is sending over footage."

Mahoney called it up on his iPad. The camera caught the woman appearing from the alley; she turned her back and hurried away while she opened a black umbrella. We backed the footage up and froze it on our best look at her, which gave us about an eighth of her face. She wore Doc Martens boots, black tights, black jacket. Her hair was short, spiky, and blond.

"Judge Franklin's killer had hair like that," I said.

Mahoney nodded. "I say it's her. Same athletic build. But I'm not sure we've got enough of her face here to use recognition software."

"We've got her DNA on those clothes."

"We do indeed."

The fact that we had DNA on the killer bolstered our spirits on the flight home. But now, as I shaved and finished my shower, all I wanted was to set all work aside and be with my family.

I dressed in jeans, a Howard University track team hoodie, and sneakers and went down the stairs. The balsam fir was already upright in its stand in the front room, and everyone was moving in boxes of ornaments and lights. Willow trailed them with Sampson close behind.

Willow saw me and her eyes grew wide and excited. "Uncle Alex! We're going to decorate the tree now!"

"I know! I'm glad I didn't miss it!" I said, entering the front room.

Bree gave me a disapproving look. "You need sleep."

Nana Mama said, "Look at the bags under that boy's eyes."

"I'll take a nap this afternoon," I said.

"No work?" Bree said. "Promise?"

"Work doesn't exist for at least forty-eight hours."

"Good," my grandmother said. "You want eggs?"

"I'll get them myself, Nana. I just want to grab a cup of coffee and enjoy the day."

And I did.

And we did.

The simple acts of playing our favorite Christmas music, stringing the lights, and hanging familiar ornaments took me away from dead federal judges and blond assassins. Trimming the tree, listening to my kids chattering and joking, watching Willow's excitement—it all anchored me in a way I guess I needed because when we were finished, I felt deeply content and at ease.

I made good on my promise and took a long, much-needed nap. When I got up, Bree and I went for a run with Damon and Jannie; Ali led the way on his mountain bike.

We ran past the White House, admired the National Christmas Tree. Everyone we encountered was smiling and happy despite the raw wind. Before dinner, we gathered around Nana Mama for another tradition as she read us the story of the Nativity as told in the Book of Luke.

"'And there were shepherds living out in the fields nearby,'" she read, "'keeping watch over their flocks at night. An angel of the Lord appeared to them, and the glory of the Lord shone around them, and they were terrified. But the angel said to them, "Do not be afraid. I bring you good news that will cause great joy for all the people. Today in the town of David a Savior has been born to you; he is the Messiah, the Lord. This will be a sign to you: You will find a baby wrapped in cloths and lying in a manger."'"

Willow went to the carved Nativity scene that sat on the little table by the fireplace. "Like this baby?" she said.

Nana Mama smiled. "Exactly like that baby," she said. "That's what we really celebrate on Christmas, Willow. Jesus's miraculous birth."

For Christmas Eve dinner, we surprised my grandmother with steamed clams and king crab legs, her favorites. Afterward, we sang songs until Willow fell asleep in her father's arms.

The next day, Bree and I went to church early with Nana Mama and heard the story of the Nativity. Back at home, we opened presents with the kids. Willow was out of her mind with all the toys she got and all the attention showered on her, especially by Rebecca Cantrell, the U.S. attorney for Northern Virginia and Sampson's new girlfriend.

Rebecca stayed with us all day, ate roast turkey with us that evening, and proclaimed it the best Christmas she'd had in years before kissing Sampson and Willow and leaving around nine. I tried to stay awake to watch a movie the kids wanted to see, but I fell asleep during the opening credits and soon after went to bed.

After a deliciously long sleep, I awoke to find Bree dressed, sitting in a chair in the corner, and looking at me with a fretful expression on her face.

"I guess it's him, then," she said, sounding disappointed.

I sat up, blinking. "I think I'm coming in at the end of this conversation."

"We promised not to talk work for two wonderful days, but now I need to."

"Okay," I said. "Can I get some coffee?"

"Right there on your nightstand."

I looked over and saw an insulated go-cup with a thin trail of steam rising from it. "You do need to talk."

Bree nodded and spilled the details of her trip to Hunting Valley and her discussion with Theresa May Alcott.

"After hearing about the DNA report, I felt like I had zero grounds to be there," Bree said. "I felt like I'd poked someone with a stick on their worst day, and I pride myself on not being that kind of person, you know?"

"I do," I said. "And I hear and see how upset you are, but we're investigators. We ask questions at difficult times. When you went, you thought you were doing the right thing by confronting her."

"I got the same notice about the DNA results she did, but I didn't look at the Google Alert before I went in."

"Would you have done things differently if you had?"

"I don't think I would have gone inside at all. I mean, what's the point? Even if he was M, he's dead, and he kept it from her. The only person I was trying to help with my questions was me so I could prove I was right."

"How many people has Maestro killed over the years we've been chasing them?"

She shrugged. "More than a hundred."

"You don't think more than a hundred dead people played a part in your thinking? Because I know they always play a part in my mind when I'm thinking about M. Always."

"They do for me too," she admitted.

"There you go, then," I said. "You went to Cleveland with a nobler purpose, caused a little unintentional agitation in service of that purpose, and now you move on."

She shifted in her chair, her brow knitting. "And give up on identifying M?"

"Maybe give it a rest. It might help you get some perspective."

She thought about that, nodded, and came over to the bed, smiling. "Thanks."

"Anytime."

Bree bent over to give me a kiss, but my cell phone started playing Ned Mahoney's jingle before our lips could meet. "I have to answer that."

"I know," she said, drawing back. "Rain check?"

"Definitely," I said, and answered the call. "Ned?"

Mahoney said, "We've gotten a disturbing tip that we have to run down no matter the political implications."

29

BETWEEN DECEMBER 26 AND January 2, the nation's capital is usually dead. Congress is in recess, the federal agencies are operating on skeleton crews, and the president is off skiing or golfing with family somewhere.

But today, three days after the FBI received an anonymous tip on its hotline, the offices Mahoney and I entered on Capitol Hill were crowded with young people working at breakneck speed. Cell phones were ringing constantly and everyone was shouting over one another.

"Welcome to the office of President-Elect Sue Winter," said the harried woman with curly ginger hair who met us at the elevator. "And who are you again?"

"FBI, ma'am," Mahoney said.

"Oh," she said, clearly taken aback. "No one told me the FBI was coming."

"And you are?"

"Hester Little," she said, extending her hand. "I work for the transition team."

"In what capacity?" he said, shaking it.

"Assistant to the assistant director of transition personnel," she said, squinting. "I'm sorry, the person at the front desk said you were looking for a job."

"Not at this time, Ms. Little," Mahoney said, smiling at her and stepping back. "We'd like to talk with the director of transition personnel."

The assistant to the assistant director's face fell. "I'm afraid that's kind of impossible. She's meeting with the inaugural team at the moment."

"Where?"

"Here."

"Then you should go and kind of get her out of that meeting," Mahoney said, the smile fading. "This is a double-homicide investigation and the FBI's highest priority."

"Really?"

"Really."

She hurried away.

A few moments later, Ms. Little returned, apologized, and led us through a maze of desks to a conference room.

An extremely irritated-looking woman with close-cropped black hair came into the room through another door. "This better be good," she said. "I'm losing ground by the minute."

"Edward Mahoney, FBI. This is my colleague Dr. Alex Cross. We're working the murders of federal appeals court judges Franklin and Pak."

That sobered the woman. "Sorry, I'm Allegra Dennison, director of transition personnel. How can I help?"

I said, "An anonymous caller said that the incoming administration had been considering nominating Judge Franklin to the U.S. Supreme Court."

Dennison frowned. "There's no opening that I know of."

Mahoney said, "But there must be lists you keep, files of possible candidates."

"I'm sure," she said. "But we're not in the habit of discussing those with the public."

"We're not the public, Ms. Dennison," Ned said, getting that hard-ass edge to his voice again. "We're the law."

"Yes," she said, holding up her palms. "And I am not here to obstruct you in any way, Mr. Mahoney. I'll tell you that as far as I know, Judge Franklin was not on any transition-team list of possible Supreme Court appointees."

"Okay," I said. "What about Judge Pak?"

"Pak? No. He was a longtime supporter of President-Elect Sue Winter, but no."

"Supporter?"

"The president-elect knew Mrs. Pak in college and attended the Paks' wedding. Both Judge and Mrs. Pak made regular donations to her campaigns over the years."

"Huh," Mahoney said. "And that didn't get Pak on a list?"

"If it did, it has not crossed my desk," she said firmly. "I want to put this rumor to rest. The office and work of the transition team is in no way, shape, or form connected to the tragic deaths of Judge Pak and Judge Franklin."

CHAPTER

30

DECEMBER SLIPPED AWAY AND January began bitter cold for the nation's capital.

The Cross family Christmas tree came down on New Year's Day. Damon left on January 2 to see his new girlfriend in Nashville before going back to Davidson. A few days later, Jannie returned to the dorms at Howard. And not long after that, Ali's Christmas break was over.

At breakfast after dropping Ali off at school, Bree said, "I can't believe how empty the place feels with just us."

Alex nodded. "There was a whirlwind and now the calm afterward."

"I'll miss it until next Christmas," Nana Mama said.

"Wish me luck getting in," Alex said as he left.

"Getting in where?" Nana Mama asked Bree.

"The office of President-Elect Sue Winter," Bree said. "He and Ned spoke to her transition team about something and got nowhere, but they realized that there were more parts to the incoming administration, like the inauguration team and the permanent team that will eventually surround the president in the White House. That's who they're trying to talk to."

"Sounds complicated," Nana Mama said.

"It's not my cup of tea either."

"Going to work over at Bluestone today?"

"Alex said I can use his attic office, so I'm going to stick around and get a few things done without distractions."

After cleaning the kitchen for Alex's grandmother, Bree got her laptop and climbed the stairs to Alex's hideaway. He had a nicer office in the basement where he saw patients from time to time, but Bree liked the attic office more. Wood interior. Slanted roof that made you duck. A sturdy, wooden desk with neat stacks of files. Dozens of cardboard boxes crammed with the relics of his early investigations. And it smelled like Alex.

That made Bree smile. She turned on the light, shut the door, sat down at her computer, and spent some productive time answering emails from clients and finishing a report on her most recent assignment, a missing person who had sadly been identified as a plane crash victim.

She knew she should do some background reading on a case of possible corporate fraud her boss had asked her to look into, but instead, she sat there trying unsuccessfully to suppress a worm that kept invading her thoughts.

Okay, he's dead. But that does not mean he wasn't M.

Telling herself that it had been over a week since she'd

obsessed about M and Maestro, she decided to give herself thirty minutes, an hour, tops, to review the case, looking for loose threads that might give her a different angle.

She scrolled through her files, saw a note she'd left for herself to find out why Ryan Wheeler had become Ryan Malcomb instead of Ryan Alcott. His aunt had tried to explain, but it still struck Bree as a little odd, the way the billionaire had pleaded ignorance and reacted dismissively when asked if her nephew had ever tried to track down his biological parents.

But was *she being dismissive? Or was she trying to make me lose interest?*

And what about Sean Wheeler? What had become of him?

Bree started to dig around in Idaho's online court system. She found records—likely falsified—showing Ryan and Sean Wheeler had been born at home with the Wheelers listed as parents. Not long after, she found a filing in Boise in which eighteen-year-old Ryan Wheeler had petitioned to have his birth name, Ryan Felix Malcomb, reinstated. Bree muttered to herself, "That helps. But why do it in Idaho? Unless he was actually born in Idaho?"

She started digging into Ancestry.com, then stopped. She went back to the Idaho court records and searched for Ryan Felix Malcomb.

Almost immediately, up popped a reference to a filing in a Latah County, Idaho, court petitioning the judge to open the adoption records of Ryan Felix Malcomb. The petition was approved when Malcomb was twenty-one.

Bree tried to open the file but was halted by a digital seal that had been requested by Ryan Felix Malcomb shortly afterward. She felt thwarted. Why unseal and then almost immediately reseal?

Because he didn't like what he found?

Bree felt that was a fair bet, but without access to the file, what good was it? She was about to move on when she noticed that the unsealing petition and the resealing petition had been filed by two different attorneys.

The unsealing petition had been filed by a Moscow, Idaho, lawyer. The resealing petition had been written and filed by a counselor from Salmon, Idaho.

She looked up the Salmon attorney and found an obituary from nearly ten years before. Why Salmon?

Bree went to the Ancestry.com birth records and typed in *Ryan Felix Malcomb Idaho.*

She got a hodgepodge of references to various Felixes and Malcombs but couldn't find the one she was looking for until she added *Salmon* to the search.

Soon a birth certificate appeared on the screen, and Bree smiled. "There you are. And that birth date looks on the money. Your dad was William Malcomb, seventeen, and your mom was Lucille Wallace, sixteen."

He had changed his last name to his biological father's.

Why?

She checked her watch, saw it was almost noon. She'd spent close to three hours looking into Malcomb, and she told herself to stop. She had to start working on the corporate-fraud investigation.

Bree meant to save Malcomb's birth certificate to her Ancestry.com folder but accidentally scrolled up to the next birth certificate in chronological order.

She stared at it and saw links to other documents. She clicked on several; the implications dawned on her slowly at first and then very, very fast.

Bree stood up and pumped her fist. Feeling vindicated, she whispered, "That, my friend, changes the story! That flips everything on its head!"

CHAPTER

31

I GOT HOME THAT evening feeling like we were being stalled by the Office of the President-Elect staffers.

Ned Mahoney and I had been told we had an appointment with Matthew Shearson, the personnel director for the incoming administration. But when we arrived, we were informed that Shearson had gone to Arizona with the president-elect and would not be available for two days.

Mahoney demanded to see someone higher up the food chain but was told that the entire senior staff had gone to Tucson with Shearson and President-Elect Sue Winter for an intensive work retreat before the inauguration preparations. Ned called the acting FBI director after we left, and she told us she would put pressure on Shearson to call us at his earliest opportunity.

We hadn't heard a thing since.

The frustration must have shown on my face when I entered the kitchen because Bree immediately came over and hugged me.

"Rough day?"

"If you call a state of inertia rough, yeah."

"Sit down. Ali and I are making tacos."

I noticed my youngest child stirring shredded chicken in a pan. "Smells good," I said.

Ali grinned. "I put the spices in. Well, Nana told me which ones."

"Where is Nana?"

"Right here," she said, coming in and yawning. "Sorry, I just did another one of those AP English lectures online and they wipe me out."

"But they do those kids a lot of good," I said.

"And they still wipe me out," she said, taking a seat at the table. "You have to have a lot of energy to keep their attention, and I have only so much these days."

"What did you teach?"

"*Invisible Man* by Ralph Ellison," she said.

John Sampson came in with Willow, which surprised me because they'd moved back into their home after the gas leak was fixed.

"I invited them for tacos," Bree explained. "I want to show you and John something later."

We spent dinner discussing *Invisible Man*, the story of an educated Black man in the 1950s struggling in a racially divided country that refused to see him as a full human being.

Nana Mama pushed away her plate and yawned. "Unfortunately, the story is as pertinent today as it was when it was published more than seventy years ago. This old lady is going to watch a little television and then it's lights out and toes up!"

"Willow and I will come with you, Nana," Ali said, grinning. "I don't have to do dishes because I cooked."

"Well, lucky you!" she said and got up. "Do you both want Nana's brownies?"

Willow nodded excitedly. "Yes, please, Nana."

"With vanilla ice cream," Ali said.

"After all those tacos?" I asked.

"Always," Ali said.

Sampson and I cleaned up while my grandmother got Willow and Ali brownies with vanilla ice cream, then led them off to the front room. As soon as they were gone, Bree went and grabbed a manila folder.

"I found something today that reminded me to expect the unexpected at every turn."

She opened the folder and showed us printouts of various documents from Idaho court records and Ancestry.com.

"I thought you were taking a break from Ryan Malcomb," I said.

"I was. I did," she said. "More than a week. You were right. It gave me a new perspective. Just look."

Sampson was turning the pages. "Malcomb was adopted. Tried to find his real parents."

"And then he had the adoption files resealed?" I said, reading over his shoulder. "How did he get that done?"

"Money under the table," Bree said. "Had to be."

Sampson turned another page. "The birth certificate for Ryan Felix Malcomb. No doubt about where he came from now."

"Salmon, Idaho?" I asked.

"Yes," Bree said, grinning like Willow had in anticipation of dessert. "Now look at the next one."

John turned another page in the file.

We both stared at it.

Sampson whistled.

"Right?" Bree said.

"Sean Malcomb Wallace," I said. "Is that the brother?"

"Different name, but definitely the twin. Took the last name of the mom's family, I guess. But look closely at the page that follows. The DNA tests."

We did. I didn't quite understand it until I saw a notice below each one: *You have an identical twin in the database.*

At that point I got confused. I looked up at Bree. "But you've known about Ryan's twin for quite a while now."

"Alex," she said impatiently, "think of it another way. They are, or were, genetic copies of each other. All the evidence says Ryan Malcomb died in that crash outside Elko—the ID, the vehicle, even the DNA. But now there's doubt."

Sampson nodded, starting to smile. "You think Sean Malcomb was in that vehicle and not Ryan."

"If they were identical twins, sharing the exact same DNA, then I think it's possible, especially with someone as nefarious as M."

"So, what? Did Ryan take on Sean's persona?" I asked. "If so, where is he?"

"I'm still looking under every name he might have used."

Sampson said, "What about the parents of the twins? Ryan might have contacted them after getting the papers unsealed. Or Sean might've."

Bree brightened. "That's an angle I didn't consider. I mean, you're right—if they're alive, they just might know what became of Sean Malcomb Wallace."

CHAPTER

32

Athens, Georgia

PROFESSOR NATHAN CARVER OF the University of Georgia School of Law finished up a lecture on the separation of powers in the U.S. Constitution. Forty-five, a full-blooded American Indian, and a stirring speaker, Carver engaged with several inspired students afterward, then excused himself. He had to meet an old and dear friend for dinner.

The professor hurried to an off-campus bistro, where Elaine Holmes, a fellow graduate of the law school and a very successful attorney in Washington, DC, was waiting.

"Elaine, you look fantastic!" Carver said after giving her a kiss on each cheek.

"It's a miracle what makeup and a good dye job can do these days," she said. "But look at you! You've lost weight!"

"Twenty-five pounds since the divorce," he said proudly.

"And I've gained five since mine," Holmes said. "Dating anyone?"

"Tried a couple of times. I don't think I'm ready yet."

"My three attempts have been nightmares. Did you know men put up fake photos of themselves on dating sites as often as women?"

"I can't imagine," Carver said, laughing.

Faking a shudder, Holmes said, "I don't have to. I saw them in the flesh."

They shared a bottle of wine and ate dinner, caught up on each other's lives. Though she was paid insanely well, Holmes had grown to hate her job and was itching for something new.

"I still love my job…" Carver said.

"Why do I sense a *but* coming?" Holmes asked.

"Just a little nonsense I can't talk about at the moment."

"Nonsense?"

"Something that is extremely unlikely to happen, hence it's nonsense."

"You'll tell me if it proves more than that?"

Carver cocked his head at her and smiled. "Actually, you'll be the first to know."

The professor felt a nice little tension between them, a little spark, especially when she asked if he was interested in a nightcap at one of their favorite hangouts as students. But then he remembered how raw he'd felt when his ex-wife had followed through on the little tension, the little spark, and their marriage had come apart.

"I'm good for tonight, Elaine," he said. "Early classes."

She nodded a little sadly. "I understand. You get up to DC, you call me."

"I'm coming next week, as a matter of fact," he said. "I'll text you the particulars. I'd love to get together. I had fun tonight."

"I did too," she said, brightening. "We'll go out to one of my favorite spots."

They hugged a little too long on the sidewalk, had an awkward peck of a kiss, and promised they'd see each other next week.

Carver walked home beneath leafless oaks feeling pleasantly drunk and better about his personal life than he had in a long time. *Elaine Holmes. Who would have thought? Well, why not? She's smart as hell. Good-looking. Funny. Single. And I'm not a bad catch.*

He felt a little dizzy and in need of water and sleep as he turned onto the quiet street a few blocks from campus where he lived. It was well past eleven. Many of the brick homes were dark. The sidewalks were empty.

As he walked up his driveway, he heard a car door open and shut behind him on the other side of the street.

He didn't turn because he was thinking, *I could do a lot worse than Elaine Holmes. And I could not do much better. Or any better.*

Carver felt a little goofy inside, a good goofy. He thought, *I wonder if I should text her something before I go to—*

"Professor Carver," a woman said in a thick accent.

He frowned and felt a little wobbly as he turned to find a woman in her thirties, short blond hair, wearing jeans and a dark hoodie. She was standing about twenty feet away.

"I'm sorry," he said. "Do I—"

She said something, raised a suppressed pistol, and fired two shots.

33

THE MORNING AFTER BREE told us what she'd discovered, she, Nana Mama, and I were having breakfast in the kitchen when John Sampson came by.

He poured himself a cup of coffee and said, "I think we owe it to ourselves to go to Nevada, Bree. I think there's something there."

Nana Mama said, "Vegas?"

"Elko," Sampson said. "Northern Nevada. And then Salmon, Idaho."

"Sounds cold, and I'm already cold," my grandmother said and drew the lapels of her quilted day coat tighter.

Bree looked at me. I held up my hands. "I've got a full plate with the appellate judges' murders."

"I know you do," she said. "I also think John's right. There's something out there."

JAMES PATTERSON

"Why not go? What's the issue?"

"Work and the fact I got very little out of going to Cleveland."

Sampson said, "Get time off. Forget Cleveland."

"What about Willow?" I asked.

"Billie's daughter is coming down from Philadelphia to look after her baby sister."

"So you were planning on going even before you got here?" Bree said.

He nodded. "I figured you would go, and there was no way you were going in search of M's origins without me, so I talked to the chief. He's giving me time off without pay."

Bree smiled. "So there was more kale in the old Crock-Pot."

"Scraping the bottom, but yeah."

I said, "It's settled, then. When are you going?"

"ASAP," Sampson said. "Before the trail gets colder."

Bree pulled out her laptop and she and John were looking for flights to Reno when Ned Mahoney knocked and immediately rushed in. "What's wrong with your phone, Alex? I've been calling for the last twenty minutes."

Frowning, I checked my phone. "I had it on Do Not Disturb."

"Let's go," he said. "The head of personnel for the transition team called me. Wants to see us straightaway."

After we all promised to keep each other posted on our whereabouts, Bree and Sampson went back to finding flights, and Ned and I headed to his car. Fifteen minutes later, we were being shown into the offices of a distraught Allegra Dennison.

"I wanted to tell you this in person," Dennison said, closing the door. "I was wrong the other day. Judge Franklin apparently was being vetted. But not by us. Not by the transition team."

"By people in the Office of the President-Elect?" Mahoney said, sitting forward.

She shook her head. "By a group of private advisers to President-Elect Winter. Big donors. Many with law backgrounds. They were evidently charged with creating a short list of possible nominees for Winter to consider if a Supreme Court seat opened up."

"Is that unusual?" I asked. "To have that kind of group?"

"Absolutely not," Dennison said. "These kinds of teams are put together whenever an incoming administration prepares to take office. They've got panels vetting people for all the cabinet and West Wing positions as well."

"Why didn't the staffers in the Office of the President-Elect tell us this?" Mahoney said, his frustration showing.

"I can't answer that. But as I understand it, the panels are supposed to be informal, a way to let big donors make recommendations and feel involved while the final decisions are made elsewhere."

I said, "Okay, so how do you know Franklin was on the list?"

"A friend of mine who's working with the group mentioned it."

"Who else was on that list? Judge Pak?"

"I don't know."

"We need your friend's name and the names of others on that team."

"Geneva Roche at the Trafalgar Group on K Street. She'd know them all."

34

WE REACHED THE TONY offices of the Trafalgar Group around ten that morning, presented our credentials, and asked to see Geneva Roche.

Roche, a sharp and well-put-together brunette in her forties, came right out to greet us. "I had a feeling I'd be hearing from someone in your organization," she said. She led us into her huge office and shut the door.

Mahoney got right to it. "We were told the late Judge Franklin was on a short list of possible Supreme Court candidates."

Roche made a sour face. "I would not call it a short list."

I said, "What would you call it?"

"An endlessly revised long list. It changes daily at this point and will throughout the administration." Roche explained that she had worked in the White House two presidents ago, and lists of possible candidates for various appointments were constantly evolving and being updated.

Mahoney said, "Was Judge Bitgaram Pak of the Ninth Circuit ever on that constantly evolving list?"

Roche raised an eyebrow. "Yes. The president-elect knew Pak. She had him put on the list right after she clinched the nomination so we could dig in quickly."

"And?"

"An investigation was ongoing, but he was high on the list. Top five."

I realized she did not know about the unconventional sex life and the gambling but said nothing. "How high on the list was Judge Franklin?"

"Top five."

Mahoney said, "You don't find it odd that two people on that list have recently been murdered?"

Roche swallowed. "Two, I found a little odd. Given where Judge Pak lived, you could see it happening. Not Judge Franklin, though. And certainly not Nathan Carver. So three—I find that *very* odd."

We both shot forward.

Ned said, "What do you mean, three?"

I said, "And who's Nathan Carver?"

She looked at us incredulously. "Professor of constitutional law at the University of Georgia. He was shot outside his house last night. I thought you knew."

"We do now," I said, reeling as I considered the implications. "And Professor Carver was on this list of recommended candidates?"

"Our number one, as a matter of fact."

"We need the list and we need to know the groups that have access to it," Mahoney said.

Roche thought a moment, then named the president-elect's office, the vice president–elect's office, the incoming attorney general's staff, and the advisory panel itself.

"But these lists do float around a fair bit. Names are mentioned, debated. The group gets feedback and then vets the information. The order of preference changes. Like I said, at this point, it's all fluid."

"Whatever," Mahoney said. "I need the names of everyone on that advisory panel."

Roche shifted uncomfortably. "These are the kinds of people who prefer to stay in the background. And I know them. They would not be involved in —"

"Look, we'd let them stay in the background if three potential nominees to the Supreme Court hadn't been murdered. The names, please."

Roche wasn't happy, but she turned to her computer and printed out a list of fifteen names. We recognized many of them — big-time donors and supporters of the president-elect, titans of industry, law, finance, and Hollywood.

But it was the last name on the list that stopped us cold.

35

BREE AND SAMPSON BOARDED a United flight to Denver; there, they would pick up a jet to Reno.

They sat next to each other on an exit row the flight attendant gave to Sampson because of his height. Bree tried to call Alex, but it went straight to voice mail and he wasn't answering texts.

"He and Ned must be onto something," Bree said, putting her phone in airplane mode.

"Doesn't surprise me," Sampson said. "Those two are like hounds when they're together." He said it with a little wistfulness.

"You miss working with him full-time. With Alex, I mean," she said.

Sampson shrugged. "We'll work together again soon. I'm sure of it."

"I am too. And I'm glad you're coming with me."

"I thought *you* were coming with *me*."

Once the plane was airborne, Bree noticed how pensive Sampson was. "M?" she said.

John nodded, a cruel expression appearing on his face. "When he taunted me about Billie's death, said he'd killed her so I had to go through the nightmare of having her exhumed, I swore that I would not stop until I had this guy in my sights."

"I remember," she said. "And I feel the same way. One hundred percent. If there's something there in Nevada, we'll find it."

He nodded without looking at her. "I need to find it."

Bree felt the urge to change the subject. "How's Rebecca these days?"

His tight jaw loosened, and a smile came to his lips. "She's busy but good. We talk almost every night and try to see each other on the weekends when she can spend time with Willow."

"And Willow likes her?"

"Adores her," Sampson said. "Says I should keep dating her."

Bree laughed. "You *should* keep dating her."

"No argument there."

"No, I mean, don't make it entirely about the three of you—you, Willow, and Rebecca—even though that is very, very important."

Sampson's jaw tightened again. "Okay?"

"I'm saying keep the romance going," she said. "You're at the very beginning of a relationship, John. You have to feed the romance, and to do that you have to find time to be alone, and you have to be, well, creative."

"Creative?"

"Surprise her with something thoughtful or playful. It doesn't have to be much. Just enough to say, 'I see you. I hear you. I was thinking about you.'"

"I say that?"

"No, your gesture does. But that's your intent."

"Oh," Sampson said, clearly puzzled. "I'm going to have to think on that."

He was quiet for much of the rest of the flight. Bree tried to work on the corporate-fraud case but fell asleep. When she woke up, he was busy writing in a notebook. He finished up and put the notebook away.

"Took your advice," he said.

"How's that?"

"You know, being creative with Rebecca. I wrote her a little love letter. I'll get an envelope and a stamp and mail it in the morning."

"Good for you," Bree said and giggled. "A love letter? From John Sampson? My, how times have changed."

He laughed. "Happens to the best of us. Especially when we get good advice."

It was snowing in Denver when they landed. Their flight to Reno was delayed by five hours.

She finally got Alex on the phone around eleven o'clock his time. "You picked up!" she said.

"Crazy day," Alex said, shouting to be heard over the sound of a jet engine. "I'm sorry. We just landed in Athens, Georgia."

"Athens?"

He told her about the recently murdered Professor Nathan Carver being on a list of possible Supreme Court nominees along with Judge Franklin and Judge Pak.

"Guess who's a part of the panel that came up with the list?" he said.

"You got me."

"Theresa May Alcott."

Bree shook her head. "Really? Is that a coincidence?"

"Ned seems to think so," Alex said. "He said it would be stranger if someone with that kind of financial and political clout *weren't* on the panel."

"I'm not buying that."

"Neither am I. It feels off. Like we're working two sides of the same story."

"No proof of that yet, even if Alcott's on that panel," Bree said. "Have they alerted the other people on the list that they might be in danger?"

"Mahoney made it his first priority," Alex said, his cell phone crackling. "Before we caught our flight south, he assigned agents to protect everyone on the list and investigators to look at everyone who had access to it."

Sampson was gesturing to her. "We're finally boarding for Reno," she said.

"I'll talk to you tomorrow?"

"In the evening," she said. "Love you."

"Love you too. Tell John good hunting."

36

BREE AND SAMPSON WERE up before sunrise and left Reno, Sampson driving, heading east on I-80 in a white Jeep Cherokee they'd rented at the airport. Several hours later, they switched, and Sampson drank gas-station coffee while Bree drove into a glary winter sun.

"I should have bought a protein bar or something back there," she said.

"I have one, I think," Sampson said, reaching into his pack. He rummaged around in it. "What's this doing here?"

Bree glanced at something in his hand. "What?"

"Willow's little Jiobit, the GPS beacon I used to keep track of her in Disney World."

"Maybe your little girl's trying to keep track of you," she said.

Chuckling, John dropped the fob back in the pack, found a Clif Bar, and handed it to Bree.

She took a few bites, washed it down with water, and looked out to her left across a high desert landscape with peaks beyond. "Look at that!" she said. "Those mountains out there with the snow dusting the top. You don't see that in DC."

"I think I said something like that when Alex and I rode on horseback into the Bob Marshall Wilderness," Sampson said, craning his neck to see the mountains and smiling. "I think we'll go up into something like that to see the ranch Malcomb wanted."

"Oh," she said. "I don't think I brought boots."

"Neither did I," he said.

They refueled and bought insulated rubber boots in Elko before heading north up Nevada 225 toward the Independence Mountains. Both of them wanted to see where Ryan Malcomb had died before they did anything else.

Shortly after noon, they turned off the highway and headed west through dry, rugged sagebrush terrain toward the trees and the edge of the national forest, where the road became a series of tortuous switchbacks. They encountered no one else.

When they got above four thousand feet, flurries fell. At forty-five hundred feet, the road was covered in an inch of snow, and Sampson put the Jeep in four-wheel drive.

"There it is," Bree said. "Has to be." She pointed to a steel guardrail that was badly bent. Seeing no one behind him, Samson pulled over and parked.

They got out, went to the rail, and looked over. Far below, they could see the burned skeleton of the van Ryan Malcomb had been driving.

"They should have brought that up," Bree said.

"How?" Sampson said. "A construction helicopter?"

"Why not?"

"Cost, I'd imagine. But what do I know?"

"Should we keep going up?" Bree said. "See this ranch he was all hot to buy?"

"We've got the boots. Might as well use them."

By the time they reached the locked gate to the Double T Ranch, the snow was falling steadily; it was already five inches deep. They got out and saw no tracks on the other side of the gate. Signs flanking it read NO TRESPASSING. Sampson ignored them and started climbing the gate.

"John?" Bree said.

"I've come a long way," he said. He straddled the top and then jumped down to the other side. "We haven't seen anyone since we left the highway. I'm going to see why Malcomb was so interested in this place, and the snow will cover my tracks."

Bree debated with herself and then followed him. They trudged up a two-track lane through stands of pine.

A mile in, they emerged into a spectacular series of alpine meadows surrounded by forested ridges frosted in the snow. In the distance, they saw a big log house.

No lights were on. No smoke curled from the massive stone chimney.

Bree said, "You can see why someone with as much money as Malcomb would want to own something like this."

"Maybe," Sampson said. "But maybe it was just a cover. I mean, c'mon, the guy was in a wheelchair most of the time. How would he enjoy this?"

"I don't know. A big ATV?"

"Could be," he said. "Let's go to Elko and ask questions."

They started back through the thick stands of pines, and when they rounded the first corner, a grizzled creature of a man stood there.

He ran the action on his pump shotgun, snapped it to his shoulder, and aimed right at them.

37

BREE AND SAMPSON THREW up their hands.

"Who are you and what the hell are you doing here?" he demanded.

"I'm a homicide detective," Sampson said. "Washington, DC, Metro."

"And I'm a private investigator and former chief of homicide at DC Metro," Bree said. "We're looking into the death of Ryan Malcomb. We heard he was interested in buying this ranch."

"And you figured you could ignore the signs telling you not to trespass because of that?"

"I admit it was a moron move," Sampson said. "We just wanted to see why Malcomb was interested in owning a place like this."

"Sheer beauty, maybe?" the man said.

"We saw that," Bree said. "Can you lower the gun, sir? We are unarmed."

He hesitated, then lowered the shotgun. He pivoted away from them and racked the shell out of the chamber. He turned back and said somewhat sarcastically, "What's there to investigate? It was officially an accident. Read the report myself."

"Your name?" Sampson said, holding out his hand.

"Eldon," he said. He removed his mitten and shook Sampson's hand. "Eldon Boyt."

Bree said, "You the caretaker, Mr. Boyt?"

He nodded. "I look in on the place for the owners."

"Brazilians."

"Correct."

Sampson said, "You've met them? The Brazilians?"

"Never had the pleasure," Boyt said. "Absentee owners."

"Did you meet Ryan Malcomb when he flew in here to see the ranch?"

He shook his head. "I was over in Denver. My mom's been sick."

Bree said, "Why do I get the sense that you're skeptical of the accident ruling?"

He squinted at her. "You work for an insurance company these days?"

"Something like that."

After a moment of hesitation, he said, "Follow me."

Boyt limped back down the snowed-over two-track road and put in a code to open the gate. He got in an old red Ford F-250 parked by their Jeep, led them back down the mountain, and parked just shy of where Malcomb's van had gone over the guardrail.

The caretaker got out and retrieved an aluminum snow shovel from the back of the pickup. He shoveled and carefully scraped up several inches of snow, from the impact point at the rail back into the road, revealing thick skid marks arcing from the right lane to the left.

Boyt said, "I used to drive a tow truck out of Elko. We had all the interstate chaos. You see enough pileups, you know that for someone to lay down rubber this thick, he's gotta be driving like a bat out of hell before he hits the brakes to avoid whatever he was trying to avoid."

"What was Malcomb trying to avoid?" Sampson asked. "An animal?"

"The only animals that can move up and down something this sheer are mountain goats and wild sheep, and neither live in this range."

"A rock broke free of the cliff and landed here?" Bree asked.

"If there was one, it wasn't mentioned in the report. It just says he must have been traveling at an excessive speed, lost control somehow, and hit the rail. But look at the skids. To me, it says he was avoiding something big that was sitting right here, blocking the lanes."

"Like a vehicle?" she asked, trying to see it in her head.

"Now you're thinking," Boyt said. "Like a vehicle parked sideways."

CHAPTER

38

Athens, Georgia

AT ELEVEN O'CLOCK THAT morning, Ned Mahoney and I were getting ready to search the office of the late Professor Nathan Carver; we were joined by the dean of the law school, the chief of campus police, three FBI agents from Atlanta, and two local homicide detectives.

"We're going in there first," said one of the detectives, a young, short powerlifter named Donny Forbes. His partner, Keely Warren, towered over him.

"Fat chance," Mahoney said. "This is a federal investigation into the deaths of multiple people across multiple state lines. Have you gone house to house in the neighborhood?"

"Yesterday," Detective Warren said defensively. "No one saw or heard anything. People across the street weren't even home. We spoke with a friend Carver had dinner with the night he was killed. Elaine Holmes. From DC. She's devastated."

"You get any security video?"

Forbes flushed and clenched his hands. "Not yet. Like Detective Warren said, the people across the street weren't home, and they won't be back until this afternoon."

"But they have a camera?"

"I think so. One of those doorbell things."

"What about after Carver left the restaurant? Anyone follow him?"

Warren said, "That was top of our list for this morning."

"Let's keep it that way," Mahoney said. "We'll handle the search here."

Forbes looked like he wanted to argue, but Warren walked off and he followed her. Mahoney asked the dean to open the door.

Professor Carver's personal workspace was spare and neatly arranged. A single file sat on one side of his desktop computer, a slender leather folio on the other side.

The file contained drafts of a paper he was writing. The folio held a copy of the first public printing of the U.S. Constitution and the Bill of Rights inside a plastic sleeve.

"He loved that," said Anne Banks, the dean of the law school, misting up when she saw the document. "That folio copy was Nathan's most prized possession. He called it his 'certificate of freedom' and he argued endlessly over the meaning of every word the Founders wrote."

As they searched, Dean Banks described the late law professor as a tireless writer and teacher who received excellent reviews from the students. Time and again, Carver had been offered positions of power in the judiciary. "He always declined," Banks said.

"Did you know he was being vetted as a possible U.S. Supreme Court candidate?"

The dean nodded. "I was told by someone working for an

advisory panel to Winter. I have her name somewhere. I was supposed to be quiet and discreet in my responses."

Mahoney raised his eyebrows. "What did you say about Carver?"

"That Nathan's understanding of constitutional law was unparalleled and that he would make a fine centrist justice, an asset to the court."

I said, "And did Carver know he was being considered?"

"Not until last month. After the election, someone on the advisory panel called him."

"Who?"

"I can't remember. I'm horrible at names. She owns a big soap company."

An out-of-sync gear suddenly snapped into place. "Theresa May Alcott?"

"That's her," Dean Banks said. "Nathan said she was very nice. Very gracious."

Mahoney said, "What did they talk about?"

"It was short and sweet. She said he was under serious consideration, and if he was interested, she invited him to come to Washington next week for a sit-down with other members of the advisory group."

"Was he interested?"

"To my surprise, yes. More than interested. But then again, he'd just gone through a nasty divorce, so why not?"

"How nasty?" I asked.

"Even though the divorce was her idea, Sheila made every step of the process an unnecessary ordeal."

"Is there any way she's the killer?"

Dean Banks shook her head. "Sheila was always squeamish around guns. She hated that Nathan was a hunter. And she left a year ago, moved to Seattle."

Mahoney took notes. "Did you have anything negative to tell the panel?"

"No," Banks said.

"No skeletons in his closet?"

"If there were, I never heard of them, and I've known Nathan for twenty-five years."

I looked at Mahoney. "I'll call Roche."

I went into the hall and phoned Roche. She answered on the second ring.

"How can I help, Dr. Cross?"

"You said Nathan Carver had been at the top of your list."

"He would have been the first American Indian justice, and I think the president-elect would have given him serious consideration if a seat on the court opened up."

"We forgot to ask you if the panel found anything negative about him during the vetting process."

"Nothing to disqualify him. He drank, but never to excess. He was passionate about his students but never lecherous. He was a fitness nut, if that's a negative. And he liked to hunt. Deer mostly, and usually with a bow. But he owned guns and believed in the Second Amendment, although with limits."

"On guns."

"Correct. I believe he was in favor of restricting the size of magazines."

"We heard Theresa May Alcott called Nathan Carver to tell him he was under consideration and invite him to Washington."

"Was Mrs. Alcott the one? It's hard to keep track. They all got to do it with various candidates. One of the fun perks of a volunteer job."

"Did she notify Pak or Franklin?"

"No," she said. "I know that for a fact."

"And Carver was supposed to fly up next week to meet the panel?"

"Quite possible," she said. "Honestly, I've been busy with my work and prepping for the inauguration since Christmas, so I haven't been keeping a close eye on all the comings and goings of the advisory panels."

"Especially since the possible candidates are always changing."

"Exactly why it's not always at the top of my to-do list. But one of my top to-dos today is to meet with a new client, and that new client is here, I'm afraid."

I thanked her and hung up as Mahoney rushed out of Carver's office.

"Pigs are flying," he said. "Detectives Forbes and Warren say they may have the entire shooting on that doorbell camera."

CHAPTER

39

Independence Mountains, Northern Nevada

BREE AND SAMPSON TOOK multiple photographs of the skid marks on the road where Ryan Malcomb's van had flipped into the canyon.

Eldon Boyt, the caretaker of the ranch Malcomb had been visiting, called them over to the bent guardrail and gestured at the snow-covered hulk of the van several hundred feet below.

"I climbed down there the other day," Boyt said. "It's scorched but not burned to hell the way it would have been with a full tank of gas."

"Okay?" Bree said.

Boyt popped a stick of gum in his mouth, chewed a few times. "I know the guy was from back east and all. But most people don't drive into mountains this rough with only about a quarter tank aboard."

"Not a mountain boy," Sampson said. "Maybe he forgot to fill up."

Boyt said, "Or maybe someone put just enough gas in the tank to burn the body beyond recognition."

"But not beyond DNA identification," Bree said.

They thanked Boyt for the information, drove back to Elko, and arrived at the county sheriff's office shortly after four in the afternoon. They identified themselves and asked to see Deputy Patty Rogers about Ryan Malcomb's case.

Deputy Rogers, a big brunette in her late thirties, met them at the front desk a few moments later, visibly irritated. "What are you doing here?" she said. "I told you it was an accident."

"We looked at the skid marks up on that road," Sampson said. "They don't add up to an accident."

"Oh, really?" she said, hands on her hips. "I've been investigating auto accidents for ten years. How about you?"

"Washington, DC, homicide detective for twenty. I know a thing or two about physics and skid marks."

"Look, what is it that you think happened?" Rogers said.

On the ride down to Elko, Bree and Sampson had decided to lay their cards on the table if necessary.

Bree said, "For the past few years, along with the FBI, we have been investigating a vigilante group known as Maestro. It's run by a mysterious guy known only as M. We have recently come to suspect that Malcomb was involved in Maestro."

"And maybe was M himself," John added.

Rogers looked at them suspiciously. "And, what, you think this Maestro group somehow turned on Ryan Malcomb and killed him?"

"Maybe," Bree said. "If that was even Malcomb in the wreckage."

The deputy snorted. "Who the hell else could it have been? DNA does not lie."

"Ryan Malcomb had an identical twin with identical DNA," Bree said.

"Okay, now, that's interesting," Rogers allowed. "But I suspect they did not have the same dental records."

Bree's heart sank a little. "They have a match on dental?"

"As I understand it," Rogers said. "But check with Dr. Bevan, the ME. And I know he confirmed that Mr. Malcomb had a high level of alcohol in his system."

"We'll do that," Sampson said.

"Dr. Bevan works out of the hospital," the deputy said, reaching out to shake their hands. "Let me know what he says. In the meantime, I need to check in with my sergeant, get out on patrol, and wait for the next accident investigation."

Rogers winked at them and wished them well. They left, and she watched out the window to identify their vehicle, then got what she needed from her locker, pocketed it, and walked to her cruiser.

Inside, windows up, air conditioner on, she took out a burner phone she had never used and dialed a number she had never called.

On the third ring, someone picked up. No hello.

"Is this the sweeper?" she asked.

"Janitorial services. Yes."

"They said to call on this phone if there was ever a problem."

"Is there?"

"I'd say so," Rogers replied. "A big one."

CHAPTER

40

YOU LIVE LONG ENOUGH, you practice your trade long enough, and you develop skills that help define your identity. Playing the piano, say. Or blacksmithing Damascus-steel knives. Or cleaning up when a mess has been made.

Brian Toomey had all three of those skills, but for the last, he went beyond mere competence; he transcended tradecraft and produced art. Toomey was, in his own modest estimation, one of the best janitors in the world. He was certainly among the highest paid.

The moment he hung up with the sheriff's deputy, the janitor went into motion. Toomey grabbed his computer and his packed go bag off the second bed in the Airbnb where he'd been patiently waiting. He left behind everything else, which wasn't much.

Toomey got in a drab green Toyota Tundra with Utah plates

and started driving as he dug in the bottom pouch of the pack. Within minutes, he was cruising through the parking lots surrounding Northeastern Nevada Regional Hospital in Elko. He found the white Jeep Cherokee rental the deputy had described near the emergency department entrance.

Toomey threw his truck in park, went to the Cherokee, looked around, and pressed a magnetic GPS beacon to the inside of the rear bumper. Then he walked to the passenger side and took out an oval translucent sticker microphone with a hair-thin wire attached to a dull black transmitter that was smaller than a fingernail.

The janitor peeled the paper off the microphone's adhesive, used a box cutter to raise the windshield's weather stripping, slid the wire and transmitter beneath it, and pressed the stripping down hard.

He was back in the Tundra less than forty seconds after he'd left it. He drove in a loop through the lot, parked in a spot where he could watch both exits, and got out his laptop.

The janitor activated his personal hot spot, navigated to a private browser, signed into a website that further concealed his IP address, and made a phone call. He listened as the line rang, clicked as it was transferred, and rang again.

After four transfers, a woman answered.

"It's the janitorial service in Elko," he said.

"Unanticipated complications?"

"Yes," Toomey said, and gave her the gist of the situation. After several moments she said, "How much do they know?"

"Only the birth date and birthplace at this point."

"Their present location?"

"With the coroner here in Elko, checking autopsy reports."

"They won't find anything there we don't want them to find."

"Good. I have a tracer on their vehicle and an audio bug."

"Smart."

"That's what you pay me for. Deep-cleaning, then?"

There was a pause. "You said one is an active-duty cop?"

"Sampson is with DC homicide. Stone is private."

"Hold on while I seek guidance."

Toomey got his 8x42 Leica binoculars from his go bag and looked across the parking lot to make sure the Cherokee was still there.

His contact returned. "You didn't say Stone was married to Alex Cross."

"Didn't know and don't know him."

"FBI and police consultant. Very dangerous. He used to be Sampson's partner."

"You still want my services?"

"Affirmative. Just maintain contact for now but remain ready to sweep up. And we will fly the Utah cleaning team to Twin Falls ASAP in case you need backup."

"Smart."

"That's what they pay me for," she said, and hung up.

The janitor scrubbed his laptop's history and cache, retrieved a Slim Jim from his go bag, turned up the heat, and settled in with his binoculars to wait.

41

DR. WAYNE BEVAN, THE Elko County medical examiner, was finishing a report when Bree and Sampson were led into his office by his secretary. The two explained that they were looking into the death of Ryan Malcomb.

"You reporters?" said Bevan, a tall, lean man in jeans and cowboy boots. "The last bunch left a week ago."

"We're just going over the details," Bree said.

"Insurance company?"

"Something like that," Sampson said. "We were told you had a match on Malcomb's dental records."

Bevan nodded, scooted his chair over to a cabinet, and pulled out a thick file. "DNA was a match, but it never hurts to get corroboration." He opened the file, turned over several documents, and came up with a photograph of a corpse. Its skull was fractured in multiple places and splintered in others.

The medical examiner said, "Because of the height he fell from, the airbag did nothing. He took the steering wheel just above the maxilla. Snapped his neck. He died instantly."

"His teeth are almost all gone," Sampson said. "How did you make the match?"

Bevan got out a photo that showed the teeth he'd found in the mouth during the autopsy.

Bree pointed to a tooth with metal sticking out where the root should have been. "Are those implants?"

"Two of them," he said. "Lateral incisors. Malcomb's dental records show he didn't have adult lateral incisors. He had the implants in his twenties."

"Do you have copies of those records?" Sampson asked.

"I'll get copies made for you," he said.

Bree said, "Could we get copies of your autopsy report as well? And the tox screens?"

"All in the public record," the medical examiner said. "Tox screen too. He had a load of booze and a little fentanyl in him, I can tell you that. You want the DNA report also?"

"Yes, sir," Bree said. "Just so we've dotted our i's and crossed our t's."

Twenty minutes later, they returned to the Cherokee.

"What now?" Sampson asked.

"We go to Salmon, start tracking Sean Malcomb Wallace there."

"But you heard the man—the dental records support the DNA report," Sampson said. "I mean, what are the chances that Sean Malcomb Wallace had the same missing teeth and implants as his brother?"

"I don't know," Bree said, throwing up her hands in frustration. "But I didn't come all the way out here just to give up on day one. You know I was air force military police before I joined Metro."

"I did know that."

"They taught us that when in doubt, dig deeper than you think is reasonable."

Sampson sighed and started the Jeep. "Salmon it is."

They got on I-80 heading east, then took U.S. 93 north toward Idaho. As John drove, Bree reviewed the medical examiner's reports on the autopsy, the DNA test, and the tox screen. Death was attributed to massive blunt-force trauma.

The DNA report was conclusive on Malcomb's identity. And the tox screen showed that at the time of the accident, the tech entrepreneur had had a blood alcohol level that was twice the legal limit and more than a trace of fentanyl in his system.

"There's something off about this tox screen, though," Bree said as they neared the Idaho border and night began to fall.

"What?"

"I don't know exactly," she said. "I just have a feeling I'm missing something." She got out her phone and called Alex. The connection was weak and crackly, and the call went straight to voice mail. "This is Bree. We're heading to Idaho. Love you." Bree looked at the reports in her lap and almost put them aside. But something clicked in her mind.

She studied the tox screen one more time. "There it isn't," Bree said.

"What's that?" Sampson said, glancing over at her.

"Malcomb had muscular dystrophy," she said, tapping on the report. "I read a profile of him from a couple of years ago and he said he used drugs to delay the progression of the disease and control some of the symptoms. The treatment is almost always steroids, like prednisone."

"No steroids in the tox screen?"

"No test done yet. Has to be specially ordered."

"But they think it's an open-and-shut case and it's unnecessary."

"Yeah," she said, feeling even more frustrated.

CHAPTER

42

Athens, Georgia

FOR SOME REASON, THE way Detective Forbes downloaded the footage from the doorbell camera to his thumb drive had corrupted it and the camera's hard disk.

It was by no means a total loss, but we had to upload and send the pertinent footage to my friend Keith Karl Rawlins, a computer expert who, like me, worked as a consultant for the FBI. It took Rawlins a good six hours to isolate and repair the video footage and another two to get the audio to jibe.

Mahoney, Detectives Forbes and Warren, and I were eating in a cafeteria at the Athens police department and thinking about calling it a night when the file finally came back. We went to their office and pulled it up on Warren's computer.

Professor Carver appeared across the street from the camera, on the sidewalk. He seemed a little off balance, a little tipsy, as he went up his driveway.

Similar to the previous video, we got only a two-second look at the assassin. She appeared in a dark hoodie, moved left to right down the middle of the street, and squared off in front of the driveway in a combat shooting stance, her back to the camera, Carver's back to his killer and the gun.

Her shoulders moved. He turned around to look at her with puzzlement in his eyes.

She shot him square in the chest, knocking him backward on his driveway. She took five quick strides, stopped beside him, and shot him in the face.

"Cold bitch," Forbes said.

Mahoney said, "I could not agree with you more, Detective."

The killer moved quickly across the driveway and vanished from the screen a moment later. We rewound the footage and watched it all again, pausing whenever a frame showed some of her face.

The best view we had was as she left Carver and moved diagonally back to the sidewalk. We froze the image when we could see the color and cut of her hair clearly. Her nose, cheeks, and eyes were blurry for some reason.

"Blond," Mahoney said. "Short spiky hair. It's her again."

I said, "But what's with her face? Can you zoom in on it?"

Detective Warren gave her computer a command, and the killer's face occupied the entire screen. She was wearing what appeared to be a semitransparent plastic mask that distorted her features from the top of her lips to above her eyebrows.

"She's smart," Warren said.

"And efficient," Forbes said. "She doesn't waste any time, does she?"

Mahoney nodded. "She's always like that. Decisive. No hesitation."

We watched it yet again. I saw the killer's shoulders move before Carver turned.

"She said something there," I said. "Just before Carver faced her."

Warren frowned, played with the controls, said, "Well, there you go, the volume was almost off."

She rewound it, turned the volume all the way up, and hit Play. We could suddenly hear the brisk breeze that had blown that night and some distant sirens.

When Professor Carver appeared, we could hear him chuckling a little as he turned unsteadily onto his driveway and started up the grade. The killer came into the frame in total silence, moving like a cat stalking prey. She squared off, called, "Professor Carver."

Carver hesitated, then pivoted to face her. Those sirens got closer. She said something else to him and shot him twice; the suppressed rounds sounded like pillows being plumped.

"Did anyone get what she just said to him?" Warren said.

"Garbled," Forbes said.

I shook my head. Mahoney did too. He dug in his pocket and came out with a white AirPods case.

"Connect me to your computer. Play it again but try to damp down the high tones of those sirens. Maybe I can make it out."

Warren connected him and adjusted the equalizer on the computer to limit the upper range. She hit Play and Mahoney listened closely, his index finger to his lips.

"Again, but squelch it down more this time," he said, glancing at me with some concern.

Warren further adjusted the equalizer and hit Play. When Carver turned to face his killer and her shoulders moved again, I saw Ned lose color.

He tore out his right AirPod. "Detectives, I'm going to have to ask you to leave the room for the time being. I'm sorry, but this is a national security issue now."

I was shocked. Warren and Forbes seemed taken aback and a little angry.

"The two of you did good, real good," Mahoney said, seeing their reaction and getting out of their way so they could leave. "I will write a letter recommending a citation for both of you. Your nation thanks you. And I promise to explain when I can."

"We get it—we're small-town," Forbes said. They left, shutting the door to the office.

"What does she say?" I asked.

Mahoney took out his other AirPod and handed me the pair. "Listen for yourself."

I put them in. He rewound the video and hit Play.

With the high-frequency noises dampened, I could hear Carver chortling and the light steps of the killer following him.

"Professor Carver," she said clearly after squaring off to shoot him.

The constitutional law professor turned.

Before she shot him, she said, "Maestro knows what you've done. It's over."

43

BREE WAS ASLEEP IN a motel room in Hailey, Idaho, when her phone rang.

She found it, answered. "Alex?"

"Sorry not to call last night, Bree," he said. "There was a major development in the murdered-judges case that you and John need to know about."

"Tell me," she said, sitting up.

"We caught the assassin on camera and on audio. Before she shot him, she said, and this is a quote: 'Maestro knows what you've done. It's over.'"

"C'mon!" she cried as she got out of bed. "Is that right?"

"It was hard to hear, but there's no mistake."

Bree put her hand to her forehead. "My God, the heat on you and Ned is going to go sky-high."

"Deadly, mysterious vigilante group targets possible Supreme Court nominees? I'd say so. Ned and I are on our way back to DC to brief the acting director."

"And John and I are going to Salmon, Idaho, to try to track down Malcomb's brother," Bree said. "We found an address for his father, William. What did Professor Carver do to merit assassination?"

"Unclear. We have possible motives for Franklin and Pak, but not Carver."

"I think you need to look at Theresa May Alcott," Bree said. "She's on that advisory board. She's the link to Malcomb. She may also be the link to Maestro."

"We're on the same page—we're heading to Cleveland after we see the director. How did yesterday go for you two?"

Bree told him about Eldon Boyt's theory of the crash on the mountain road and about the dental records.

"Two matches, Bree," Alex said. "That makes him dead in any court in the world."

"I know, I know," she said. "But I wish they'd tested him for steroids. We'd know for certain it was him."

"You'll have to figure it out another way. How's the weather there?"

She looked out the window. "Ooh, snowing. There's like six inches on the ground. But our rental is a Jeep Cherokee with four-wheel drive."

"Call me tonight?"

"I'll try around eleven your time."

They said they loved each other and hung up. Bree texted Sampson to make sure he was awake, then showered, dressed, and repacked her overnight bag.

John had the Jeep warmed up when she left the room. He also had two coffees and two breakfast burritos waiting.

As they ate and drove north on State Highway 75, past the Sun Valley resort area, she told him about Maestro's involvement in the assassinations, which stunned Sampson.

"That's just cold and brazen," he said. "What do they think they're achieving by killing these people?"

"I have no clue. But I told Alex they should focus on Theresa May Alcott as the potential link to Maestro."

"Good idea. But more important, this shows that Maestro is not stopping even if Malcomb was M."

"Or they're not stopping because Malcomb is M and he is very much alive."

They passed the turnoff to Alice Lake a half hour later. Bree pointed to it. "That's where Malcomb's adoptive parents were murdered."

"I remember that," Sampson said. "Looks like the road in is snowed over."

"Let's get to Salmon. I have a good feeling."

The snowstorm intensified north of Sawtooth City and the going became slow and treacherous on the mountainous two-lane highway. They did not reach Salmon and the address of William Malcomb and his wife, Cherise, until nearly three thirty in the afternoon.

It was a ramshackle dump, half prefab home, half plywood-walled addition, with no siding and tin on the roof. When they pulled in, an angry black standard poodle barked at them from the end of a chain.

As they got out of the Jeep, a wizened-looking woman in a stained red snorkel parka stepped out onto the sagging porch. She clutched a lit cigarette in one hand and a red go-cup in the other.

"Damn it, Fifi! Shut up!"

The poodle did so immediately; she sat and stared at them through the falling snow. The woman said, "Who are you? You were not invited."

"We're detectives from Washington, DC," Sampson said. "We wanted to ask you some questions if you don't mind."

"I do mind," she said. "About what? I ain't done nothing. I haven't been nowhere in three damn days."

They walked toward her with their hands up. "Just a few questions," Bree said. "Can we come inside?"

"Hell no," she said. "And that's far enough."

Bree could see that the woman was younger than she'd first thought. Scrawny, with sallow skin and missing teeth. Her eyes were glassy and her hands trembled. Bree figured her for a meth addict.

"Are you Cherise?" Sampson said.

"That's right."

Bree said, "We were actually hoping to talk with William."

The woman cackled. "You wanna talk to my Billy? Well, that's no problem. Follow me."

Cherise shuffled off the porch, kicked aside the snow, and headed toward a barn, cackling, puffing on the last of her cigarette, and taking sips from the go-cup. She went past the barn door and around the back.

She led them down a short, snowed-over path to a clearing by a creek. She pointed to a fresh grave mound marked by a white wooden cross with a red MAGA hat nailed to it that fluttered in the snowy wind.

Her next cackle was more subdued and sad. She said, "Talk all you want to Billy, 'cause that's him there. Died last month. Pneumonia got him before the congestive heart failure could."

CHAPTER

44

Washington, DC

MAHONEY AND I WERE stewing outside the FBI director's office and had been since our arrival two hours before. During our flight from Athens, there had been a firefight in Houston that left several agents dead, so the director had her hands full.

We were finally led into Marcia Hamilton's office around three in the afternoon. A former special agent with the Bureau, Hamilton had gone on to become a crusading U.S. attorney in Chicago. Tall, athletic, and in her late forties, Hamilton came from behind her desk to greet us, the crisis of the moment showing in her face.

"I'm sorry for keeping you waiting," she said, shaking our hands. "These are the first agents to die on my watch, and we're still in a standoff."

"We understand," Mahoney said.

I said, "How many, ma'am?"

"Seven." She sighed. "They thought they were raiding a chop shop run by a gang operating across state lines. They got in there and found a massive fentanyl operation guarded by at least twenty well-armed men, and it got ugly fast. But bring me up to speed on what you found."

Ned had her put on headphones and listen to the assassin's final words to Professor Carver: *Maestro knows what you've done. It's over.*

Hamilton was confused. "I'm sorry, but I've been in this job only six weeks. Maestro?"

We gave her a brief history of the vigilante group, our efforts to find M, the group's leader, and our suspicions about Ryan Malcomb and Paladin, his company.

"And you think Malcomb orchestrated the murders of the three people on the advisory board's list?"

"Not necessarily Malcomb, but Maestro, yes," I said.

We explained that the circumstances of Malcomb's death were suspicious and we were open about Bree and Sampson looking into it.

Mahoney said, "Alive or dead, with or without Malcomb, Maestro has to be our total focus now."

Hamilton said, "I have a hard time believing that the NSA can't track this group down."

I said, "That's the problem. To do that kind of massive data search, the NSA uses a contractor—Paladin, Malcomb's company."

Mahoney nodded. "If we request the search, we tip our hand."

"That has to change."

"Using Paladin. Yes, ma'am. I agree."

"There's no one else, no other company, that can do this kind of thing?"

"Not like Paladin," I said. "They have proprietary algorithms."

She thought again. "Okay, Mahoney. Where next?"

"First thing, we're going to double the protection on everyone on that advisory board's list," Ned said. "And then we're going to talk to the only person on the list linked to Ryan Malcomb."

"Who's that?"

"Theresa May Alcott, the soap-company billionaire."

Hamilton visibly lost color. "Theresa May Alcott? I know her. From Cleveland. You can't possibly think she'd be involved in this brutal vigilantism. She's a huge philanthropist and a big donor to Winter."

Mahoney said, "We know that, and I did not say she was involved in the murders. I just said she's the only person on that advisory board we can link to the guy we suspect ran Maestro, Ryan Malcomb. Her nephew."

"Who is dead."

"Correct."

Hamilton fell silent, then said, "You've put me in a difficult situation, gentlemen."

"How so, ma'am?" I asked.

"I am the acting FBI director. I would like to be the actual FBI director for the next ten years, and you're asking me to focus an investigation on one of the biggest supporters of the president-elect. A woman I have dealt with extensively on various civic boards over the years."

Mahoney said, "Yes, ma'am. At the very least, we want to talk with her as soon as possible."

"Well, I think she'd be in Jackson Hole this time of year. She loves to ski."

"Permission to use the jet again to go there?"

She smiled sadly. "Permission denied, Mahoney. I'm about to use it to fly to Houston. You'll have to go commercial."

CHAPTER

45

BREE AND SAMPSON LEFT Cherise Malcomb with her go-cup and Fifi and headed north at her suggestion. Cherise said she was no friend to her, but she knew her late husband's ex-girlfriend, Lucille Wallace, now Lucille Danvers. She and her husband ran a country store about twenty miles north on U.S. 93.

Cherise also said she knew about the twins being given up for adoption when Billy and Lucille were teenagers and that there had been under-the-table money involved. But she claimed that had all happened long before she met Billy Malcomb, when that money was barely a memory.

Cell service was horrible in the narrow canyon, and the snow was dumping at two inches an hour as dusk fell and they approached tiny North Fork, Idaho, where the two main channels of the Salmon River met and took a hard turn north. The

Danvers Country Store was at the south end of town, a log-faced two-story building with a neon Rainier Beer sign in the window.

They parked and hurried through the snow to the porch. They kicked the snow off their boots and went inside.

A woodstove blazed in the corner to the right. To the left, a woman in her sixties wearing a blue fleece pullover sat at the counter behind the cash register, alternately staring at her phone and scribbling something on a pad of paper.

"Hold on a second," she said to Bree and Sampson. "Be right with you. I'm addicted to this thing."

They grabbed chips, homemade turkey sandwiches, and drinks and brought them to the counter as she said, "Ha! There it is!"

She looked up at them, beaming. "*Quilt* is the Wordle of the day!"

Bree smiled, liking the woman immediately. "My husband's grandmother plays it."

"I just started last month," she said. "I play this and that Spelling Bee. Love them. And the doctor says it's good for the stuff going on with my memory."

Sampson said, "Business slow?"

She laughed as she rang up their purchases. "A real snoozer until you two walked in. What brings you up this way in the dead of winter?"

"Are you Lucille Danvers?" Sampson said, and she nodded.

Bree said, "We came to see you, Mrs. Danvers."

"You did?" she said, the smile fading a little. "About what?"

Sampson said, "We're detectives investigating a traffic death near Elko, Nevada."

"Yes?"

"The victim's name was Ryan Malcomb."

Lucille Danvers stared blankly at them for a moment, then her hand traveled slowly to her mouth. She got up from behind the counter, waddled fast to the front door, turned the sign from OPEN to CLOSED, and drew down the blind.

She burst into tears. "Was it my Ryan? Please tell me it wasn't."

"I'm sorry, ma'am," Bree said, going to her and giving her a hug.

"Even though I had them for only a day, I never stopped loving those boys," she said as she blubbered. "Even after I married Big Ed and had my girls, I never stopped loving them."

When she calmed down, she told them the adoptions had been handled by an attorney her mother knew. She and Billy were each given ten thousand dollars to stay quiet about it.

Bree said, "Who was the attorney?"

"Mel Allen in Salmon. He's dead. Twenty or maybe thirty years ago. I can't remember so many things these days."

Sampson said, "And you never heard from the boys?"

"No," she said sadly. "I got updates over the years from Mel, a few pictures of them and their family, letting me know they were okay and reminding me to keep quiet about the money and all."

Bree told her that Ryan Malcomb had petitioned the court to unseal his adoption papers, that he had known who his biological parents were. That saddened Mrs. Danvers even more. "He knew who I was and didn't contact me? I wonder why."

They showed her a photo of Malcomb, and she was stunned. "I know him," she said. "He came to the store several times over the past four or five years, said he was rafting and fishing in the area. Sometimes he was fine. Other times, he couldn't walk very well."

"He developed muscular dystrophy as a teenager," Sampson

said. He gave her a brief rundown of Malcomb's accomplishments and wealth but left out his possible involvement in a deadly vigilante ring.

Mrs. Danvers was amazed. "He did all that? My son?"

"Yes, ma'am," Bree said. "And we're trying to track down his brother."

"Like I said, I don't know anything. I can't help you."

"Mrs. Danvers," John said, "by any chance do you still have those photographs of the boys and their family?"

"Big Ed doesn't know I have them," she said softly. "But he's in Twin Falls tonight with our daughter and granddaughter. I'll go up and get them."

She left and a few minutes later returned with a large manila envelope. She pulled out a plastic sleeve containing three snapshots.

Bree and Sampson recognized the Wheeler family from the coverage that had surrounded their murders. In the first and oldest picture, a formal family portrait, Norman and Patricia May Wheeler, sister to Theresa May Alcott, were proudly holding their babies.

The second, taken when the boys were roughly five, showed them with life preservers on sitting on a dock on what Bree assumed was Alice Lake. It was remarkable how much the twins looked like each other. The only real difference was their expressions: One twin was laughing. The other was staring at his laughing brother coldly.

In the third picture, the twins were seven or eight with buzz-cut hair; they were back on that dock again. One was holding up a big trout, and the other stared off, his fists clenched.

"That's all you've ever seen of them?" Sampson asked.

"Well, except for the one who came in here over the...you know what? I think I remember he paid with a credit card last time he was in," Mrs. Danvers said. She sat down behind the register and fiddled with a laptop computer. "I think it was Labor Day last year. Or was it the year before?"

"Mrs. Danvers?" Bree said. "It doesn't—"

"No, my memory is shot in some places, but I remember him, I—"

She seemed to freeze for several moments, as if lost somewhere.

"Ma'am," Sampson said. "We're sorry we took up so much—"

The woman pivoted in her chair, her eyes glassy. "I remember now. He bought a dozen jars of huckleberry jam. My huckleberry jam." Mrs. Danvers smiled in deep satisfaction. "My son. He bought all my jam."

"That's nice," Bree said.

Her brow knitted. "What did you say his name was again?"

"Ryan Malcomb."

She brightened. "Well, that should be easy." She turned to the computer again. "I'll show you. Big Ed keeps track of inventory. And every credit card payment goes to Quicken."

Sampson looked at Bree and gestured to the front windows. It was almost dark. Snow peppered the glass.

"Mrs. Danvers," Bree said, "with the weather, we should be going."

"Won't take but a second," she said. "I know I'm—"

She seemed to freeze again.

They stood there for several more awkward moments before Bree said, "Mrs. Danvers, we're going to leave our cards here. If you find what you're looking for, you can let us know."

The woman smiled uncertainly and nodded. "I lose track of what I'm thinking about."

"We understand," Sampson said. "Are you alone, ma'am?"

She looked up at the clock—it was almost half past five. "Oh, my daughter Kate will be along at six to help me close."

"Well, then, you've got our cards."

The older woman smiled at them. "My son bought all my jam. Wasn't that nice?"

46

SAMPSON AND BREE LEFT the Danvers Country Store as full darkness fell and the snow came down in torrents. Bree glanced around before they climbed off the porch, saw Lucille Danvers back at her laptop.

"Poor lady," Sampson said. "She's young for that."

"Too young," Bree agreed as they crossed to their Jeep. "And I don't know what to make of Ryan Malcomb coming here several times."

"And buying all her huckleberry jam," Sampson said, unlocking the doors. "She really lit up at that."

"She did, didn't she," Bree said, smiling as she climbed into the passenger seat. "I was glad we didn't have to tell her our suspicions about Ryan's secret life as M."

"Better leave her to the good memories she has," John said.

"Agreed."

"Do you have cell service?"

"Nothing."

"We'll try in Salmon. I saw a Stagecoach Inn there and a diner next door."

"I saw it too. Said free internet on the sign."

"Here we go, then."

He put the Cherokee in gear and tensed as he drove south into the storm. The wind was blowing the powder in big swirls.

"Hard to see the road," Sampson said, slowing down.

"Take your time."

They drove on in silence. Alex's oldest friend stared into the mesmerizing haze of the headlights cutting through the driving snow.

Bree glanced at him. "Are you all right, John?"

"What?" he said. "Why?"

"It's ten degrees out and snowing, and you're sweating and holding on to that wheel like it's a life preserver or something."

"Hey, I am DC born and raised, my good friend," he shot back, annoyed. "I have never driven in a storm like —"

Ahead of them on the highway, red and blue lights flashed in the snow.

"Uh-oh," Bree said. "Accident?"

"Can't tell," Sampson said, slowing to a crawl.

They got close enough to see the red lights were flashing on top of a massive snowplow with its hood up. There were men in heavy overalls and hoods working on the engine. A pickup truck with flashing blue lights was parked in front of it.

A smiling guy wearing a heavy parka, a sheepskin bomber hat, and an orange reflective vest and carrying a flashlight stomped through the snow to them. Sampson lowered the window.

"Hey there," the man said. "Brian Toomey, Idaho Department of Transportation. Our plow shit the bed on us where she stands. But the boys think they know what's wrong with her. We'll have the temperamental bitch up and going soon."

Bree rolled her eyes.

Sampson said, "How far to Salmon from here, Mr. Toomey?"

"Fourteen miles, give or take," the janitor said, pulling a pistol from his parka pocket and pressing the muzzle to the side of Sampson's head. "And if you ever want to see your family again, you'll do exactly what I tell you to do. Right, John Sampson? Right, Bree Stone?"

CHAPTER

47

Over Colorado

THE FOLLOWING AFTERNOON, MAHONEY and I flew west on a Delta non-stop to Salt Lake City, the only seats we could find on short notice that would get us anywhere close to Jackson Hole, Wyoming. I was signed into the plane's Wi-Fi and kept checking my texts and emails, hoping to see something from Bree or Sampson.

"Anything?" Ned asked.

"Nothing," I said, growing increasingly concerned.

"Salmon, Idaho, is pretty remote. Cell service can't be great."

"Granted, but Bree specifically told me yesterday morning that she would call me at eleven p.m. DC time. We're many hours past that."

"I hear you," Mahoney said, then paused. "You said they rented a Jeep, right? What company did Bree rent it from?"

"She usually uses Hertz, I think," I said. "But I don't know for sure."

"After we land, I'll put in a request to have Hertz ping their car's GPS locator."

"That will help," I said. "At least we'll know where they are."

We landed at two p.m. mountain time, picked up a Chevy Tahoe with snow tires, and headed north. I still hadn't heard from either my wife or my best friend, so I accessed Bree's credit card accounts on my laptop and found payments for her airline ticket, a room in Reno, a room in Hailey, Idaho, and gas in Sun Valley the morning before.

"Looks like Sampson must have rented the Jeep," I said. "I have no idea who he gets points with."

"We'll start with Hertz and Avis," Mahoney said. "And we can contact Verizon, see where their towers last picked them up."

"Good idea," I said. "I'm going to call the Idaho state police, find out if there's been an accident."

It began to snow shortly after we crossed into Wyoming. Cell service became spotty, but Mahoney managed to get through to Hertz, Avis, Sixt, and Verizon. Neither Hertz nor Avis had any record of Bree or John renting a Jeep. Sixt said they'd get back to us. Verizon agreed to look for Bree's cell data but said it would take several hours to gather.

We reached the bustling town of Jackson at six thirty p.m. after a hair-raising drive through a whiteout. After we checked into an overpriced motel, we decided there was no time like the present and drove to Alcott's spread on the east side of the broad valley of Jackson Hole, up against the Gros Ventre Wilderness.

As we approached the Double Diamond Ranch, a steel barrier rose up out of the snow, blocking the road. A ball camera rose from the steel barrier and looked at us.

Mahoney got out, walked up to the camera, and showed his FBI credentials.

A male voice said, "What is this about?"

"The judicial appointment advisory panel Mrs. Alcott serves on for the president-elect."

"Can you come back in the morning?"

"No. This is a federal murder investigation. It's urgent."

After a long pause, he said, "Come past the barns and the stable. Park below the big house near the riding ring." The ball camera retracted into the steel barrier, which dropped below the grade of the road.

We went up a windy, snowy drive, past barns, a large stable, and an exterior riding ring, and finally spotted the house up on a knoll.

We parked and climbed heated stairs to the front porch of the sprawling log and stone structure. On the double doors was a carving of a bull elk fighting a grizzly bear. One of the doors opened before we knocked.

A big Polynesian guy in shorts, sandals, and a Las Vegas Raiders hoodie took a step back to let us in. "I'm Arthur," he said. "I work for Mrs. Alcott. If you don't mind, I'd like to make a copy of your identification materials before we go further."

We handed them to him. Arthur returned a few minutes later.

"Mrs. Alcott will see you now," he said. "But do me a favor?"

"If we can," I said.

"Take it easy on her," Arthur said. "Mrs. A. has been through a hell of a lot the past few weeks. She has no family left now, and it is crushing her."

CHAPTER

48

ARTHUR LED US THROUGH a foyer to a sunken timber-frame living room with massive beams and posts and a huge boulder set into the wall on one side. A fire blazed in a glass-fronted box in the middle of the boulder. A chimney made of similar stone rose above it.

Theresa May Alcott sat in one of two dark leather club chairs staring into the flames, a cut-glass tumbler in one hand and an unlit cigarette in the other.

"Theresa," Arthur said. "Your visitors are here."

She swiveled in the chair to face us, then stood up. Dressed in brown suede pants, tooled cowboy boots, and a sheepskin vest over a denim top, Mrs. Alcott had a striking, almost regal presence. She set down the drink and the cigarette on the table between the chairs and came over.

"I'm Theresa May Alcott," she said, extending her right hand. On her left, she wore a large diamond engagement ring and a wedding band despite the fact that her husband had passed years before.

We introduced ourselves and thanked her for seeing us.

"Sounds like I did not have much of a choice," she said, the slightest slur to her words. "Can Arthur get you something to drink on a cold winter night?"

"No, ma'am," Mahoney said. "Not while we're working."

"Find them something appropriate, would you, Arthur?"

He nodded and left. She showed us to a couch and returned to her chair.

"That's a beautiful fireplace," Mahoney said. "I've never seen one like it."

"Because there isn't," she said. "It was custom-made for us in Finland. It's soapstone, which holds the heat and radiates it. My husband loved it."

I glanced at the other club chair, the empty one. "We wanted to speak with you about the judicial advisory board you sit on."

"I was surprised but pleased and honored that President-Elect Winter asked me to serve."

"You're a big supporter of Sue Winter."

"I have been for a long time," she said, picking up her drink and sipping from it. "She's brilliant. She's warm. She listens. She thinks outside the box. Sue will make an outstanding president."

Mahoney said, "Getting back to the advisory panel. Were you aware that three people on the panel's list of possible Supreme Court candidates have been murdered in the past month?"

Mrs. Alcott was either genuinely stunned or an accomplished actress. Her jaw dropped, and she set the drink down. "No. No, I did not know that. I...had a recent death in the family, someone very close to me, and I haven't been keeping up with the news. Or with anything, for that matter."

I said, "Speaking of that death in your family, did you ever talk to Ryan Malcomb, your late nephew, about the list?"

"Ryan? No. Absolutely not. The panel was instructed to work discreetly. Who are the dead on the list, please?"

"Judge Franklin of the DC Circuit, Judge Pak of the Ninth Circuit, and Professor Nathan Carver."

At that last name, her eyes went wide in disbelief and her hand traveled to her throat. "No. I spoke to Professor Carver myself. He was my number one. Oh my God. This is awful."

Mahoney said, "Did your nephew know you were on that committee?"

"I don't believe so," she said. "Why do you keep bringing up Ryan?"

"We'll get to that. But I find it hard to believe you wouldn't at least mention that you had been invited onto a prestigious panel by the president-elect."

Mrs. Alcott made a dismissive gesture. "I don't want to sound like an ass, Mr. Mahoney, but my late husband and I have played in these circles for years. I might have mentioned it to Ryan in passing, but we never talked about it."

Arthur returned with a tray with hot water, tea bags, and cookies. After he left, I decided to take the discussion in another direction. "Did you know Ryan was looking for a ranch in Nevada?"

"Of course. I advised him to look for a large physical asset as an anchor to his growing wealth."

"He wouldn't have inherited this place?"

She smiled sourly. "No. My husband's will stipulated that the house and the immediate two thousand acres around it would be

THE HOUSE OF CROSS

sold after my death. The rest will go to the State of Wyoming. Why all the questions about Ryan?"

"Just tying up some loose ends," Mahoney said.

I said, "My wife, Bree Stone, came to talk to you."

Alcott raised her chin. "I felt she was incredibly rude and insensitive to badger me like that at Ryan's funeral."

"She told me she regretted intruding."

The billionaire said nothing.

I said, "Tell us about Sean."

Her lips twisted as if she'd tasted something bad in that last sip of whiskey. "I told your wife about him. He was extremely smart. Maybe smarter than Ryan. But he was far more difficult as a child. Insolent. Defiant. Violent. Brooding."

"Bree said he had a history of mental illness. Can you tell us what his diagnosis was?"

Alcott looked disgusted. "He had most of the psychiatrists we went to wrapped around his little finger; he was able to turn on the charm and brilliance when needed. But after he had a psychotic break at age sixteen, we sent him to a residential facility, where he was diagnosed with various psychiatric illnesses."

"Can you describe the psychotic break?" I asked.

She hesitated. "He was home from prep school. It was Christmas, and out of nowhere he attacked Ryan, tried to kill him with a butcher knife. My husband and a friend stopped him."

"This happened without provocation?"

"Ryan was having a down day and was in his wheelchair. In Sean's disturbed mind, that was enough. He hated all the attention his brother got. For his illness and for his brilliance."

Mahoney said, "And how did Ryan feel about Sean?"

"Ryan was protective of Sean, tried to keep him out of trouble."

"Until he left at eighteen," I said.

Alcott nodded. "On his eighteenth birthday. Had us transfer his inheritance to a new account, told me he never wanted to see me again, and left in the Range Rover I'd bought for him for his high-school graduation."

"And you never heard from him again?"

"Not directly. I did get a notification from my insurance company that he'd sold the Range Rover in Salt Lake City about a week after he left and canceled the policy."

"And Ryan?" I said. "Did he lose touch with his brother too?"

"As far as I know," Alcott said, her hand trembling slightly as she reached to pick up the cigarette and a lighter. "We made it a practice to avoid the subject of Sean."

She thumbed the lighter on, lit the cigarette, and took a puff.

CHAPTER

49

THE BILLIONAIRE BLEW THE smoke out. "Is that all, gentlemen?"

I said, "My wife was over in Elko, Nevada, and then in Salmon, Idaho, looking into Ryan's death, along with a DC homicide detective. They've both gone missing. You wouldn't happen to know about that, would you?"

Mrs. Alcott gazed at me, expressionless, for several moments. "Absolutely not, and I'm sorry to hear she is missing. Why would she go to Elko and Salmon?"

"We're asking the questions," Mahoney said. "What do you know about Maestro?"

Her eyes flickered with confusion. "Which one?"

"The vigilante group Maestro," I said. "The one run by a mysterious figure known as M."

She stubbed out her cigarette, blew out the last of the smoke. "I have no idea who or what you are talking about."

Mahoney said, "Maestro is behind the killings of the three judicial candidates on that list, Mrs. Alcott. We have the assassin on video saying, 'Maestro knows what you've done. It's over,' before she shot Professor Carver."

"She?"

"Yes."

"Well," Mrs. Alcott said, picking up her drink again. "That's horrific, but I know nothing about this Maestro. And if you wish to speak with me further, I think I will have an attorney present. Arthur!"

The big Polynesian appeared.

"Our guests are leaving us."

"I am sorry to hear that, Theresa," he said as we stood up.

Mahoney said, "One more question before we go? One that does not require an attorney present?"

Mrs. Alcott scowled but nodded.

"Did Ryan have congenitally missing teeth?"

"Yes," she said. "Both upper lateral incisors. He had bridge-work done."

"Bridgework?"

Alcott said, "Well, bridgework and then implants later."

"And Sean?"

"The same."

"Bridgework and then implants?" I asked.

That seemed to throw her. "As a teenager, he had bridgework. After he left, I don't know."

We thanked her for her time and left the room, following Arthur. At the door, I said, "How long have you worked for Mrs. Alcott, Arthur?"

"Since her husband died. I owed him."

"For what?"

"My life. Mr. Alcott saved me when I got caught in seaweed in a free dive. I'd already drowned, but he saved me. I owed him, so I serve her."

I said, "What did you think of her late nephew?"

Arthur blinked slowly. "A great man. Like his uncle."

Seeing we would not get more out of him, we hustled back out through the storm to the Tahoe. I immediately checked my phone. Nothing from Bree or Sampson.

It was nine o'clock mountain time. Eleven back east. She was officially twenty-four hours late in calling.

As we drove down the winding road from the ranch, Mahoney said, "That was a key question, whether Sean had missing teeth the same as Ryan."

"Certainly keeps Bree's theory alive. And I got the impression Alcott believes Ryan was in touch with his brother."

"Agreed. She knew more than she was letting on. Maybe even about Maestro."

"And M," I said. "And she kind of hedged with the bridges and implants."

"I remain suspicious."

"I do too," I said, yawning. "But if we don't hear from Bree or John soon, I'm voting we eat, sleep, get up early, and drive to Idaho to pick up their trail."

"I don't know if Director Hamilton will like that. We sold this trip to her on seeing Alcott."

"And we did see Mrs. Alcott and we did hear enough and see enough to know we can't clear her of involvement in Maestro or the judicial killings."

Mahoney nodded. "Okay, Idaho, first thing."

His cell phone rang. He answered it, said, "This is he." Mahoney listened, nodded, and then thanked whoever it was.

"That was the Bureau's contact at Verizon," he said. "They have Bree and Sampson in Hailey, Idaho, then Salmon, and the last time they had a record of either of them was at seven yesterday evening in North Fork, Idaho."

I had a sinking feeling in my stomach. "Which means they've really been out of contact for more than a day."

"What do you want to do?"

"Get our stuff from the motel, find coffee, and drive through the night to North Fork. Something is wrong, Ned. I can feel it."

Mahoney hesitated and then nodded. "High-test coffee for me."

Ned drove toward the lights of Jackson. I pulled out my phone and called up one of my favorite pictures.

It had been taken several years before, when Bree and I and Sampson and his late wife, Billie, were in Jamaica. We were all standing on a cliff in Negril with the Caribbean behind us and umbrella drinks in our hands.

I looked at Bree and John, so damned happy it radiated from their faces. I felt a terrible pang in my heart.

Where the hell are you?

CHAPTER

50

A BOUNCE AND A slam roused Bree from a drugged sleep.

She tried to say something, realized she was gagged, and moaned against the fabric. Breathing through her nose, she tried to open her eyes but found she was blindfolded.

Her wrists and ankles were bound tight. She lay on her left side on some kind of carpet and had been lying there long enough for her arm, shoulder, and hip to feel numb.

She rolled onto her back, aware that her head was splitting, that she was thirsty, and that there was an engine roaring dully somewhere. Bree swallowed against her parched throat, and her ears popped, which made her understand that someone had put plugs in them.

The drugs hit her again, made her woozy enough to want to sleep.

Whatever she was lying on bounced again; she was slammed against the carpet again, became more alert again, and finally got that she was in some kind of vehicle. Her instinct was to get the blindfold off, the gag out of her mouth, and the plugs from her ears.

But when she tried to raise her hands, she felt a tug at her ankles and could reach no higher than her throat. Her bonds were tied together somehow.

She fought a rising sense of panic. She could not give in to hysteria.

It won't do you any good, Bree. You've got to calm down. Remember your training.

In the air force, she had taken an officer survival-training course. One of the first things she'd been taught was that no matter what, you had to remain calm. Assess your situation. Think clearly.

She forced herself to ignore how much she wanted the gag out. She forced herself to try to work out where she was and why.

But the drugs in her system made her swoon again. Eventually, she began to piece it together: The snowplow blocking the road. The man from the highway department pulling a gun.

He knew us. He knew who we were.

She recalled the gunman getting in the back seat of the Cherokee and ordering Sampson to drive.

John! Where is he?

And then she remembered the man injecting her neck with something. It had all gone to darkness until that bump.

How long have I been out? Where are they taking me? Is John here?

Bree rolled over again, felt the wheel well of the vehicle, a van of some sort. She rolled onto her back again, breathed through her nose, and caught the stale odor of sweat.

They bounced again and again. She slammed down each time.

Even through the earplugs she could hear the chassis squeaking in protest as they passed over washboard terrain that caused the vehicle to shake and vibrate, the feeling pounding into her bones, making her joints ache.

I need water, she thought before one of those swoons came again. This time the dizziness was accompanied by nausea, and she was certain she was going to puke.

She got frightened. If she vomited behind the gag, she was as good as dead.

Swallowing against the metallic taste flooding the back of her throat, she rammed her heels down hard enough to make a thump that she heard even through the plugs. She did it again and again.

Then she squealed and kicked her heels.

The vehicle slowed to a stop. She heard doors open and slam shut.

A bubble of cold air surrounded her, made her feel less sick. Then more doors opened. She felt hands on her. The hands dragged her out of the vehicle into a frigid wind and then sat her upright.

Fingers wrenched the gag from her mouth. "Water," she croaked.

She felt the ties being cut. The blindfold came off next, and she was looking into the glare of sunlight reflecting off snow.

She squinted, turned away, and saw Toomey, the man who'd said he was from the highway department; he was standing there with a Glock in one hand and a plastic water bottle in the other. He gave her the bottle and Bree drank greedily, grateful for the way it washed her throat and filled her stomach.

Finished, she became aware of two men standing nearby in snow camouflage. They carried automatic weapons.

One of them took several steps to his right, revealing Sampson, who was sitting on a log, also drinking water, also looking dazed. Feeling more lightheaded than woozy now, she reached up under the wool hat she wore and pulled out the earplugs. She heard birds cry.

Her hands were cold. No gloves. She put her hands in her parka pockets, felt around. Her phone was gone.

Bree looked at Toomey. "Who are you? Where are you taking us?"

He gestured to an untracked trail leading into dense forest.

"I'm the janitor. Get moving."

CHAPTER

51

AS IF FROM DOWN a long tunnel, John Sampson thought he heard Toomey, the man with the highway department, say that he was a janitor. His vision was fuzzy, so it was not until Bree stood up that John realized she was there.

One of the armed guys in snow camo urged him to his feet. Sampson stood but felt dizzy and almost went down.

"Put some snow on your face," Toomey said. "That'll wake you right up."

John scooped up snow and rubbed it on his face. Almost instantly he felt more alert.

"You good?" Toomey said.

Sampson nodded, looked to Bree, and nodded again.

The janitor led the way into the forest, breaking trail in ten inches of new snow, with Sampson behind him, one of the gunmen trailing Sampson, then Bree, then the second guy with an automatic weapon.

Still feeling the effects of the drug, Sampson had to keep blinking to prevent the tunnel of trees, brush, and snow they were passing through from closing in on him. Ten minutes into the hike, Sampson became alert enough to know he needed to keep track of where they were going by remembering where he'd been. Sampson had once been a sergeant in the U.S. Army. This was Survival, Evasion, Resistance, and Escape 101.

Count your steps. Determine your course direction. Look at everything around you, but don't be obvious about it.

There was snow hanging heavy from the trees, so it was not until they'd passed through several clearings that Sampson got a decent enough look at the weak winter sun to estimate it was close to midday and that they were headed roughly northwest. He also figured by the angle of the sun that they'd come north a considerable way since they'd been abducted.

They walked for more than two hours and took more than ten thousand steps through a dense forest. The year before, in Montana's Bob Marshall Wilderness with Alex, Sampson had studied the trees. In the Bob, they'd been mostly pine. Here they were fir and growing in pockets, some the height of Christmas trees and others old-growth giants.

Sampson figured they must be in the Cascades by now.

The trail ended at a large lean-to tucked in the woods. Six men also wearing snow camouflage waited with snowmobiles. Two of the snowmobiles had pull sleds attached.

Toomey gestured to the sleds. "Get in."

"We're hungry," Bree said.

"You'll eat soon enough," he replied. "Now get in the sled. Or die."

Bree trudged to one sled. Sampson went to the other.

"Lie down," one of the gunmen said.

Sampson lay down and was surprised that his long frame fit.

"Hands," the gunman said, and zip-tied his wrists together and then the ankles of his rubber boots. He used a long, thick zip tie to bind the top to the bottom, limiting Sampson's ability to raise his arms.

"My hands are going to get frostbite," John said.

Another one of the gunmen threw a heavy wool blanket over him. A third buckled and cinched straps across his chest, pinning him to the sled.

Then they got out a heavy, black wool hood and pulled it down over his head. There was some kind of toggle in the fabric that allowed them to tighten the hood around his neck.

The snowmobiles started. The sled began to move. They were soon racing over the snow so fast he started to panic, feeling claustrophobic behind the mask; he wanted to see where they were going. He tried to keep track of the times they slowed and took sharp curves and when they climbed and when they descended.

But it was soon a blur. He started to wonder how long they'd been gone and whether they'd been missed. He remembered that Bree had said she was going to call Alex at eleven his time on the evening they were taken. How long would Alex wait until he decided something was wrong? Twelve hours? Twenty-four? And how long had they been unconscious?

Then he thought of Willow. He told himself, *No matter what happens, I promise, I will not let you become an orphan.*

Then he thought of Rebecca Cantrell. *And Rebecca, I have only begun to realize this, but I love you.*

CHAPTER

52

THE WEATHER AS WE drove southwest from Jackson to Idaho was foul, creating the worst road conditions I'd ever seen: Snow. Sleet. Ice. Winds gusting to fifty.

We made it out of the Tetons without much trouble, but once we reached Idaho, it was a whiteout again. We crawled into Idaho Falls at two in the morning, got a hotel, and slept through the rest of the storm.

When we set out again, the roads were slick and treacherous all the way north to Leadore. It was nearly four in the afternoon when we finally made it to Salmon and five when we reached North Fork, where Verizon said Bree had last used her cell phone.

My wife and my best friend had been out of touch for more

than forty-four hours when we parked in front of the Danvers Country Store and went inside. An enormous man, easily six foot eight and three hundred pounds, was stocking shelves.

We all introduced ourselves, and I showed him pictures of Bree and Sampson, said cell phone records indicated Bree's phone had last been used in the store's parking lot.

"Must have been lucky," Big Ed said. "Cell service is horrible."

"Have you seen them?"

"Not me," Big Ed Danvers said. "My wife, Lucille, did. She's got early-onset Alzheimer's and about had a nervous breakdown after they left. She's still got the lows. She's upstairs."

Mahoney said, "Can we speak to her, sir? It's important. Both John and Bree went missing after they were here."

Big Ed hesitated. "You going to make her sadder?"

I said, "I sure hope not, sir. That is absolutely not our intent."

Ned said, "We believe she can help us."

He led us through a door, up a flight of stairs, and into a large apartment. Mrs. Danvers was in her pajamas and robe, curled up on a sofa, watching a movie.

Big Ed said, "These folks are with the FBI, Lucille. They want to know about the two who came the other day to ask about the twins. I'll be downstairs."

We sat down. Mrs. Danvers looked like she'd rather be thrown out in the snow than talk to us, but she sat up. "What about them?" she asked. "Those folk weren't real?"

I said, "They were real, Lucille. Bree is my wife. John is a close friend. They are both detectives. And the last place we know where they were was here two nights ago."

"Oh," she said. "There was a horrible storm going on."

"We know, but there are no accident reports," Mahoney said.

"Mrs. Danvers, can you tell me what you talked about that night?"

She showed us the copies of photographs of her twin boys with their new family. "They said Ryan was dead."

"Yes, ma'am," I said.

"They showed me a picture they said was him as a man and I remembered him. They wanted to know about when he was here."

"He came here?"

"Yes. I mean, I thought it was him," Mrs. Danvers said, then appeared confused. "I thought he bought all my jam, but I looked and looked in our records. I couldn't find Ryan Malcomb in the credit cards on Labor Day…"

Mrs. Danvers fell silent, staring at the floor, worrying the sleeve of her robe. Mahoney was about to say something, but I waved him off.

"You wonder," she said finally, "about genetics and all and what gets passed on even before life has happened. You know what I mean?"

Ned said, "Not really, ma'am."

"William Malcomb? My late boyfriend and father of the twins? His family had a history of mental illness. His uncle Tate ended up in the ward for the criminally insane at the state hospital after he killed a family up in Bonners Ferry."

"You think a gene for that was passed to the twins?" I asked.

"Like I said, you wonder."

"Ma'am, if it's any consolation, I'm a criminal psychologist, and there's no evidence that there's a gene like that."

"Oh," she said, brightening a little. "Well, that's good. I…" Mrs. Danvers looked confused again.

"Ma'am, did my wife and friend say where they were going next?"

"Salmon? I mean, I think that's what they said."

Ned got up and I did too, feeling sorry for her and feeling like we were spinning our wheels.

"Thank you, Mrs. Danvers," I said. "We'll be going now."

53

LUCILLE NODDED BLANKLY AT us, then seemed to focus. "I didn't find Ryan in the Quicken. He didn't buy all that jam last Labor Day weekend."

Mahoney said, "Yes, ma'am, you told us that."

"Wasn't him," she said, puzzled. "Another name, you know. All that jam, but I…" Without warning, she began to weep. "Whatever his name was, he's dead. I only knew him for a day, and they said he was dead."

"I'm sorry for your loss, Lucille," I said.

Looking forlorn, she nodded and wiped at her tears. "I have three daughters. Seven grandkids."

"That's a blessing," Mahoney said.

"It is," she said.

We wished her well, said goodbye, and went down the stairs to find Big Ed looking worried. "How is she?"

"Calm now, thinking about her grandkids," Ned said.

"Thank God for that," he said, sounding worn out. "She's been getting worse. Was she able to give you the information you were looking for?"

"Unfortunately, no," I said, and then stopped as fragments of our conversation with his wife fell into place. "Well, maybe. Can you do us a favor?"

"I'll try," he said.

"Could you look in your Quicken records from last Labor Day weekend, see if you can find the name of someone who bought a lot of jam?"

"All of Lucille's huckleberry jam," Big Ed said, opening a drawer. "She wrote his name down on your wife's card."

He handed me Bree's business card. I flipped it over and saw a name in Lucille's careful print: *Ian Duncanson.*

It didn't ring any bells. I showed it to Mahoney, who shrugged.

I pocketed Bree's card and we thanked Big Ed and left. Outside, a bitter wind had kicked up, so we hustled to the car and Ned fired up the heater.

"Who do you think Ian Duncanson is?" Mahoney said.

"Lucille said she recognized Malcomb from the picture Bree and Sampson showed her," I said. "And she did say he bought all of her jam. So maybe Ian Duncanson is an alias that Ryan Malcomb used or maybe Ryan Malcomb did not buy all that jam but his long missing twin brother did."

Ned's eyebrows shot up. Before he could reply, his phone rang.

He grabbed it, looked at the screen, said, "No caller ID." He answered anyway. "Mahoney."

After a few moments, he said, "You're going to have to repeat that. I'm in the middle of nowhere and you're cutting in and out."

He listened, then nodded at me. "Write this down."

I got out my notebook.

Mahoney said, "Northeast of a place called Huckleberry Hollow, mile marker eleven on the road to Salmon."

I scribbled it down. Ned thanked the caller and hung up.

"That was Sixt car rental," he said. "They found the Jeep and notified the local sheriff to sit on it until we got there. And what's with all the huckleberries?"

CHAPTER

54

BENEATH THE WOOL HOOD and the blanket, Bree shook uncontrollably as the snowmobile dragging the sled she was on slowed and then accelerated rapidly up a steep hill. The sled went airborne and slammed down, blowing the breath out of her.

She choked and gasped, her body shivering and trembling, but finally calmed down enough to breathe. She'd never been so cold in her life. Her toes and fingers had lost feeling. She was sure she was developing frostbite and did not know how much longer she could take it.

Finally, after what seemed like a five- or six-hour trip, they stopped. There were voices, and the hood was pulled off.

Bree blinked against the light, turned her head against the bitter wind, and saw armed men in balaclavas, goggles, and snow camo removing the straps that held her to the sled. It was late in the day. There were flurries falling.

Bree's ankles were cut free; two of the men lifted her up, but they left the wrist cuffs on.

Her feet felt frozen and then burned painfully as she took a few cautious steps in the knee-deep snow. When the men were sure she could stand, they walked away from her and got on their snowmobiles.

Bree, still shivering, saw Sampson about thirty yards from her, also shaking from the cold. His goatee was coated in frost.

The one who'd abducted them, Toomey, gestured toward a stand of fir trees. "Take the trail. Find the old metal building and do it fast. It's going to get brutal out here."

He whistled. The six snowmobiles started up and sped off, leaving Bree and Sampson in the fading light. John began struggling against his wrist restraints.

"John," Bree said. "It's too cold. We will die if we don't seek shelter."

Sampson gave up and stomped toward her. "Let's go, then."

He got ahead of her and broke trail down the path through the firs. It was dimmer in the trees, but there was more light when they got out of the woods. Sampson stopped, shaking his head. Bree stepped around him and gasped, not at the intensity of the frigid wind but at the scene before them.

They stood near the edge of a high cliff overlooking a stunning alpine valley with towering, jagged peaks on two sides and a broad, frozen river running through it. The last of the sun was playing on storm clouds that quickly swallowed the crags and blew toward them on a wind building up to a gale.

Bree tried to see if she could spot some kind of building down in the valley. But how would they get down there if they could see it?

"There it is," Sampson said, nodding to their right.

She saw it then—a low building with a metal roof about two hundred yards from them and back from the rim of the bluff. Sampson broke trail through the snow again and within minutes they were at the door.

The knob turned. He pushed the door open, and they stepped inside.

There were windows below the eaves of the building that caught the last good light of the day and cast bluish beams and deep shadows across the space. They shut the door, which cut the wind, but they could still see their breath as they walked deeper into the structure, saw pieces of steel cable, several massive rusty gears on the concrete floor, and multiple iron things that looked like the seats of strollers mounted on railroad wheels.

"What is this place and where are we supposed to go?" Bree asked.

"Looks like part of an abandoned mine to me," Sampson said, going to one of the gears and rubbing the plastic wrist restraints against the edge. "Those have to be ore cars."

"How did they get into the mine?" Bree said, scanning the cavernous space that was getting darker by the minute.

Before John could respond, they heard a loud creaking noise near the far end of the structure. A light appeared from the floor itself, and an octagonal glass cylinder rose up out of the concrete.

"The weather report has just been updated," said a man in a reasonable voice. "With the windchill, it will soon be sixty-two below zero. Even out of the wind as you are, you don't stand a chance of lasting through the night. Get in, Bree Stone and John Sampson. Or die and we'll cremate you both in the morning."

CHAPTER

55

WE REACHED MILE MARKER eleven on the road to Huckleberry Hollow, Idaho, and spotted the flashing blue lights of a Lemhi County sheriff's patrol rig, a beefy Dodge Ram 3500 lifted to allow for a set of huge, studded tires. It was parked in a turnoff by a bear-proof trash bin. Beside the pickup was an SUV covered in five inches of snow.

Mahoney pulled up alongside the sheriff's truck, rolled his window down, and held up his FBI credentials. The pickup window lowered, revealing a jowly man with a flat face and a big neck that made him look like a bulldog. In his late sixties, he was wearing a heavy parka and a black wool hat.

"Sheriff David Tucker," he said.

We identified ourselves.

"I haven't touched it, haven't been near it. Just eating my supper, waiting on you."

"We appreciate that, Sheriff Tucker," Ned said.

"I can put my rack lights on it if you think it will help."

"I do. Thanks."

Tucker put his rig in gear and turned it around. He put his overhead lights on the Jeep, and it was as bright as day as Mahoney and I swept off the snow so we could try the doors.

The sheriff got out, stood to one side, and watched.

Both front doors opened. The keys were in the ignition.

I got a sick feeling when I saw Bree's purse on the floor of the passenger seat and Sampson's day pack in the rear. Their luggage was still in the hatch.

"That's it," I said, trying to fight my growing panic. "They've been taken. Maestro has them. They probably got too close to the truth."

"Who is Maestro?" Tucker asked.

"Vigilante group," Ned said. "That's who they were here hunting. Maestro and its leader, someone who calls himself M."

While Mahoney told Tucker in more detail why Bree and Sampson had come to the area and what they'd found out at the country store in North Fork, I went through Bree's purse with latex gloves on. I found her driver's license, cash, and all her credit cards, but her cell phone was missing. I searched Sampson's pack and found his wallet, laptop, car keys, a sealed envelope addressed to Rebecca Cantrell, and a carefully folded crayon drawing of flowers from Willow with the words *You are the best daddy!* But no phone.

I got emotional and found myself praying for their safety. I reached into the bottom of John's pack and came up with a little pink fob. Willow's Jiobit fob.

That was strange. It was supposed to be in Willow's backpack in DC.

I tucked that, Willow's drawing, and the envelope for Sampson's girlfriend in the chest pocket of my parka for safekeeping, then shut the car door. "You'll have to have criminalists go through this vehicle."

Tucker said, "I'll call the state crime bureau. They can be on their way first thing tomorrow."

Mahoney said, "What were you about to say about Alice Lake, Sheriff?"

"I was there," he said. "First to respond to the Wheeler murders. I was a young green deputy with Blaine County's sheriff's department. Let's get inside where it's warm and I'll tell you the whole thing."

Mahoney climbed up front. I got in the back of the cruiser and shivered; Sheriff Tucker got in and turned the heat on full blast.

He described being on call almost forty years before and being dispatched to the Wheeler home on Alice Lake. The sons had found their parents murdered.

"It was a shitshow, top to bottom," Tucker said. "I took one look and, I'll admit it, I had to throw up."

"Happens to everyone the first time," I said. "Lot of blood?"

"Hell, whoever did it had to have been spattered head to toe with blood. But the Wheeler kids, the poor little bastards, were clean, and they were destroyed by the killings. One of them, Ryan, kept saying that he should not have kept his music playing all night, that if he or Sean had heard something from the boathouse, they could have called the police."

"And Sean?"

"Kid was catatonic. Hardly able to say a word. Completely traumatized. Whatever happened to him?"

Mahoney said, "As we understand it, he had mental problems

after the murders that his aunt tried to deal with. When he turned eighteen, he vanished with his inheritance."

Tucker said, "And, what, you think Sean Wheeler became this character M?"

"We don't know what to think, and the trail is thirty years old."

"No leads whatsoever?"

"Just a possible name," I said. "Ian Duncanson."

I saw the sheriff blink and frown in his rearview mirror.

"Oh, Christ," he said. "Is that possible?"

I said, "Out with it, Sheriff Tucker."

"Let me make sure," he said. He got on his radio and called his dispatcher. "This is Sheriff Tucker, Cat. Can you do me a favor and look up the name of the guy who disappeared hunting couple of months back? The guy from Boise."

Cat came back a minute later. "Duncanson. Ian Duncanson."

CHAPTER

56

THE DOOR OF THE octagonal elevator closed on Bree and Sampson, and the elevator dropped for close to fifteen seconds before it slowed to a stop.

Sampson figured they were at least a hundred and fifty feet below the abandoned metal building. The door slid back with a whoosh, revealing a massive bald guy in his early forties and a fit woman with short sandy-blond hair who looked to be in her late thirties. They were about ten feet away in a hall with rock walls. Both held pistols loosely aimed at them.

"My name's Lucas Bean," the man said in a clipped British accent. "This is my colleague Katrina White."

White said in a Slavic accent, "You should know that the elevator and the interior and exterior doors are all biometrically controlled. You cannot open them. If you're going to ignore that fact and be a problem, the restraints stay on. Will you be a problem, Chief Stone?"

Bree shook her head.

Bean looked at John. "What about you?"

"Not for the moment," Sampson said.

"Fair enough," Bean said, raising his gun. "Easy as you exit. Detective Sampson first."

Sampson studied the bald man as he stepped toward him. The way Bean held his pistol and the way he stood—ankles and knees apart and flexed, his balance rolled toward the toes—said athlete to Sampson at the very least and likely a special forces operator of some sort.

White moved her gun off Bree and aimed at Sampson.

"Hands out," Bean said.

John extended his wrists. Bean held his gun in his left hand, reached into the pocket of his pants with his right, and came up with a folding knife. He flicked it open and neatly cut Sampson's wrists free.

"Thank you," John said. Bean wagged his pistol to the side, and John stepped away.

"It's a privilege that can easily be revoked," Bean said. "Chief Stone?"

Bree stepped out. White's gun swung toward her head. Bean cut her restraints.

She immediately rubbed at her wrists.

Bean said, "You will want to get off your heavy clothes and take showers before eating."

"Not hungry," Sampson said.

"I suspect you will be soon enough," White said.

"What does that mean?" Bree demanded. "Who are you? Why are we here?"

Bean said, "All in good time, Chief Stone. Please remove your parkas and boots here. And don't bother to look for your phones. We have them."

"Good luck getting in," Sampson said. "They're encrypted."

"We already have them open."

Sampson wanted to put his fist right in the man's smirking face but kept his cool as he removed his parka and boots. After both he and Bree were in their stocking feet, Bean waved his gun again.

"Down the hall, second door on the left for Chief Stone, third door on the right for Detective Sampson."

John led the way, noting the echo in the hall and the small black boxes set next to the first two steel doors built flush into the rock walls. No handles.

He looked over his shoulder after he passed the second door on the left, saw White step up to the box, flip the lid up, and press her right eye to a retinal scan. The steel door slid back with a quiet whoosh.

Bree looked inside, then over at Sampson. She nodded; John nodded back and started toward the third door on the right. White said something he did not quite catch because of the echo in the hall.

Bean used the retinal scan to open the door to a small bathroom with a shower. "Sorry about the ceiling height," Bean told Sampson. "Towels and soap on the sink. Slippers in your size. Nothing in there you can use as a weapon, so don't try. Knock twice when you are done and I'll get you to your room."

Sampson hesitated, then ducked inside and slowly stood; he had barely two inches of clearance. The door slid shut.

Lucas Bean stood in the hall for a long moment before pulling out a small radio. "Edith?"

A moment later, a woman with a hoarse voice and a British accent said, "Right here."

"Tell the boss they're buttoned up. If you're sure, I'd say the trap is set and you're good to transmit."

"I'm sure," she said. "Here we go, then. Three-second distorted sat burst with a full degree deflection off the towers above Kimberley. Should put them at least fifty miles off target."

CHAPTER

57

BREE KNOCKED TWICE ON the steel door. She had to admit that the hot shower had killed the chill in her fingers and toes, and the wool slippers were cushy, warm, and exactly her size.

The door slid back. Katrina White stood off in the hallway, still holding her pistol. "Better?" White asked.

"Yes," Bree said.

"Exit and move to the elevator, please."

"What about Sampson?" Bree asked as she started down the hall toward the elevator.

"Ahead of you. Men don't need as much time as we do."

White used the retinal scan to open the elevator door. They entered, and she tapped something on a touch screen; the elevator rose for five seconds and stopped. The doors opened.

"Fourth door on the right," White said and gestured with the gun barrel for Bree to exit.

Bree walked down a rock-walled hall similar to the one just below, her captor trailing her just out of reach. *A pro,* Bree thought. *She's handled prisoners before.*

"We hope you still like your steak charred and rare," White said.

How did she know that?

"Who hopes I still like it?" Bree asked as they reached the fourth door on the right and White stepped up to activate the retinal scan.

The door slid back as White said, "The management. We hope you enjoy your meal and have a nice rest."

Bree looked into a room, which held a bunk and a toilet. It was no bigger than a prison cell. "Why are you doing this?" she asked.

"Because all of us have had to go through it," White said. "It's just protocol."

"For what? For who? Maestro?"

The woman wagged the gun. "All in good time, Chief Stone."

Frustrated, knowing she had no choice, she went into the cell. The door slid shut.

There was a dinner tray with covered plates on a stool in the corner. The smell of a freshly broiled steak filled the tiny room, and she was suddenly famished. Bree lifted the plastic lids on the dishes and found a perfectly charred New York strip steak, roasted fingerling potatoes, broccoli, cauliflower, and a glass of wine.

She immediately felt all sorts of conflicting emotions. On the one hand, she was looking at one of her favorite meals, and that gave her some comfort. On the other hand, it was creepy that they'd known it was her favorite meal.

Then again, Bean made it sound like they were already in our phones. Which means they have access to all sorts of data about me and my past.

She stood there a moment, debating whether to eat the meal. She was terribly hungry, but she feared the food or wine might be drugged.

Nice little prison you've gotten yourself into, she thought as she looked around the room and back to the food. *God, it smells so good.* Bree thought of her air force survival training, thought about her situation and what her instructors would tell her to do. *They'd tell me to eat. If I'm not strong, I can't escape.*

It felt so right, she picked up her plastic fork and knife and cut the steak. She put it in her mouth and almost swooned, it tasted so good.

She hesitated again but then took a sip of the wine. If it was drugged wine, she thought, it was excellent drugged wine.

Even though the fork and knife broke halfway through the meal, Bree ate every bit of the food and drank the rest of the wine. When she was done, she looked around her cell.

The bunk was made of impact-resistant fiberglass like a kayak and was bolted flush into the wall. The faucet and toilet handles were welded in place. The light switch was controlled with your finger. The two bulbs that lit the room were behind a wire screen overhead.

It was as White had said before Bree entered the shower room: there was nothing here to use as a weapon.

Though she could not spot a hidden camera, she assumed the room had one, which was even creepier.

And if it was true that everything mechanical in the place was controlled with biometric devices, how could she get out? How could she even find Sampson?

After a few more minutes of this kind of fretting, she felt

anxious and almost helpless, which Alex always said was a terrible, debilitating emotion.

I won't be helpless, she thought and yawned. *I will act with purpose. I will take care of the only thing I can take care of: me.*

With that, Bree forced herself to turn off the light. She groped her way to the bunk, pulled back the blanket, kicked off the slippers, and climbed in, telling herself that she had to sleep if she wanted to think clearly.

But her brain refused to slow down, refused to stop asking the same questions over and over: *Where's Alex? Does he even know we're missing?*

CHAPTER

58

MAHONEY AND I DRAGGED ourselves into a Best Western after a long, hard, frustrating day.

Ned threw his stuff on the bed, turned on the television, and flipped through the stations to CNN. We'd picked up sandwiches, potato chips, and beer on the way here, and I cracked a beer and ate a chicken breast on rye that wasn't half bad, given that we'd bought it at a gas station called the Town Pump.

The cable news was mostly focused on the upcoming inauguration of President-Elect Sue Winter and her nominees for secretary of the treasury and secretary of commerce. None of it interested me in the slightest.

Bree and John had been missing for more than two days. And Ned and I believed that they might have been taken by Maestro because they'd learned that Ryan Malcomb's twin had gone missing in the wilderness.

I'd read up on that case during the car ride in from Salmon. In almost all the stories about his disappearance, Ian Duncanson was described as a single, reclusive code writer and investor in his late forties who lived on fifty acres north of Boise.

He'd disappeared during a solo elk-hunting trip in early November in a vast roadless area between Boise and Sun Valley. The only picture they had of Duncanson was nearly ten years old, but if you took away the shaggy hair and the beard, he was a dead ringer for Ryan Malcomb.

CNN had been running a piece on the president-elect's likely attire on Inauguration Day but now it cut back to the anchor.

"We're sorry to interrupt that fascinating segment, but we have breaking news," the anchor said. "CNN's legal correspondent Imogene Lawrence has learned that fifty-two-year-old U.S. Supreme Court justice Margaret Blevins collapsed in her chambers around eight o'clock this evening and was rushed to the hospital. Imogene, what can you tell us?"

The screen jumped to the reporter on the steps of the U.S. Supreme Court.

Lawrence said, "Justice Blevins evidently lost consciousness in her offices where she was working with her clerks on a dissenting opinion to an upcoming ruling. She was treated on scene and rushed by ambulance to George Washington University Hospital. We have no official word on a cause, but aides close to Blevins said she appeared to have suffered some kind of seizure.

"News of Justice Blevins's condition comes on the heels of public confirmation earlier today that her fellow justice Albert

231

Mayweather has had a recurrence of his cancer," the reporter went on. "Though it is too early to tell definitively—and we at CNN wish both justices a full and speedy recovery—President-Elect Winter may be in a position to alter the balance of power in the high court very early in her administration."

Mahoney's phone rang. He looked at the ID and lost color, then picked up and put the call on speaker. "Director Hamilton, I'm here with Dr. Cross. How are you?"

"Great," she said. "Have you heard about Blevins and Mayweather?"

"Just saw it on CNN."

"I want you to end your wild-goose chase out west and get back to Washington first thing tomorrow," she said.

"Ma'am, with all due respect—"

"This is a direct order, Mahoney. The incoming attorney general wants you to brief him face to face and ASAP. I will be there as well. If Winter has to nominate a new justice, she has to know all about this Maestro group trying to influence the pick."

He sighed. "I'll try to book a flight right now."

"Notify me when you have your itinerary."

"Yes, ma'am."

He ended the call as my phone rang. It was Keith Karl Rawlins, the FBI cybercrimes consultant.

"KK," I said. "To what do I owe the honor?"

"Bree's cell lit up about an hour ago," he said. "It was on for maybe four seconds. I got a rough location, but you're not going to like it. I'm sending you the GPS coordinates now."

I pumped my fist. "Thanks, KK. I owe you."

Mahoney was on his laptop, trying to get a flight to DC through Salt Lake City, when I hung up and said, "Rawlins found Bree!"

"Where?"

My phone chirped to alert me to a text. "We're about to find out." I got my iPad, called up Google Earth, and typed in the coordinates. The app took us almost due north, across the Canadian border and deep into the mountainous wilderness of British Columbia.

I zoomed in on the exact spot: a high mountainside amid big fir trees.

"There's nothing there," I said, disappointed. "No buildings. Nothing. My God, how the hell did she get in there? It's like seventy miles from nowhere. And it can't look like this now. The place must be buried in ten feet of snow, maybe more."

Mahoney said, "Well, we don't know that she's there at all, Alex. Maestro could have thrown the phone out of a plane."

"Or she could still be right there," I said, closing my iPad and grabbing my carry-on and heavy parka.

"Where are you going?"

"I'm taking the Tahoe and going up there. You can get a ride to the local airport in the morning."

"Do you have your passport?"

"I do," I said. "I always carry it as backup ID."

Mahoney didn't like this. "How the hell do you plan on getting in there?"

I went out the door. "I'll figure that out when I get to the closest town."

CHAPTER

59

EVEN THOUGH SAMPSON FELT drowsy from the food and wine, he forced himself to assess his situation.

He started with the assumption that he was being monitored and decided he did not care if they watched him probe the room for weaknesses. Although it was clean and reasonably well appointed, it was a cell, plain and simple. There was no secret toggle or pressure plate he could find to open the door from the inside. The steel sink's faucet knobs were welded on. The toilet top was bolted down. He could not get at any of the moving parts. There was no mirror.

The bunk below the mattress was one piece and made of a dense fiberglass material, the edges rounded like a surfboard's. The hardware that held it to the wall was seamless, with recessed screws and permanent hinges.

The wine had come in a flimsy plastic cup. He'd been given plastic cutlery along with a paper plate. The knife broke when he was halfway through his steak — which, although he hated to admit it, was excellent. By the time he was finished with the meal, the fork's tines were all broken. He knew prison inmates made shanks out of small pieces of plastic, but he saw no way to craft a knife.

There was the issue of the biometric controls on everything. And even if he could somehow circumvent the retinal scanners, get out of his cell, get the elevator working, and make it outside, they'd taken his parka, boots, hat, and gloves. In the slippers, at night, he'd probably freeze to death in the sixty-below windchill before he even figured out where he was.

A hollow feeling started to build in his gut. His breath came quicker, and he realized his muscles were tense.

John knew what was happening. He felt trapped, cornered. The most primitive parts of his brain were activating, pushing him toward a fight-or-flight response.

Can't let that happen. You're going to make bad decisions. Got to get control if you want to survive.

Sampson's SERE training instructors had consistently stressed that the most important weapon he had in captivity was his mind. If he could not control his thoughts, his emotions, keep them from dragging his brain into its most primitive state, he would spiral down, make impulsive decisions, and be doomed.

He remembered one of those instructors, a tough master sergeant named Frank Eagleton, telling him that to avoid despair when being held, to stay active and alert, you had to focus on the moment at hand rather than on the unknowable future or the unchangeable past.

But try as he might, he could not stop his thoughts from

straying to his past with Willow and his future with his daughter and Rebecca Cantrell.

Up bubbled a rush of regret, guilt, and sorrow. He'd willingly come along on this trip with Bree. He'd put himself in harm's way as much as she had. And why hadn't he sent the love letter?

And now here he was, a prisoner of his decisions.

Willow had had no say in the matter. Neither had Rebecca. And they were the ones most likely to suffer the long-term consequences.

Sampson shut off the light, climbed into his bunk, and wallowed in his predicament, feeling weaker and less sure of himself and his chances for survival.

But then he saw Sergeant Eagleton clearly in his mind — that big jaw his survival instructor had had, the way it jutted out when he spoke.

The enemy is everyone and everything that might prevent you from coming home alive and with dignity, Eagleton said. He tapped his temple. *I say again: Your number one weapon against any enemy is your mind. The question is, are you going to let your mind use you or are you going to use your mind in a way that allows you to resist and fight back?*

Again, Sampson thought of Willow, how she danced her way to him when he picked her up at school, and of Rebecca, how she made him smile every time she walked into a room.

I'm going to use my mind, he told himself over and over again. He closed his eyes and began to drift toward darkness and dreams. *I am going to resist and fight back.*

CHAPTER

60

WHEN I REALIZED THAT it was going to take me way too many hours to drive to Kimberley, British Columbia, the town closest to Bree's last cell phone transmission, I pulled over in Dillon, Montana, and slept from one a.m. to six.

I got to Butte by eight, went straight to the airport, and chartered a turboprop plane. It cost a small fortune, but I didn't hesitate. I was sure Bree's and John's lives were at stake.

We were in the air by ten; we landed to refuel and clear immigration and customs in Bonners Ferry, Idaho, then flew two more bumpy hours to Kimberley. We landed at one p.m., and I was shaken from the turbulence we'd flown through and a little wobbly from fatigue as I climbed out of the plane into bitter cold and snowy weather.

There was two feet of the white stuff on the ground and the

pilot said the snow was supposed to continue falling overnight. I cleared Canadian immigration and customs, glad that my FBI credentials meant that I could keep my weapon as long as I went straight to the local Royal Canadian Mounted Police office to declare and register it.

I rented a Ford Bronco at the airport and drove to the mounted police offices on Archibald Street. The place looked more like a one-level cottage than a police station with its white shake shingles and bright blue trim.

I knocked on the bright blue front door and went in. A woman in her mid-thirties sat at a desk alone beyond a small counter. She wore a green wool cap over a mane of startlingly red hair, a black puffy coat, and glasses, and she was typing furiously on a keyboard.

"How can I help you?" she asked, not looking up from her work.

"I'm looking for someone with the Canadian Mounted Police."

"You're looking at her," she said, turning from the computer. "Officer Molly Fagan."

I identified myself. She came over to look at my credentials.

"I didn't know the FBI had consultants," Officer Fagan said, squinting at them. "You have any real authority, Dr. Cross?"

"I'm federally deputized, but I almost always work with active agents who make the formal arrests."

"Unconventional, but what do I know. How can I help?"

"I need to register my service weapon," I said, setting the hard case on the counter. "And I need some advice."

"Weapon first," Fagan said, turning all business.

I opened the case, and she filled out a form, including the make and model—a Glock 19—and the serial number, then counted the rounds in the two clips. By the time I signed the form, the clock on the wall behind her said ten past two.

"And the advice?" she asked.

I told her that Bree and Sampson had vanished almost fifty-six hours before, that I believed they'd been taken by Maestro, a vigilante group involved in the deaths of U.S. Supreme Court candidates, and that there'd been a four-second transmission from Bree's cell near this location.

As I was finishing, a big guy in his late thirties came in wearing a heavy down parka with a fur hood. He shook off the snow and pulled back the hood, revealing a broad, bearded, smiling face and short hair, both beard and hair tinged with gray.

"Brutal out there, eh?" he said.

Fagan looked over at him. "Give me a minute, sir."

"Brian Toomey," he said, unzipping his coat to reveal a blue jumpsuit. "I'm the new janitor? From Wolcott Secure Maintenance?"

"Since when?" she said, frowning.

"Last week," Toomey said, removing the jacket.

"I was off last week," Fagan said. She glanced at me and slid his way. "Identification? Federal?"

He hung up the jacket, nodded, got out several cards. "Everything's there. Or at least it was last week when I showed them to Officer Craig, eh?"

After several moments, Fagan handed them back. "Ontario?"

He smiled. "I'm a regional supervisor for Wolcott back there and they said no problem when I asked them for a short-term transfer out this way for the winter. For the snowmobiling, eh? Incredible, eh?"

"The year for it," Fagan agreed, and came back to me.

The janitor put in earbuds and tapped his phone. His head began bopping as he slid on latex gloves.

"You have the coordinates from your wife's phone, Dr. Cross?" Fagan asked.

61

"I DO," I SAID, sliding a piece of paper with the coordinates across the counter to her.

The janitor moved about, gathering papers to be shredded and bagged.

Officer Fagan told me to come around to her desk; she called up Google Earth and typed the coordinates in. The app zoomed in on the mountainous heavily forested area Mahoney and I had studied the night before.

The Mountie looked up at me with a frown on her face. "Are you sure? That's the middle of nowhere, the back of Kianuko Provincial Park."

"The burst was short, but the FBI cybercrimes expert was positive on the location."

"Is there even a cell tower in there?" she asked, scrolling around.

"No idea," I said. "I just know that's where the transmission came from."

Fagan shook her head. "Look at it. There's nothing out there for thirty or forty miles in any direction, and I guarantee you the area is buried at the moment."

"How can I get in there?"

She shrugged. "Snowmobile or helicopter, but there's no way they'd let you land one in the provincial park without formal permission, and that is a total hassle to get."

"Can you zoom out?"

The Mountie did, giving us a higher aerial view of the terrain. I scanned the scene, saw mile after mile of uninterrupted wilderness.

"Can you zoom out farther?" I asked, and she pulled back more.

"What's this?" I pointed far west of where Bree's cell had gone off.

"Lumber camp and sawmill. It's just outside the park boundary. You can get to it, but you'll have to drive all the way around to Sirdar and you'll need a strong sled."

"Snowmobile?"

"That too."

I kept scanning. Along the north boundary I saw a small square that was shaded gray. "This?"

"Private inholding, including an old cabin and horse barn," Fagan said. "A woman in Toronto inherited it, but she's in the process of selling it to the park service."

"Any other inholdings?"

"Several, all old mining claims," she said. She brought up five different inholdings, all small, no more than four or five acres, and none with any structures on them until the one farthest south, a remote triangle of property a good fifty miles from the signal.

She zoomed in on the area, revealing the caved-in roof of a metal building. "Used to be an old silver mine. Abandoned in the 1960s. Some outfit out of Edmonton bought the rights and went back in there about ten years ago, hunting for rare earth metals and silver. Test borings never panned out. The project was abandoned."

"And these?" I asked, tapping on two structures about nine miles apart between the GPS coordinates of Bree's last phone transmission and the city of Kimberley.

"Those are well inside the park boundaries, old trapper cabins from before the formation of the park. A snowmobile-rental place out of Meacham uses the closer one for day riders to stop and get warm. There's a woodstove in it."

"I'll start there," I said. "Rent one of those snowmobiles in Meacham."

The Mountie looked at me skeptically. "You ever driven a snowmobile?"

"Not yet."

"Then I am going with you to protect the Canadian government's interests."

"Great," I said. "Let's go."

She narrowed her eyes. "Dr. Cross, I completely understand your eagerness to get out and see if your wife is there. But we've got only two hours of daylight left and a storm that's still puking snow. We won't even get close before dark. Storm is supposed to end during the night. We'll go first thing in the morning."

CHAPTER

62

AT FIVE A.M., OFFICER Fagan pulled up outside my motel room and honked. I was finishing up a text to Mahoney, telling him where I was and where we were going.

He had texted me while I slept fitfully to tell me that the acting director of the FBI had used the briefing with the incoming attorney general to pitch herself as the best choice for permanent director while simultaneously distancing herself from Ned's Maestro investigation.

I didn't need to be there, he'd written. It was performance art, with me taking a lot of heat. I don't know if I'm still on the case at the moment. I'll let you know tomorrow.

Fagan honked again. I grabbed my pistol in its holster, put on my down coat, gloves, and hat, and went outside. She was at the wheel of a big Ford pickup attached to a trailer that held two Arctic Cat snowmobiles and a pull-along sled.

The storm had ended. The temperatures had plunged to twenty below zero.

"How far in is it, Officer Fagan?" I asked as I climbed into the pickup, shivering.

"Call me Molly. I figure it's seventy kilometers. More than forty miles, anyway. There's a burrito and a coffee there for you in the sack on the floor."

"Forty miles in this cold?" I said as she pulled out and I found the coffee. "How are we going to stay warm enough to get all the way in there?"

Fagan motioned with her thumb to the back seat. "I've got extra insulated coveralls, boots with heaters, mitts with heaters, goggles, face masks, and a pack and a helmet for you. An avalanche transceiver too. I think they'll all fit you. They belonged to my predecessor. He was big like you. The pack includes emergency medical gear, everything from bandages to blood coagulators. I also brought a hunting rifle with a scope for you and a twelve-gauge Ithaca pump-action gun with slugs for me."

"Expecting trouble?"

"I just like to be prepared, which is why the under-saddle compartments of both sleds are filled with survival gear: double-wall tents, sleeping bags, freeze-dried rations, and fire starters."

"So we're not going to die from exposure?"

"Not if we can help it."

We bounced down a rough road and parked at the trailhead beyond Meacham. The moon was three-quarters full and the stars were brilliant. I got the avalanche transceiver positioned correctly on my chest and struggled to get the insulated coveralls over my pants and parka.

The boots were clunky and very warm. The mitts came up to my elbows. The helmet was equipped with a two-way radio.

The coldness of the air took my breath away and with all the clothes I wore, I could barely manage a waddle when we got out of the truck and pulled the helmets on. Fagan backed the snowmobiles off the trailer and showed me the controls.

"Don't over-gun the accelerator if you feel her bogging in deep powder," the Mountie said over the helmet radio. "Just stand and get your weight forward. The engine will do the rest."

"Okay," I said, the uncertainty plain in my voice.

"Stay behind me and you'll do fine. But with this new snow, we'll have to be really careful when it gets steep and deep."

With the guns in plastic scabbards attached to the snowmobiles and an extra twenty gallons of fuel in green jerricans strapped in Fagan's following sled, we set out on a trail heading south-southwest an hour before dawn. With all the new snow, I was glad she was in front breaking trail. But her sled blew so much powder snow behind it, I had to slow down and let a gap form so I could see. I was lucky. The terrain was mostly flat in those first ten miles. Once I got the hang of the accelerator and learned how to shift my weight opposite the direction of a turn, I was almost keeping up with Officer Fagan as the first light showed in the east. The sun rose, transforming the trail through the snow-coated conifer forest into a shimmering, dazzling, and bitingly cold tunnel.

Bree and John are not equipped for this kind of cold, I thought. *If they were out in the storm the past two nights, they're dead.*

Fifteen miles in, the way got steeper and the snow deeper, and my inferior riding skills were exposed. I had to stand, sit, and throw my body around to wrestle the sled up the incline, and I was sweating hard when we reached the top of a plateau.

The wind was howling. It cut through the coveralls and the down coat, made it to my wet wool sweater and vest. I started to shiver, and I was shaking from cold an hour later when we came to an intersection of trails about twenty miles in, halfway to the GPS coordinates from Bree's phone transmission. One trail went almost due north.

"I have to get warm," I said, teeth chattering.

"That first trapper's cabin is ahead a kilometer or so. We'll get in there and get a fire going, dry out."

"A kilometer," I said. "I can make that."

We continued on the trail and reached that cabin we'd seen on Google Earth. There were seven snowmobiles already there, riderless and idling. Smoke was coming out of the chimney.

"They already have a fire going for us," Fagan said. "Let's talk to these folks and see what they know. Leave your sled running."

It sounded like a great plan to me, and I hurried after her. Inside, we found three women and four men huddled around an old-fashioned potbellied stove, their helmets and gloves off.

"I'm Officer Fagan with the Royal Canadian Mounted Police," she said after pulling her helmet off.

With the arms of his coverall tied around his waist, revealing a very buff torso, a bald, cocoa-skinned guy wearing a spandex beanie smiled as he stood up. In a British accent, he said, "Lucas Bean. You coming to rescue us, then?"

"Do you need rescuing?" Fagan said.

"We did last night," one woman said in a British accent. "Got trapped in that other cabin in the storm. Had to sleep in our gear. It's not as airtight as this place."

Bean nodded. "We had enough food to last, though. And water. And gas."

"Heading out?" Fagan said.

"Soon as our fingers thaw," the woman said.

I said, "You see anyone else back in here?"

"In that storm?" Bean said. "Not a chance."

"Are you all from other countries?" Fagan said.

"From all over," Bean said, smiling again. "Looking for new trails to ride, and I think we got in a wee bit over our heads."

"A *way* bit over our heads, Lucas," another woman said firmly.

There was something slightly awkward about Mr. Bean and his friends, but then again, they'd passed the night in an uninsulated shack with cracks in the wall at twenty below zero. While they dressed to leave for the trailhead at Meacham, we stood around the woodstove until I could feel my feet and hands again.

After drinking a cup of hot coffee, I told Officer Fagan I was ready to push on. The Mountie damped down the firebox and we went outside and found Bean and his group getting ready to ride out.

"Serious power sleds," Bean said, gesturing at the RCMP snowmobiles.

"Meant to get us there and back again," Fagan said. "Be safe, Mr. Bean."

"You as well, Officer Fagan," he said, tugging on his helmet. "You as well."

63

AROUND ELEVEN THAT MORNING, with the sun nearing its zenith in the impossibly blue skies, we were on what Officer Fagan described as a "rarely used side trail," roughly one mile and several thousand vertical feet from where Bree's cell phone had transmitted more than two days before.

Fagan was not kidding that the route was rarely used. She had to duck down behind her windshield to avoid getting whipped by the thin saplings overgrowing the trail.

I did the same, feeling the saplings grab at the sled runners and the sleeves and legs of my coveralls. More than once, I thought one of my boots had gotten snarled in the brush and would pull me off the machine.

Finally, we crested a knoll. Fagan stopped her sled at the edge of a ravine and faced the steep, snowy flank of a mountain on the other side.

She got out binoculars and looked all around us. "Far as we can go," she said, climbing off the snowmobile and lifting the seat.

"Where do you think she was?" I asked, getting off my sled into knee-deep snow.

"I think I can show you," the Mountie said. She pulled out a padded bag with a ballistic cloth exterior and unzipped it, revealing a compact Swarovski spotting scope and a tripod. After several tries, she fit them together and aimed the scope up the mountain.

"That's roughly where I put the transmission location," Fagan said at last, standing back. "You're looking at it at sixty-five-power magnification."

I shuffled forward in the deep snow, peered into the scope, and saw thick firs, sheer rock, and ice high up the side of the crag. My stomach turned over.

"She could not have been up there," I said. "Not alive."

"I know," Fagan said. "But I knew you wouldn't believe me unless you saw it with your own eyes."

"It had to have been a mistake," I said. "Or Maestro tossed her phone out of a plane. Or her." The thought almost made my knees buckle.

"Go back?" she asked.

"Where's that lumber camp?"

"Far. We'd never make it back tonight. Like I said, you're better coming at it from the west side of the park."

"What about that abandoned mine?"

"It's a ways too, but I know a spot where you can look at it from up high."

Three hours later, as I was feeling like I'd wrestled a tiger while running a marathon, Fagan finally stopped her sled. We were up high, looking almost due south across a great expanse of snowy wilderness.

Again the Mountie set up her spotting scope and looked through it. After several minutes, she stood back and said, "You should see the outline of the old mine building there."

I pushed up the visor of my helmet and looked through the scope. I saw a distant snow-covered hilltop and the suggestion of a building wavering like a mirage. I was about to stand up when I caught movement near the building.

I put my left mitt over my left eye to see better. At first I saw nothing, then I clearly spotted movement.

"There's someone there," I said.

"There is not," Fagan said.

"Moving right to left away from the building. Take a look."

I stepped back to let her peer through the scope again. She was there for several long moments before she said, "I do see something moving. I can't say it's a man."

"What else could it be?"

"Moose? Elk?"

When Fagan stood up, I said, "Can we get closer? Check?"

The Mountie thought a moment. "I think there is a trail to the mine. But it's older than the ones we were on. And as I remember, there's warnings for sleds to stay out because there's still mine debris on it—tailings, pieces of pipe, and old cables that could snag our runners."

"We need to check."

Fagan looked up at the clear blue sky and finally nodded. "We'll be back at the Meacham trailhead around midnight, but I'm game if you are."

"More than game," I said.

She took us south for another hour. The sun was getting low in the southwestern sky when we reached a series of long, linked, snow-covered alpine meadows and stopped to refuel.

"We get to the end of this chain of parks, we should be able to get a good view of that old mining area before dark," she said. "Then it's a long slog out."

"I'm ready for it."

Fagan shifted in her saddle as if to start again, then pulled off a mitt, unzipped her coverall, and got out her binoculars. She pushed up her visor and peered ahead down through the meadows and then behind us.

"We've got company," she said.

"Really?" I said, pivoting on my machine. Seven snowmobiles about a half a mile behind us were roaring our way.

"Son of a bitch!" the Mountie said.

"What?"

Fagan stuffed her binoculars inside her coverall, pointed at the plastic scabbard on the side of my sled. "Get your rifle handy, Dr. Cross. It's that same bunch from earlier today. And I think they've all got automatic weapons."

64

FOR A SPLIT SECOND I hesitated, needing to be sure, but when Officer Fagan put her sled in gear and took off south, the decision was made. I followed in her tracks, wanting to look back but not daring because the snow was soft in the meadow and I was struggling to keep my machine going.

"You have ten rounds three hundred Win mag," the Mountie said over the helmet headset. "Eighteen rounds nine-millimeter?"

"Correct," I said.

"I have eight rounds in the Ithaca, and eighteen rounds nine-millimeter."

"Not enough if they mean us harm."

"Roger that, so we are going to have to put distance between them, find some high ground for an ambush where I can use my satellite phone, alert dispatch."

She banked her sled toward the southwest corner of the first meadow and accelerated, throwing a plume of powder snow in the late-day sun that made it hard to—

Even though I had my helmet on, the flat crack of automatic-weapon fire behind me was unmistakable. I ducked and cranked the throttle, no longer caring whether I could see or not, hoping I was throwing up enough snow to mess with their aim.

And then we were in fir trees on a lane that led to the second meadow.

"They're close enough to shoot at me," I said.

"I heard," Fagan gasped. "Stay with me. We'll hit the second meadow, peel away west, then loop around to cover in the east toward the rim of the canyon. We'll have a bit of high ground, and the sat phone will connect no problem."

"Your country," I said, seeing the lane ahead break free into the second meadow, which had many more scattered trees than the first. I followed the Mountie hard west toward the sun, which was now right in our eyes, making it difficult to see. "If they follow, they'll be as blind as we are going through here."

"Exactly, so that knoll there, then," she said, turning her sled toward a rise in the meadow where trees had burned down a long time ago.

I said, "You go to the rim and call. I'll go up the knoll and cover you."

"Done."

The Mountie rounded the back of the knoll and headed east toward the rim of the canyon. I climbed the knoll, stopped the machine just below the crest of the rise, and looked over our back trail. After unstrapping the scabbard, I pulled out a Winchester Model 70 stainless-steel rifle with a Leopold scope, ran the action, and watched a 180-grain .300 magnum round seat snugly in the chamber.

Beyond my sled, the snow was deep. I struggled the last few feet to the top, then flipped up my helmet visor and scanned the tree line in the slanting light.

It was pushing zero. My breath hung in the air like fog.

For several moments, there was nothing but the fading buzz of Fagan's machine. I looked behind me and realized I could see quite plainly that butte where the old silver mine had been and where we'd seen movement. It was no more than two miles away.

But the light was fading. I didn't have an hour of it left and—

Three snowmobiles came from the north and exited the lane between the alpine meadows, following in our tracks. I took two steps forward in the snow and eased in behind the stout and charred stump of a burned fir tree.

"They're here," I said into my helmet microphone.

"Come back?" Fagan said, barely audible over static.

"They're here."

"Can't…you. Try to…"

There was nothing but a hiss in my ear as the sleds slowed no more than four hundred yards below me. I swept aside the snow atop the stump and laid the hunting rifle over the top.

The sleds stopped. The drivers looked around.

I peered through the telescopic sight. As Fagan had said, they had automatic weapons hanging from chest harnesses.

I heard other machines and looked northeast along the tree line. The other four sleds were leaving the woods in the far corner, headed south.

A northwest wind had picked up, spinning snow devils across the landscape. I looked to my right far off the knoll, trying to spot Fagan toward the rim of a canyon she'd said was right there, no more than five hundred yards away. In the rising wind and blowing snow, it was impossible to make out for certain. I was on my own until the Mountie came back in range.

My eye went back to the scope, and I moved it on the first rider. My finger went to the trigger. Given that we had already been shot at, I believed I would be acting in self-defense. As far as I was concerned, there was no legal issue if I was forced to shoot under those circumstances.

But a hunting rifle against machine guns?

Was I better off running? Without Fagan and with darkness coming?

The lead driver of the three pressed the ignition on his sled. He started fast, following in our tracks, but slowed some two hundred and fifty yards from me, caught in that blinding late-afternoon sun and swirling snow.

65

THEY WERE GOING TO round the knoll in a matter of moments. They were going to see where our tracks had split and where I had gone uphill.

I felt I had no choice at that point. I flipped off the safety and slowly swung the gun and scope to the lead driver; I saw the crosshairs cover his chest at two hundred yards and squeezed.

The trigger was crisp and light. The shot came as a surprise to him.

I knew he was dead even before I'd run the bolt and saw the second driver trying to get off his sled and find cover. I shot him through his left side before he could dismount.

The third driver sprayed bullets uphill in my direction, forcing me to duck while I ran the action again, and I started to ease up over the top of the stump. But then I heard his machine at my nine o'clock and realized he was trying to flank me, trying to come around the knoll.

I spun around and took five quick bounds back down the hill. I threw the rifle over the handles of my snowmobile and found the third driver in my sights. He saw me and tried to get his gun up.

But he was less than a hundred yards away. My shot caught him square and hurled him off his machine.

My heart slammed in my chest. My breath came in gasps.

I'd just killed three men. Or women. I didn't know. And I'd been forced to do it for reasons I did not understand.

But then, standing there in knee-deep snow in the bitter-cold aftermath of a gun battle, it hit me. I did understand. And I knew who they were.

They had never been tourists. They were Maestro soldiers.

And they're protecting that mine! I jumped onto my sled, shoved the rifle in the scabbard, and started the engine. I swung the nose of the machine around and gave it throttle, meaning to head straight downhill.

But it drifted sideways in the deep snow, pushing me toward the third driver's snowmobile. I went with the drift, realizing I could get his weapon and ammunition. I stopped next to his idling machine and found him dead on his back.

I refused to raise my visor; I pulled a knife from a sheath on the harness and cut free the gun, a short-barreled H and K nine-millimeter, and three high-capacity backup clips. I'd no sooner returned to my snowmobile when I heard rapid-fire shooting.

My helmet radio crackled to life.

"Cross, they're on me!" Fagan yelled. "I'm heading south."

"Coming!" I twisted the throttle, spun southeast, and barreled that way through the loosely set trees toward another rise in the terrain, this one dominated by a massive, needleless snag of a fir tree.

I caught sight of Fagan about three hundred yards away at my ten o'clock, heading toward that dead tree that seemed to claw at the sky. Four Maestro sleds were suddenly at my eight o'clock at an equal distance, three hundred yards and closing on the Mountie.

They were too far to shoot at her with the short-barreled submachine guns. And they were moving at such high speed, I doubted I could hit one of them if I stopped to use the long rifle.

"I'm close to you, Fagan," I said. "Off your right shoulder. Satellite phone?"

"Negative on the call. Batteries all but shot."

One of the Maestro drivers sped up and started closing the gap.

"He's right behind you, Fagan!"

I lifted the H and K and shot wildly at him left-handed while trying to keep the sled going. Fagan stopped behind a fir tree and fired the twelve-gauge twice at the driver.

She hit him both times with double-aught buckshot, once in the visor and once in the chest, hurling him off his sled.

"Turn back on them, Dr. Cross," Fagan said. "There's only three left."

Before I could argue, she'd gotten her snowmobile turned around and was heading toward the other Maestro men. I struggled to do the same without losing the submachine gun. I finally just sat on it.

By the time I got turned around, the Mountie was cutting away hard northeast about one hundred yards from me with the remaining drivers flanking her, firing at her. She twisted in her saddle, trying to return fire with the shotgun one-handed, then seemed to realize her mistake.

Fagan swung her head around and dropped an F-bomb in the headset before she and her sled vanished off the rim of the canyon into the dying light.

CHAPTER

66

THE WIND PICKED UP out of the northwest then, whistling and bitter. In seconds, dark clouds took the sun, some thirty minutes from setting.

Shadows and snow swirls swept across the winter landscape.

And still I sat there on my idling snowmobile, staring at that gloomy spot where Officer Fagan had vanished from sight.

I had only the vaguest idea of our location.

The Mountie had been tracking us on some mapping app she had on her phone that did not require an active connection. I had no such app and my phone had lost service right after we left Kimberley.

But the compass app on my phone had to work. And we had just refueled. As long as I could locate the tracks of the Maestro soldiers, I reasoned, I could eventually find my way back to the warming hut. I'd light a fire. I'd spend the night and—

Two of the drivers who'd been chasing Fagan appeared on their machines. They were close to where she'd gone over, moving from my left to right about one hundred and fifty yards out.

I did not give them a chance to spot me. I killed the ignition, threw the hunting rifle over the handlebars, and shot the near rider as he passed through an opening in the scattered trees, then picked off the second.

I shoved the rifle back in the scabbard, and took off south toward that ridge with the big dead tree. I slowed to a stop near dense Christmas trees in the corner of the clearing, the snag silhouetted ahead and above me in the gray light.

I got behind the sled, watching my back trail over the top of the rifle scope, looking for the last of the seven people who'd been hunting us. The biting-cold wind blew snow devils through the low fir trees, which shook.

New snow began to fall. I glanced farther south, toward that abandoned mine, believing that Bree and John were there, yet wanting serious backup before I went in to see for certain.

Shooting erupted to my left, muzzle flashes at a distance. Bullets snapped branches of the trees nearest to me. I reached up, thumbed the ignition, twisted the throttle, and lurched the sled forward a good twenty yards, putting thicker trees between me and the gunman.

The shooting stopped. I slid the hunting rifle in the scabbard and picked up the submachine gun, knowing he was there listening for me just as I was listening for him.

For the second time in less than ten minutes, I felt as if I had no choice in my next move. Night was falling, bringing temperatures that could eventually kill me, and I doubted I could find my way back to the distant trailhead. I could see only one real option.

Forget backup. Forget trying to get out of the wilderness.

You've got to kill this last guy and go to that abandoned mine building.

Suddenly and unexpectedly, my headset crackled with a woman's hoarse voice.

"Dr. Cross? Are you there?"

For a moment, I was sure it was Fagan.

But then the woman said, "Dr. Alex Cross? Are you hearing me at this frequency?"

I realized she had a light British accent. I debated whether to reply.

"We can hear you breathing, Dr. Cross. And there's someone here who wishes to speak with you."

There was a pause before the sweetest and most familiar voice came to me over the headset. "Alex? Are you there?"

My heart soared. "Bree?"

"Right here," she said, her voice breaking. "It's time to put the guns down. They have too many men. Even if you knew the way out of this place, they'd catch you."

I said nothing, wondering at her level of duress.

"Alex," Bree said. "It's going to be fifty below zero out there tonight."

"What do they want me to do?"

The other woman's voice came on the headset. "Leave your weapons. Follow the snowmobile and driver when they cross in front of you."

I said nothing for several moments. Finally, the woman said, "Do you wish to see your wife and Mr. Sampson again? Or do we hunt you all night?"

The situation was no-win, and I knew it. "Putting my weapons down."

"You've made your wife happy, Dr. Cross."

But I was not happy as I got out the hunting rifle and hung it by its sling on the nearest tree. I tossed the submachine gun in the snow below it, unzipped my coverall and my down parka, and dug for my shoulder harness and the Glock, which was right above the avalanche beacon Fagan had made me wear.

As I did, I felt something brush my knuckles, something small and oblong in the pocket of my parka. I got the Glock and the backup ammo out and regretfully dropped them as well.

"Dr. Cross?"

"Almost," I said, digging again. "I'm not good with coveralls and cold."

My fingers closed on that little oblong object in my chest pocket. I'd forgotten Willow's Jiobit fob was with me.

I squeezed the sides of it for several seconds, praying Sampson was right, that its GPS signal could be picked up anywhere. I debated taking it with me but decided not to; I hung it low, near the trunk, and zipped up the coverall.

I shrugged off the pack and tossed it by the machine gun. Some instinct told me I needed to remember this place. The same instinct told me to empty the sled's under-storage compartment, take out the tent, sleeping bag, and emergency gear.

If I can save Bree and just get back here, I—

"Dr. Cross?"

"Okay," I said, putting my mitts back on. "I am officially without weapons."

"Good," the woman said.

A moment later, I heard a snowmobile start up off to my left. A headlight cut the gathering gloom, slashed, and wavered like a fighting sword.

The light became the snowmobile and the final driver, who did not look over at me before accelerating toward the abandoned mine.

I looked at the cache of weapons and emergency gear in the glow of my sled's headlights. I remembered Bree's voice, knew she was captive, and knew I might not see her or John or my kids or my grandmother again. And if we all did survive, our lives might never be the same.

I understood all that and yet I followed the red taillight of the gunman's sled into the gathering storm and the night.

CHAPTER

67

THE DRIVER TOOK AN old trail off the southern meadow that led through dense forest and a wetland. It took all my strength to keep the machine from bogging down before it reached the other side and a cleared trail that ran in switchbacks up the north flank of the butte and the old mine.

I imagined cresting and seeing some kind of structure to the north. But even after we passed the hulking shadow of the abandoned building, there was nothing on the flat top but snow in my headlights, blackness all around, and that red light on the back of the sled in front of me.

On the far southwest side of the plateau, we took another switchback trail down into a maelstrom of wind and snow. I could sense a very big drop-off to my right, and I kept trying to keep the machine hard left.

Mercifully, after what seemed a long descent, the trail hit a wide, windswept shelf devoid of trees. The driver led me to the other end and slowed to a stop in front of a wall of rock, saplings and scrub brush sticking out from ice and snow.

I halted my sled twenty-five yards behind him, and I was starting to wonder what was happening when a piece of the mountain about the size of a barn door began to slide back. Light poured out and got stronger the more the door retracted, revealing a vaulted space beyond the swirling snow.

The sled in front of me drove inside onto a concrete floor and stopped. I did the same and raised my visor, squinting at the bright lights.

The door closed behind us.

I looked all around. The room was a solid two hundred feet deep and seventy-five wide, with a ceiling that had to be thirty feet high. At least twenty snowmobiles were parked to my left. To my right, a small white Bell helicopter was up on a massive dolly that was lashed in place.

"Stay where you are, Dr. Cross," the woman with the hoarse voice said through my helmet radio. "You need to be scanned."

The last driver of the seven who'd chased me was off his machine; two women in their forties and two men in their thirties came through a door on the opposite side of the space. The men carried machine guns. The women held detection wands.

The snowmobile driver removed his helmet and then a hood beneath, revealing the same buff bald guy we'd seen at the warming hut much earlier in the day. He scowled at me while unclipping his weapon from its harness.

"You don't look happy to see me, Mr. Bean," I said as the two other men and women approached.

"You killed six of my mates," Bean said, cradling the gun, his expression stony.

"They shot first. And by the way, one of you killed a Canadian Mountie."

"Not likely. I saw it. She had an accident, didn't she? Lost her way, she did. What you did, however—ambushing us—that was cold-blooded murder."

"Perspective is everything," I said evenly, watching him like you'd watch a snake at close quarters.

Before Bean could reply, the women came up wearing dark fleece leggings and tops. They studied me with some interest as they ran the wands over me, stopping on my left chest.

"Avalanche transceiver," I said.

"Show us," one of them said.

Bean turned and stalked away while I lost the helmet, the heavy boots, and the coverall. I dropped it all on the floor beside the sled, then took off my parka to show them the transceiver strapped to my torso.

One of the women cut the transceiver off while the other waved her wand over the pockets of the parka. I was happy they were empty.

When she was done, she nodded to one of the armed men.

"Let him shower, give him slippers, then take him to level four."

CHAPTER

68

FLANKED BY TWO ARMED men, I passed through a door into a narrow hallway. As we walked, I steeled myself with three internal goals.

Number one: Find Bree and John.

Number two: Escape.

Number three: Get to the guns and survival gear.

They took me into a locker room, told me to shower, and left me jeans, long underwear, a shirt, a wool sweater, and socks and slippers.

As I showered, I thought about Willow's Jiobit fob now out in the snowstorm and wondered whether its signal would carry. I prayed it would as they put zip ties on me and led me into an elevator that rose smoothly and slowed to a stop.

The door slid back, revealing a foyer of sorts with double

wooden doors on the other side. Standing there, guarded by three armed men, were Bree and John.

I felt a huge weight fall from my shoulders. They were both alive.

"Alex!" Bree gasped and came over fast to me, her wrists in restraints as well.

"Go inside, please," one of the guards said. "Dinner will be ready soon."

At that I became aware of the smell of savory meat, garlic, onions, and basil. Bree took my right arm with her bound hands.

"Are you okay?"

"Sort of. You?"

"Sort of," she said, and we started toward the double doors.

I looked over at Sampson, who nodded with a blank expression and a thousand-yard stare. I had known John long enough to understand: in his mind, in his heart, my oldest and dearest friend had gone total warrior.

That alone gave me a lot of hope when we went through the doors into another large, high-ceilinged space. Massive girders had been bolted into the rock ceiling. Dramatic lighting fixtures hung from the girders and shimmered like icicles.

The far wall was entirely covered in a crystal-clear digital closed-loop video that depicted an alpine valley surrounded by crags with a frozen river zigzagging through it. Wind blowing. Snow swirling.

The floor was stamped, stained concrete with large area rugs on top.

To our left a gas fire burned in front of modern furniture, all black and chrome. Beside the fireplace, there was an empty wheelchair with a blanket.

When I finally looked to my right, I froze and stared along with John and Bree. There was a large kitchen and dining area in the corner about fifty feet away, the space defined by an overhead trellis with more of those icicle lights hanging from it.

Three people were working in the kitchen. The lone female had her back to us at the stove. Short blond hair, green fleece top, dark tights. Lucas Bean worked beside her, wearing a gray sweatsuit, hood down to reveal his bullet-shaped head.

The other man in the kitchen was taller, slender, with wispy, sandy-gray hair. He wore horn-rimmed eyeglasses, a dark blue wool sweater, jeans, and running shoes. He leaned on a cane as he left the kitchen and hobbled toward us a few feet, then stopped and gestured to the digital mural and the snowy scene with his cane.

"Dr. Cross, Chief Stone, Detective Sampson, I wish you could see the real thing in all its glory. But it's dark now and we have the shutters down for the storm."

He came closer, his expression one of deep interest and irony, his mannerisms and speech pattern putting me in mind of the late actor William Hurt.

"They're quite remarkable, the shutters. Five-inch steel holding the integrated digital screens you see on the interior. The exterior has been sand-blasted and powder-coated to match the color of the cliff face, and they are thick enough that we can't be detected by heat-seekers. For all intents and purposes, we don't exist here. We're invisible, especially to prying satellites and such things. But here it is on a summer's day."

He picked up a remote from a table and clicked it.

The digital video changed, became the valley in midsummer with a riot of wildflowers blooming in the river bottom and eagles winging about.

"Isn't it magnificent?" he said, his eyes glistening. He frowned and shook his head. "Oh, how rude of me. Dr. Cross and I have met. But allow me to introduce myself. I'm —"

Bree cut him off. "Ryan Malcomb."

His eyes softened and he smiled as if he knew something she didn't. "Am I?"

"You are," Bree said. "I knew you weren't dead, M."

CHAPTER

69

"AM I?" MALCOMB SAID again with an infuriating smile.

Bree looked like she wanted to smack him, but she kept her cool and said, "Yes."

The smile remained as he pointed us to chairs by the fire. He limped to the wheelchair, sat in it, put the blanket across his legs, and gazed at us with renewed interest if not energy. He looked as if he'd recently been ill.

"The three of you are persistent, I'll give you that," he said. "And I must say, we knew you were an investigative all-star, Dr. Cross, but we had no idea you were a marksman as well. Six dead because of you and Officer Fagan."

I said, "The rifle was well sighted in, and your men shot first."

"Yes, that was a mistake," Malcomb said, tapping his finger

against his chin. "Tell me, does it stick in your craw that your wife was the one who figured me out?"

I shrugged, said, "I've always said she was the shinier side of the coin."

"Ah, yes, the self-deprecation," Malcomb said softly. "The need to be liked. I am well aware you are a psychologist. You know a lot about the human mind in general. But I know a lot about the way you specifically think, Dr. Cross. And you, Chief Stone. And yes, you, Detective Sampson. We've been tracking your data for years."

Sampson looked like he wanted to rush him. He said, "And you've been killing people you don't like and taunting men who've just lost their wives."

"No." Malcomb shook his head. "Never. Not me. That would have been my lesser half."

Bree said, "Sean."

I added, "Your twin brother, aka Ian Duncanson, who vanished hunting near Boise two months ago."

"What?" Sampson said, looking at me.

"True," I said.

To me, Malcomb said, "You really have gotten to the heart of the matter, haven't you?" Then the head of Maestro looked at Sampson. "What you all failed to understand was that there were two of us contacting you over the years. One M—me—was fairly helpful to your investigations. The other, my brother, less so. Cruelly less so. I personally apologize for the way Sean treated you after your late wife's passing."

Sampson said nothing.

Bree said, "You're saying your brother was part of all this? Maestro?"

Malcomb squinted. "He was aware of it, but not a part of it. In the instances I've mentioned, he just signed into our area of the darknet and went about his cruel mischief."

"How's that?" Sampson demanded.

"Sean seemed to have a troubled mind from early childhood. But he had a better brain for math and computer code than I ever did. He helped me write the algorithms that made my company, and I made him a very wealthy man. He also had a knack for hacking and for hiding things, like ownership, through Brazilian shell companies."

"Like that ranch in Colorado where your men were attacked," I said.

Malcomb dipped his head. "Like that ranch. And the ranch above the road where I met my untimely end. And this place, of course."

"Sean died in your vehicle," Bree said. "Not on a hunting trip."

Malcomb sighed. "It had to end at some point. In the past few years, Sean was deteriorating mentally, and his mere existence provided a bombproof alias for me."

"You're a great brother," Bree said.

"Better than you know. Sean's life would have been over decades ago if it had not been for me. Protecting him. Keeping his secrets secret. And yes, you were getting too close to those secrets, and to mine. That's why we had to send for the janitor. Toomey, the man who brought you here. He cleans things up for us on a regular basis."

I flashed on the janitor at the mounted police office in Kimberley. *Toomey? Wasn't that his name? He had to have heard me and Fagan talking.*

The blond woman came into the room wearing an apron. Handsome more than pretty, she said with a mild Slavic accent, "Dinner is ready, M."

"Thank you, Katrina," Malcomb said, then looked at us. "Shall we?"

CHAPTER

70

LUCAS BEAN LEFT THE kitchen and pushed Ryan Malcomb's wheel-chair through the great room to a dining area near the kitchen.

Malcomb said, "I am going to release you from your restraints so we can eat in a more civilized manner. But don't get any stupid ideas. Lucas was with the British SAS, elite counterterror. And Katrina, in addition to being an excellent cook, was trained as a Swallow by the GRU."

Katrina White was walking away from us as he said it. She was very strong and moved like a gymnast, very aware of her posture and gait.

A GRU Swallow, I thought, now very interested in the woman.

Bean came around to each of us and cut free our wrist restraints. We sat at a trestle table, Malcomb at one end, Bree and I opposite each other in the middle, and Sampson at the other end.

White brought out a sausage, broccoli, and garlic dish that smelled like heaven and spooned it out over fresh pasta. The former SAS operator poured Chianti into our glasses.

"A toast," Malcomb said, raising his glass.

We all looked at each other. Bree shrugged and picked up her glass, so I did too. Sampson gave it an awkward second and then grudgingly raised his glass.

"To a better future," the head of Maestro said.

We mumbled the words. Bean said, "Amen, M."

Malcomb sipped the wine. Bree and I did as well. It was very good. Sampson set his down. The lights flickered and died.

The darkness was so complete, it was disorienting.

Malcomb said, "No need for panic. The redundant generators are switching." He'd no sooner said that than the lights came back on, dimly at first and then with more power. The big video wall rebooted.

"Redundant generators," I said, looking around. "The work that must have gone into this place is extraordinary."

The leader of Maestro smiled again. I've always believed that there is nothing a powerful rich man likes to talk about more than himself, his accomplishments, and his toys.

Malcomb said, "The mine's previous owners did most of it. The pneumatic elevator occupies the main shaft. This room was actually a cave chamber they accidentally drilled into. The place was riddled with them, like Swiss cheese, old limestone deposits amid the granite. All our work and living spaces are located inside tunnels that were bored into the butte back in the fifties. All we had to do was come in and modify them to serve our needs."

I said, "Still must have cost you a fortune."

Malcomb's smile widened. "It is extraordinary what you can accomplish when you have billions at your disposal."

"Your aunt the bank on all this?"

The smile vanished. "My aunt is a saint. She helped fund my start-up, nothing more."

Sampson said, "Why are we here, Malcomb?"

His face fell. "I usually talk business only after the meal. At least try your food. Katrina went to a great deal of trouble to make this for you. It's a Sicilian peasant dish."

John looked like he wanted to grab his table knife and wing it at the man but he picked up his fork and forced himself to eat. Bree and I followed his lead.

Like the wine, the dish was incredibly good.

"What do you think, Dr. Cross?" Malcomb asked after I'd taken a couple of bites.

"Who knew a trained assassin could cook like a master chef?"

In the kitchen, Katrina laughed and rubbed the left side of her neck as if working out a knot. And then I placed her.

Malcomb was pleased. "Her grandfather cooked in the Kremlin."

Sampson glared at me until I blinked at him twice, paused, and did it again, a signal we'd been using forever to alert each other to play good cop/bad cop.

John stared at his plate as he ate, then set down his fork and said, "Again, why are we here, M? Why not just kill us like you tried to do last year in Montana?"

Malcomb sighed and took another sip of wine. "Montana was a strategic and tactical mistake made by one of my trusted team leaders, someone who was interested in snuffing out the last of the Alejandro cartel men who were in the Bob Marshall actively hunting you. I had little or no say in the matter."

I didn't believe him. "So why kidnap Bree and John? Why lure me in and kill Fagan?"

He tapped his index finger against his lower lip. "As I said, Fagan was an accident; she made a mistake. I brought you here because there is a problem I believe you three can help fix."

"Okay," Bree said, crossing her arms. "What's this problem?"

Malcomb shifted in his wheelchair, pushed his glasses farther up the bridge of his nose, and grew dead serious.

"The problem, Chief Stone, is that nothing works anymore. The system is broken. Mankind is out of order. We are spinning into chaos and in doing so, we are not only destroying civilization but also dooming the planet."

CHAPTER

71

SAMPSON, BREE, AND I stiffened at his description of the problems the three of us were supposed to help solve.

Malcomb could see the skepticism in our eyes and held up both palms.

"Hear me out while you eat. And know that almost everything I am going to say is backed not only by the mega-data that Paladin supercomputers crunch every day but also, I suspect, by your own personal experiences."

He cut a sausage, ate it, and took yet another sip of wine before pressing on. "We can argue about this, but aside from America's systemic racial injustices, until the past thirty years or so, law and order as it was practiced in the USA worked. It wasn't perfect, but it functioned.

"Today, that system is crumbling all around us, in part because of the massive disparity in wealth around the world. Because wealth has been gathered up and placed in the hands of the few, become scarce, people want it more than ever. And that desire for more breeds violence and corruption at every level.

"Don't believe me? Look at our cities. The homeless are everywhere and so are the mentally ill and so are criminals. You can't walk in parts of Manhattan, Chicago, LA, and Seattle because they are lawless open-air drug markets the police avoid. Go into stores in those areas, from Nike to Patagonia, and the security guards are packing Glocks because cops won't investigate robberies or thefts under a thousand dollars. Murders are spiking in urban, suburban, and rural areas. So are rapes and assaults.

"And look at the droughts and the wildfires burning all over the world. Look at the politicians who know the climate is in massive danger and yet do nothing. Look at judges taking bribes and calling it justice. Look at law enforcement cutting corners, turning a blind eye to illegal drug shipments flowing across borders in exchange for bigger stacks of cash in bigger paper bags. It goes on and on and on. And because of that, the chaos in our lives will grow exponentially in the coming years. Mankind, civilization, seems right on the simmering edge of a lawless boil. Or am I wrong?"

I said nothing. Neither did Sampson.

But Bree said, "You're not wrong."

"No, I'm not," Malcomb said, smiling grimly. "I wish I were, but I'm not. Every day brings another tale of chicanery up and down and throughout the financial industry. Souls are constantly sold to the devil. Same thing in law and in business. Ethics used to guide careers in those fields. Now it's just a course to get through on the way to a high-paying degree.

"Is it any wonder that the justice system is riddled with corruption or that corporations routinely ignore the law and pollute the earth? Shit the bed they sleep in? Or am I wrong?"

"You're not wrong," Sampson said. "But you say that underlying it all is the fact that the haves have most of the pie and the have-nots want it."

"I think that's true," Malcomb said.

"Then what's stopping you from spending your billions to change things, to fix the system?" Sampson demanded. "Why raise a private army?"

"That's right," I said. "Why go vigilante?"

"Because the way we practice vigilantism works. And because it has more impact than I'd have spending my billions conventionally. Would you like to see how it works?"

When Sampson and I hesitated, Bree said, "Yes, we would. Very much."

Malcomb looked at John and me with a tilted head until we nodded.

"Lucas? Katrina? We're all going to the control room."

Bean came around to push Malcomb's wheelchair. White took off her apron and followed us to the elevator.

The doors closed. We dropped smoothly. I watched White, knowing she was the one who'd killed the Supreme Court candidates, not understanding how she could be so at ease.

"Pneumatic elevator," Malcomb said proudly.

Bean said, "Rises and falls on air pressure. Bloody brilliant."

"Your own design?" Bree asked.

M's face soured. "My brother's idea."

I made a note to myself that Malcomb remained conflicted about his brother and about having to kill him. He'd also confessed to protecting Sean from his secrets. What secrets?

Thinking back to all we'd learned in Idaho, I began to have suspicions about the nature of at least one of those secrets. The elevator slowed, and the doors opened.

Bean pushed M's wheelchair into the top of an amphitheater of sorts, with tiers of workstations stepping down before a floor-to-ceiling curved screen showing various video feeds. Nine people manned the workstations and paid no attention as we entered.

CHAPTER

72

BEAN TURNED MALCOMB AROUND, and I noticed once again that the former SAS officer continued to study me, as if plotting where he'd aim if he got the chance and the go-ahead.

"Welcome to Maestro's remote command center," Malcomb said. "Everyone in this room has at one time worked for various top-rank intelligence and law enforcement agencies around the world. Toomey was in the Marines and CIA paramilitary. Lucas in the SAS. Sarah down there in the second row was a top controller with the Mossad. Edith here was with NSA. Where are we, Edith?"

Mid-fifties, half glasses on a chain, and a funky dresser, Edith put me in mind of a social studies teacher I knew who'd worked at a school where Nana Mama had been vice principal. Edith swiveled in her seat, dropped the glasses.

"Weather here is going to get rough again tomorrow, M," Edith said in that hoarse voice. "Weather Canada is calling for ninety centimeters. Maybe more. At the moment, the satellite connection is strong, and we are actively monitoring all scheduled missions."

"Are any a likely go?"

"Boston is possible."

"Who's over-watching?"

A man two stations below Edith raised his hand and turned to look at us. It was Toomey, the janitor from the mounted police force offices in Kimberley and, Bree whispered, the Idaho highway department man who'd taken Bree and Sampson.

"Warren was feeling sick, so I stepped in, M," Toomey said.

"Explain the mission to them."

The janitor looked up at us, said, "Irish mob just brought in the largest load of fentanyl in U.S. history. Two DEA agents and Massachusetts state police officers are part of it. Stuff is so lethal two of the mules bringing it died the day before yesterday when they accidentally inhaled the dust off the package."

Malcomb nodded. "We're inside the state troopers' phones. That's why we need to act quick. Tell them how we're doing it, Edith."

Edith put her half glasses back on, said, "We used artificial intelligence based on our own algorithms to sort through possible storage locations for the fentanyl and have narrowed them down to one. Toomey's team is on scene, waiting for confirmation."

Bree said, "And then what?"

The janitor said, "The team, dressed in hazmat gear, enters, retrieves the drug, and destroys the bulk of it before it can destroy anyone else."

Sampson said, "And the bad guys guarding the drugs? The DEA agents? The state cops?"

"They die from their exposure to the drug and are found with enough of it to reveal their entire scheme."

Malcomb said, "This is how the majority of our missions work. We surgically remove the cancer, but we don't bury the tumor."

I said, "Is that what you call the cold-blooded murder of three potential candidates to the U.S. Supreme Court?"

The leader of Maestro's face didn't twitch.

I looked over at Katrina White. "Your Swallow made a mistake."

Malcomb's eyebrows shot up. "That would be a first."

"We caught her all three times on home security cameras," I said. "Never her face—so, well done there—but at every scene, after the kill, she adjusted the left side of her neck, the same move I saw her make in the kitchen a few minutes ago. And in Georgia we were able to amplify her words. She said, 'Maestro knows what you've done. It's over.'"

Malcomb looked at Katrina. "Did you say that, my dear?"

"I did, M," she said, shrugging. "I figured they should know why they were dying."

The vigilante leader removed his glasses, came up with a cloth, and cleaned them.

I said, "Why were they killed? Why not just expose them?"

"And jam up the courts?" Malcomb said. "No. Better to remove them."

"But why Nathan Carver? What did a law professor do to warrant assassination?"

M appeared irritated at being questioned and he rubbed harder on his glasses.

"What did he do?" I said again.

Malcomb put his glasses back on and peered at me with a grin that struck me as both ironic and cruel.

"Unlike Judge Pak, who had skewed morals and judgment, and Judge Franklin, who arranged for her husband's plane to crash, it's not what Nathan Carver did, Dr. Cross," he said. "It's what the professor planned to do once he sat on the high bench."

"And what was that?"

"Overturn American Indian law top to bottom. As a professor and an activist, he has quietly advocated challenging every treaty between every tribe and the U.S. government since the Revolutionary War. The oppressed peoples would then attempt to reclaim their rights and lands, and the country would be consumed in havoc for years. We gathered more than one hundred thousand data points that said that would be his mission if he were named to the court, a total reversal of hundreds of years of precedent."

I shook my head. "For data points you had her kill him?"

"We eliminated Carver to prevent the chaos he would have caused in the country," Malcomb said. "All property ownership. All mineral rights and water rights. All oil and gas leases. All of them possibly thrown out if Carver reached the court at such a young age."

Sampson shook his head. "How can you know how much sway he'd have on the court?"

"If Pak and Franklin joined him, a great deal," Malcomb shot back.

"And you personally make all these decisions—who lives, who dies. I'm sorry, but who made you God? Other than your brother."

I could tell the vigilante leader was not used to being challenged, and he struggled not to lose his cool.

"It's more complicated than that," Malcomb said. "The algorithms—"

Bree said, "The algorithms? You have machines making these decisions?"

Malcomb blinked and rubbed at his temples. "Edith? Explain."

Edith said firmly, "There are rules, and we collectively make the decisions based on the data and the hard evidence."

Bean said, "There is a vote on every target."

The janitor said, "And no one takes their votes lightly."

"No one," Katrina White said.

Malcomb lifted his head and looked at us in a way that made me wonder if he was feeling ill rather than irritated by our challenges. "As Edith indicated, there are rules in Maestro. Strict ones. And we hold our operatives to the highest standards, which is why we brought you here instead of killing you."

Bree beat me to it.

"What are you saying?" she demanded.

"That we believe that while you are misguided, you are uncorrupted, and because of that we want the three of you to join us. Join Maestro and help us restore order."

CHAPTER

73

I WAS ABOUT TO tell him to put his offer where the sun didn't shine but Malcomb held up both palms and said, "Don't make an impulse decision. In fact, don't make any decision until you've slept on it. But please, tell me your doubts."

"Okay," I said. "As sophisticated as you are, I don't believe in vigilantes taking the law into their hands and making a mess of things."

"Name an instance where we did that."

"Executing drug cartel members and law enforcement officers?"

"Law enforcement officers who were thoroughly corrupted," Malcomb said, hardening. "And if you remember, the Alejandro cartel was winning the war for the southern border until Maestro got involved. Today, the cartel does not even exist, and the remaining narcos down there are terrified to take their place."

I glanced at Bree and Sampson. We could not argue with him

on that point. Every bit of intelligence we'd read indicated that drug trafficking along the southwest U.S. border had dropped significantly since the Alejandro cartel was destroyed.

Bree said, "And the fashion murders in New York?"

Malcomb said, "That designer and her top aides were running a human-trafficking operation in front of the whole world. Now it does not exist."

Sampson said, "And the men you had murdered around DC? The Dead Hours killings?"

M shifted in his wheelchair. "You mean the child molesters? That was actually my late brother's work. Even so, isn't the world a better place without them creeping around, a better place for your daughter, Detective?"

John thought about that a moment. "I can't dispute your goal, only your means."

"Not our means in this case. Sean's. Ian's."

Malcomb claimed that his brother figured out what Maestro was years ago and had created a digital back door to the organization's files and Paladin's supercomputers. He used that back door to target the child molesters.

"Why?" I asked.

"You'd have to ask him," Malcomb said. "Which is impossible." He tapped his lip again, his eyes slightly squinting.

"Was Sean molested as a child?" I asked, sensing my way toward the truth.

"We're not going there."

"Why not? You were his twin brother. Was he molested or not?"

The Maestro leader shifted in his wheelchair. "He was mistreated, not molested, beaten for things that he should not have been beaten for."

"By your father? Wheeler?"

"And our dear mother," Malcomb said.

"You were beaten too," I said.

His head bobbed ever so slightly. "Though never as bad as Sean. They knew I was physically weak even before my diagnosis. But we were both 'bad genes,' as they called us. Bad genes. Bad adoptions."

"They said that?" Bree said.

"Often," Malcomb said.

Years of clinical psychology work backed up my instincts at that point. I said, "When were the worst beatings? What age?"

Malcomb adjusted his glasses. "They got worse as we got older."

"And no one was coming to help. Your parents were wealthy. No one would have expected them to mistreat you."

He said nothing.

"When did it become intolerable for you?"

"For me or Sean?"

I shook my head. "The both of you. You were twins."

The corners of his mouth turned up ever so slightly. "You are very perceptive, Dr. Cross. I'll grant you that."

"Which one of you raised the idea of killing your parents first?"

Malcomb thought about that. "After our father whipped Sean with a leather belt so bad he bled, it was almost like he had no choice. He behaved and waited until his back healed completely to eliminate motive. And he and I figured out a way around the alarm system so it would look like Sean had never left the boathouse that night and climbed in naked through the basement window of the main house."

I watched him, unsure whether I believed him. "What did Sean do with the knife?"

"We had a boat lift that was mounted on four steel pipes about eight feet long drilled into the bedrock. The pipes were capped and below the surface a good two feet. We'd figured out how to unscrew the caps earlier that summer. Sean dove in the lake after it was done to clean himself, then unscrewed the cap and dropped the knife in. I assume it's still there."

"So he was a vigilante at age nine," Sampson said.

"Yes, yes," Malcomb said wearily with a weak flip of his hand before turning to gaze at me. "I'm done talking about Sean. Dr. Cross, do you know what I decided in the early days of Maestro, before I began approaching vetted, angry, and incorruptible law enforcement and intelligence agents to join me?"

"I haven't the faintest."

"I decided that Maestro would be democratic—everyone involved would have a vote, and we would act based on evidence, then punish by any means necessary to restore order."

Bree said, "Is that why you kidnapped Sean? Put him in your handicap van and saw him killed? To restore order? Or for you to disappear?"

M laughed softly, sadly. "Ian Duncanson was becoming highly erratic, and Ryan Malcomb needed to disappear. You, especially, were getting too close, Chief Stone. But more important than disappearing, I will miraculously appear next spring as my brother, bad spine and all, having survived an entire winter alone in the wilderness. I will have a story to tell, and it will all be backed up by evidence on the ground. How I fell hunting and injured my back. How I survived until I could literally drag myself to a remote cabin just as the snow started falling. How I shot a cow elk that fed by the cabin. How I—"

I could tell he was winding up and I wanted to bring him down a notch or two. "Killed your twin brother."

He was getting increasingly agitated the more we pressed him about his dead brother and seemed to struggle with his words. "As I told you, he was becoming erratic, dangerous. His skills were…the distance between genius and madness is always a hair's…"

He lost all color. His eyes left us and he gazed at the floor. And his jaw sagged.

Edith came fast to his side. "M? Are you okay?"

I thought for a second there that Malcomb was having a stroke. But then he shook his head slowly. "Late for my meds."

Bean said, "I'll take you up straightaway."

He nodded weakly, then gazed up at us. "You have twelve hours to decide."

"But how would it work?" Bree said. "Are you asking us to leave our lives behind? Our families?"

I was kind of shocked that my wife was entertaining the offer at all.

Sampson said, "The details. Otherwise, we can't make a rational decision."

He gestured at Edith. "She'll explain."

74

THIRTY MINUTES LATER, THE hydraulic door to the cell-like room where Bree had been kept slid shut behind us. There was a bunk above hers but hardly any room to move around.

And I don't think I'd ever been as frustrated with my wife as I was right then. "You're honestly thinking of joining Maestro?" I demanded.

"That comes second," Bree said before throwing herself into my arms. She pulled my head down and murmured in my ear, "I got to believe we're bugged, baby."

I sighed, kissed her, and drew back. "I love you too. But Maestro?"

"A lot of Malcomb's arguments make sense. And it's not like we'd be foot soldiers. All we would be doing is helping them from time to time."

That was how Edith sold it after Bean wheeled Malcomb off. She said that Malcomb wanted us to return to our lives as if nothing had happened other than a series of unfortunate circumstances that had separated Bree and Sampson from their vehicle during a snowstorm and ultimately resulted in Officer Fagan's crash into the canyon. Back in our respective investigative organizations, we would work for Maestro's aims and have unparalleled access to the power of Paladin's supercomputers and vast databanks to root out injustice and corruption.

"And you will be paid well enough to ensure you and your families are comfortable for the rest of your lives," Edith said. "More important, you will see the direct result of your crime-fighting efforts. The bad guys behind bars if there's enough compelling evidence on the record."

"And if there's not enough on the record?" Bree had asked.

"Debate and then a vote," Edith said. "Majority wins. Appeals are possible. You would have a say and a vote. All of you would."

In the cell with Bree, I thought about that and said, "Once you help them, you're caught in their web."

My wife yawned. "No, you're part of the web. Sleep on it before you say another thing. I'll take the top bunk."

She turned off the light, pushed me gently into the bottom bunk, and climbed in beside me. She snuggled in my arms and whispered in my ear, "We have no choice but to join, Alex. Think about it. If we refuse, he'll kill us."

Maybe it was the multiple days with little sleep. Maybe it was the strange, wired feeling that had been pulsing through me since I surrendered and followed Lucas Bean's snowmobile. Whatever it was, I had not thought the downside through, but it was clear that she was correct. We knew who M was, what Maestro really was, and its secret location. At least I did. Sort of.

Unless Malcomb believed we were total converts to his cause, we would not leave this place alive. But even that seemed off to me. I murmured in her ear, "If we agree to join, why would he let us go? What's to prevent us from turning on him and Maestro once we're out of here? Unleashing the FBI and the Mounties on the killers of the Supreme Court candidates?"

She stiffened a little in my arms, then whispered, "He's playing us?"

"I suspect in every way he can."

"What do we do?"

"Like you said, we have no choice. We bend the knee. We sell it. We buy time."

CHAPTER

75

Washington, DC

NED MAHONEY HAD DEALT with many difficult, pressurized days before. But this one had the potential to be the toughest of them all as he drove into the nation's capital at seven the next morning and answered a call from acting FBI director Marcia Hamilton.

"Director Hamilton," he said. "To what do I owe the honor."

"The inauguration is in three days," Hamilton said. "I need an arrest."

"You told me as much eight hours ago, ma'am," Mahoney said. "And nothing has changed. Maestro is still our focus, and—"

"Yes, yes, its relationship to that dead tech billionaire."

"Ryan Malcomb," Mahoney said.

"The candidates were all killed after he died."

"If he's dead," Mahoney said.

"The twins theory again." Hamilton groaned.

Mahoney gripped the steering wheel. "With all due respect,

Director, Dr. Cross, his wife, and Detective Sampson have all worked that specific angle of the investigation. And they've all gone missing. What does that tell you?"

"That they're missing," she said, and hung up.

The FBI agent wanted to put his fist through the windshield. Instead, he drove to the Cross house on Fifth. Since returning to the East Coast, he'd tried to check in with Nana Mama and the kids every twelve hours.

On the way there, he called the Royal Canadian Mounted Police in Vancouver again. His liaison said there'd been no news regarding Officer Fagan or Alex. And he was sorry to say that the weather was going from bad to worse in the next twelve hours, postponing aerial searches.

He parked on Fifth and went to the front door and knocked. Alex's ninety-something grandmother answered in her quilted blue robe.

"I'm making breakfast for Ali and Willow," she said, standing aside to let him in. "Any word?"

"No," Mahoney said, taking off his winter coat and putting it on the rack. "And the weather up there is going in the wrong direction."

"I've been watching the Weather Channel," she said. "Or, rather, Ali is."

Indeed, when they entered the kitchen where the smells of bacon and coffee were mingling, her great-grandson was splitting time between the Weather Channel on the TV and a real-time satellite view of British Columbia from Weather Canada on a laptop set on the counter. Both showed a major storm approaching.

Willow Sampson was sitting at the kitchen table eating Cheerios and looking at her iPad with little enthusiasm. She glanced up.

"Did my daddy call you, Uncle Ned?"

"Not yet, sweetheart," Mahoney said.

"But he always calls, every night, and now he hasn't called in three nights."

"I know, Willow. And I'm doing everything I can to get him to call you."

She began to cry. Nana Mama went and hugged her. "I know you're upset. We're all upset."

"Tonight's my dance recital." Willow sniffled. "Daddy's supposed to be there."

"I'll be there. So will Ali. And I know Jannie wants to come."

"And Rebecca," Mahoney said. "I talked to her last night. She said she wouldn't miss it."

At the mention of John's girlfriend, Willow stopped crying and brightened a little.

Mahoney smiled. "Tell you what: I will come back later this afternoon, pick you all up, and take you to the recital and we can meet Rebecca there. And I will make sure I bring my good camera so I can video your dance. That way, your father won't miss a thing. That's good, right?"

Willow nodded and wiped her eyes. Mahoney gave her a hug, then asked Nana Mama for a fill-up on his go-cup. While she poured him coffee, he said to Ali, "How's the storm looking?"

"Big and getting bigger," Alex's youngest child said, taking his eyes off the laptop to gaze at Mahoney. "Dad and Bree and John are going to be okay, aren't they?"

"I would never bet against your father, Bree, or John," Mahoney said and gently squeezed his neck. "If that storm changes direction, you'll let me know?"

Ali nodded. "The second I see it happen."

"Good boy. And thank you, Nana."

"Anytime, Ned," Alex's grandmother said. "You'll let us know if you hear anything."

"The second I know it," he said, and went to get his coat in the front hall.

His cell phone began to ring before he got his coat on. He heard Willow giggle back in the kitchen. He looked at the ID and groaned. *She just hung up on me fifteen minutes ago!*

Mahoney's thumb was moving to answer the acting FBI director when Ali called out, "Uncle Ned, are you still here?"

CHAPTER

76

NINETY MINUTES LATER, MAHONEY was working on a laptop on one of the FBI's jets. It had just reached cruising altitude and was heading west-northwest.

The supervising special agent in charge had a brightly colored app up on his screen and was studying the pink pin glowing there in the middle of the page. He clicked it for the tenth time since seeing it on Willow Sampson's iPad.

A smaller screen popped up, noted there wasn't a constant signal emanating from the Jiobit fob that Willow said she'd put in her father's pack. It had broadcast its position only twice, both times in the last twenty-four hours, twelve hours apart, for barely ten seconds.

But it was enough. It was—

Mahoney's phone rang. He looked at caller ID and groaned because he knew the shit was about to hit the proverbial fan.

"Director Hamilton," he said, trying to sound calm. "How can I be of service?"

"Where the hell do you think you're going, Mahoney?"

"Kimberley, British Columbia, ma'am," Ned said.

"With no approval?" she thundered. "Taking a jet?"

"I approved my own requisition of the jet. I have that discretion."

"Turn around."

"Respectfully, no, ma'am. You told me to get an arrest in this case before the inauguration. That's where I'm headed."

There was a long pause before Hamilton said, "Who are you arresting?"

"I will tell you that when I know."

"What?"

"Ma'am, as I've tried to explain, Dr. Cross, Chief Stone, Detective Sampson, and I believe that the murders of the Supreme Court candidates are tied to Maestro and the late Ryan Malcomb. They disappeared following the Malcomb angle, but now they've made contact."

"What? Did they call you or message you or something?"

"In a way," Mahoney said. "A GPS transponder has signaled a location deep in the Canadian wilderness where Cross was last seen with an RCMP officer who is also missing."

"What are the Mounties telling you?"

"That the weather is bad, that their helicopters are all grounded for the time being, and that Officer Fagan is an expert winter camper who always went into the backcountry prepared."

"So what are we looking at? A wilderness rescue? Or an arrest?"

"If we can get to that location in time and find them all, maybe both."

The agent knew the acting director was not happy. He could hear it in her voice when she said, "I want both. I want to be able to tell the president-elect that we got both."

"Yes, ma'am. I'll keep you posted."

He was exhausted when he hung up. He had risen through the Bureau's ranks swiftly and kept so cool under fire, his peers joked that he had an invisible shield around him.

But it felt like the constant pressure from the acting director was putting cracks in his invisible shield. Mahoney yawned, told himself he'd be useless if he didn't rest before landing in British Columbia, and closed his eyes.

He'd meant to nap for twenty minutes, maybe a half hour. But three and a half hours later, the copilot shook his shoulder and told him they'd started their descent into Kimberley and that winds were up, so landing was going to be turbulent.

That was an understatement. Ned had never experienced a bumpier approach and kept his mind off it by looking out the window at the vast alpine terrain of the Canadian Rockies, snow being blown off the peaks by the high winds.

When he got off, he hit warmer temperatures than he'd expected, and there was no snow falling yet. But the wind was howling as he made his way into the private jet terminal.

A big bear of a man with flaming-red hair wearing an RCMP parka came over and shook his hand. "Captain John Olson," he said.

"Nice to put a face to a name," Ned said. "Any chance of getting in there soon, Captain?"

Olson shook his head. "It's dicey with the helicopters in winds like this, and we're supposed to get hit hard with snow again starting midafternoon."

"Snowmobiles can't do it?"

"Like I said earlier, we've had more than a hundred centimeters of snow in the past few days and this wind is loading it, making the backcountry exceptionally prone to avalanches."

"So when do you think we can fly?"

"If we're lucky, tomorrow morning," the police captain said, then looked down when a ring tone came from his pocket. "Give me a second."

He dug the phone from his pocket, said, "Olson." Then one eyebrow went up. "How long ago?"

CHAPTER

77

OVERNIGHT AND WELL INTO the next day, we were kept confined. Our food came on a tray handed to us by a guard we'd never seen before.

Ten a.m. came and went, and with it the twelve hours Malcomb had given us to decide whether to join Maestro. Bree and I had spent the time since waking up discussing the idea in positive terms in case they were listening to us.

Thirteen hours passed. Then fifteen. Then seventeen.

"You think something happened to Malcomb?" Bree asked.

"You mean like a medical crisis?"

"He didn't look good last night."

"No, he didn't, he —"

A knock came at the door. Lucas Bean stood there, grim-faced, carrying a pistol with a suppressor on it. Katrina White carried a similar weapon and a laptop computer.

She put her eye to a retinal scan, and Sampson's door slid back. John appeared.

Bean said, "He wants to talk to you."

White opened the laptop. Ryan Malcomb appeared, looking haggard.

"There's been a change of plans," Malcomb said. "After a great deal of reflection last night, I am rescinding my offers of membership in Maestro. I have not been feeling well of late and believe that I made an impulsive, misguided decision bringing you here."

I glanced at Bree, saw the sudden unease in her eyes, and understood. He had to have known we would never put Maestro's aims above all.

And now what choice did he have? They were going to kill us.

Malcomb went on, his lips tightening. "You should know that we had a vote, and by that vote, the three of you should die right now. But for the first time in a long time, I have overruled them. I wish you luck. If you make it out, you deserve to live."

The screen went dark. White closed the laptop, looking unhappy, and our guard from that morning and two other people we'd never seen before appeared in the hallway, carrying our winter clothing and boots.

"Get dressed," Bean said. "He's letting you go."

Surprised, I said, "Why?"

White said, "He wants to leave your fate to the elements."

They'd given me back the winter clothes I'd brought with me and the heavy boots and gloves Fagan had lent me, but not the snowmobile parka and bibs or the helmet and visor.

"Wait," I said. "He expects us to walk out of here. No sleds?"

"No sleds," Bean said.

"It's a death sentence."

"Depends on your will to survive, I suppose. Now get dressed before Katrina and I decide to overrule M's overruling and be done with you."

Bree and I took the clothing and started to put it on. Her Gore-Tex parka looked solid. So did her heavy wool pants. But I kept looking at her rubber boots and leather gloves, wondering how insulated they were and how they'd function outside.

I wondered the same thing when we'd finished dressing and gone into the hallway where Sampson was pulling on his black wool watch cap. He was wearing his parka, rubber boots, and gloves. But his jeans struck me as marginal.

They marched us into the elevator. White used the retinal scan.

Bean leaned in, punched a button without a number, and stepped back. The doors closed, and we took off so fast we were all a little shaken when we rose up out of the concrete floor of the old mining building.

It was midafternoon. Weak sunshine shone through the high windows.

The elevator opened. Cold, but not frigid, air belted us as we stepped out.

The elevator closed and sank out of sight. A recessed steel plate slid over the shaft.

"What are we—" Bree began.

Sampson cut her off in a harsh whisper. "Outside."

Bree nodded and looked around the interior as if searching for cameras as Sampson led us to the metal doors and pushed one open. When we stepped outside, the skies were turning leaden and threatening.

I figured the air temperatures were close to freezing, a big increase from the below-zero temperatures I'd experienced riding in with Fagan, and the top of the plateau had been scoured almost free of snow by the gales that had followed the storm.

"This helps," I said, pointing at the thin snow cover. I set off quickly toward the northeast corner of the plateau. "We need to move as fast as we can now without working up a sweat. We've probably got two and a half hours of light left."

"You know where you're going?" Sampson asked, hurrying after me, surprised.

"I think I know how to get back to two rifles I stashed —"

"You're going for rifles first?" Bree said, jogging up beside me.

"My pack's there too, with food, a tent, and survival and medical gear. But my gut says if it looks like we're going to be able to walk out of here, Malcomb will send his people to stop us. We need the guns."

"I agree," Sampson said. "I think this is all a game to him."

"Except we're the game," Bree said.

CHAPTER

78

THE DARK CLOUDS BEGAN to spit snow when we were less than a hundred yards from the old switchback mining road down the north side of the butte. Until that point, we'd been blessed to move quickly across the scoured plateau. We'd been checking our six constantly for pursuers but saw none.

The moment we started down the mining road, the snow deepened, blown in against the bank by the wind. Luckily, the temperatures must have been above freezing during much of the day, and some of the more recent snow must have been relatively wet because the drifted snow there was firm enough in places to hold Bree's weight.

But Sampson and I were postholing in knee-deep and sometimes thigh-deep snow. Every step became a big effort. We were both sweating by the time we reached the first switchback turn.

"We have to strip down," I said. "Carry our clothes until we need them."

"It's getting colder," Sampson said doubtfully.

"Weren't you the one who taught me the dangers of hypothermia?"

With a scowl, he took off his parka, bunched it, and put it under his arm like a football. Bree had her parka and hat off when we started again.

By the time we reached the second switchback, we'd lost almost an hour of daylight, and the snowfall had shifted from scattered and intermittent to steady, large, wet flakes.

"How far?" Bree asked.

"Two miles?" I said. "If we can reach the edge of this big meadow before dark, I should be able to spot the lone dead tree at the far north end. It towers above everything. The guns, the pack, and our ability to start a fire are at eleven o'clock from the base of that tree in a clearing beyond some Christmas trees."

Sampson asked, "What else is in that pack of yours?"

"I don't know exactly. It was Fagan's. She said it had all the survival essentials."

"Then let's get there ASAP," Bree said, starting to shiver.

John began to break trail to the bottom of the butte, where strangely the snow depth dropped again. It wasn't until we'd reached the flat that we realized it was because the trail had been packed down by sleds before the latest snowfall.

"I followed Bean in here on another trail from the north," I said. "It was packed down in a lot of places. If we can find it, we won't be wading around in unsettled snow."

"What about there?" Bree said, pointing across the small clearing to a definite break in the line of fir trees.

"We came in the dark, but that has to be it," I said, and I was starting toward that trail when something changed in the sound of the place.

If we had not had our heavy wool hats off, we might never have heard it. But what had been muted and muffled by the falling snow now sounded like a low whining buzz.

Bree peered in the sky and said, "Drone."

"Where?" Sampson asked.

"Up there somewhere," she said, pointing through the falling snow back up the side of the butte.

"I hear it there," I said, gesturing toward a gnarled tree near the first switchback.

We all saw it at the same time, appearing from behind that tree: a large black drone with wide stabilizing fins. It swept down the mining road toward the second switchback and the final drop to the clearing.

"He's tracking us. Get in the trees!" Sampson said and sprinted across the clearing with Bree and me right behind him.

We got into the shadows on that trail through the woods before the drone came to within forty yards of the trees and hovered there, so close we could see the camera shifting, looking for us. But for some reason, it did not come nearer.

I peered down the trail and saw how intertwined the branches were about ten feet up.

"The drone can't come any farther," I whispered. "It will crash in here."

The drone spun and gained elevation, and we lost sight of it.

"We've got to move," Sampson said. "They know this trail and where it comes out. If the drone doesn't have enough power to fly there and wait for us or if the snow picks up, Malcomb is going to send his snowmobiles after us."

In the distance, coming from back up on the plateau, we heard a low growling noise that expanded and got stronger with every second.

"He's already sent the snowmobiles after us!" Bree said. "Run!"

79

THE TREES OVERHEAD FORMED a thick canopy, and the trail had been fairly well used, so we were able to move fast and hard north, hearing the snowmobiles behind us whine and then stop below the rim of the butte.

"I bet they're bogged down in all that drifted snow," I said.

"This is our chance, then," Sampson said. He surged in front of me to break trail through the snow that had made it through the tree limbs overhead.

John was one of the strongest men I knew, and his long, powerful legs blew through the snow as if it weren't there. I stayed right in his tracks, both of us cutting the way forward for Bree, who was puffing along, holding her own.

"I run all the time," she said at one point, gasping. "Why can't I breathe?"

"High altitude." I grunted. "I feel like I'm going on half a lung myself."

"Or worse," Sampson said as the trees began to thin. The powder under our feet deepened, and the snow falling intensified. "Is that your big meadow up ahead, other side of that last stand of woods?"

"Has to be," I said, forgetting how tired I was and surging after John in the now knee-deep snow.

We'd made it to the south edge of that last stand of fir trees when we heard the snowmobiles rev up a solid mile or more behind us.

"How long is that meadow?" Bree asked as we moved fast into the shadows and the cover of the woods.

"Less than a mile," I said. "Do we stick to the edges or stay on the trail?"

"The trail," Sampson said. "We'll move faster."

We could see the long meadow and had almost broken free of the trees when my foot snagged on something buried in the snow. I felt something pop, and I fell hard.

"Alex!"

"My ankle!" I moaned, looked back, and saw my boot was caught in a loop of rusted cable sticking up out of the snow. "Where the hell did that come from?"

"Probably left over from the old mining days," John said, quickly pulling on the cable and loosening the loop enough to release my boot.

We could hear snowmobiles moving again. A lot of them. One sled sounded like it was already on the flat, less than a mile back.

"You two go get the guns," I said, wincing as Bree helped me to my feet. "I'll hide in the woods here."

"We'll never make it across that meadow," Bree said. "They'll shoot us down."

"She's right," Sampson said. "We don't have a choice now. This is the last cover. The last place we can ambush them."

"Ambush them?" I said. "With what?"

CHAPTER

80

FOUR MINUTES LATER I was hunched over in brush and snow on the east side of the north–south trail, not twenty yards from the edge of the meadow. Bree was on the other side of the track with a better view of it to the south, hidden so well I could not see her.

Sampson had told us his plan, helped us prepare, run out into the meadow fifty yards, then skirted back toward Bree. He was there somewhere. I'd heard him popping sticks and branches getting into position but could not see him.

We had roughly an hour of light left in the day when the first snowmobile came into the woods about one hundred and fifty yards from us. I shifted my feet, tried to see how much weight I could put on the right ankle.

It barked at me. It was swelling.

But I could brace against it without provoking shrieking,

nauseating pain, which told me I had not broken a bone. Probably strained some tendon or—

The snowfall picked up as the sled slipped toward us at twenty, then twenty-five miles an hour. I gripped my improvised weapon with my gloved hands, waited until I'd picked up movement, waited until I saw the rider stand up like a jockey in stirrups, look over the windshield to the meadow, spot John's tracks, and come faster.

"Now!" Bree shouted.

I yanked up hard on one end of the length of rusted mining cable that had almost broken my ankle. Bree yanked up hard on the other end.

The cable came free of the snow where John had buried it, got above the sled's skis, slapped off the fiberglass nose, skittered up the windshield, and caught the rider under the chin and across the throat.

His neck snapped.

He was flung off the sled.

His helmet flew through the air.

His snowmobile kept going down the trail and out into the meadow.

I lost sight of it because Sampson leaped from the brush, charged down the trail, and tore the machine pistol from the harness of the Maestro operator, then dragged his body by the harness into the brush.

"Same thing again if we can," Sampson called softly.

I could hear the next snowmobile entering the woods from the south. Bree and I whipped the cable up and down until it vanished beneath the snow on the trail and waited once more.

This time, however, the sled stopped just out of our sight, idling. Another snowmobile entered the woods, and another, and then four more by my count. They all stopped out of sight, idling as well.

Are they trying to contact the point man? Have to be. And they aren't getting a response.

Sampson seemed to have the same thought; he ran out of cover, retrieved the dead man's helmet, put it on, and returned to his hiding place.

Three or four minutes went by before engines revved. One snowmobile and then two turned around and headed away from us.

When they reached the south edge of the timber, they split. One went east. One went west.

John stepped out on the trail, still wearing the helmet, and pointed to it, indicating that he was hearing them. He made a looping gesture.

They were more than alert.

They were circling us.

CHAPTER

81

THE SLED CLOSEST TO us started forward at half the dead point man's pace.

The others prowled behind him.

The element of surprise was gone. They were expecting something.

Sampson gave it to them. As the first and second sleds came around the corner slowly, with their drivers resting their weapons over the tops of their windshields, he opened fire from the brush with short, controlled bursts from the machine pistol.

The windshield and helmet visor of the first rider spider-webbed and shattered. He fell off the back. His sled kept going and stopped between us, almost on the cable.

John swung on the second rider, shot. The rider fell. His sled kept going, crashed sideways, and blocked the trail.

Sampson charged forward once again, ripped another machine pistol and magazines off the harness of the nearest dead Maestro rider, and wrenched off his helmet and the helmet of the dead female behind him.

Beyond him, I could hear the other sleds idling, but I'd lost track of the two that were trying to circle us. John sprinted to us. He threw the machine pistol and one of the spare magazines to Bree and the helmets to both of us.

"Comms," he said. "We'll know what they're doing. You two take this sled. Turn off your microphones. Go to the cache. Get the other guns. I'm right behind you."

We could hear the snow machines outside the woods, the ones circling. They were almost to the north side of the last trees.

"We're not leaving you," I said.

"I'll cover you both, then take the sled that's out there in the meadow," Sampson insisted. He ran around us and forward to the last scattered trees.

Hobbling, I pulled on the helmet, turned off the mic, and straddled the machine. I heard Bean's voice immediately in the speakers:

"Almost around this damned piece of woods. Blown-down trees everywhere."

Helmet on, Bree sat with her back to mine to cover our six as Toomey answered on the helmet radio, "Same here. But we've got them now."

"The other guys are coming behind us, Alex!" Bree shouted and began shooting into the trees.

I twisted the throttle. Our sled lunged forward.

The Maestro drivers in the woods shot back at us.

We blew free of the timber, passing Sampson, speeding out into the meadow, then slowed hard because the other sled was sitting right there in the middle of the packed trail. John opened fire on the gunmen in the trees, covering us.

Over the helmet radio, I heard Malcomb say, "They are getting away, Bean!"

"No, they're not, M. Not today."

"Definitely not today," someone else said. "I see them right out in front of me."

That last transmission was from Toomey. As I drove off the trail into deeper powder snow to circle the stopped sled, I looked to my right and saw the janitor about two hundred yards away and coming at us.

"Got them too!" Bean said.

I looked left, and there was the former British SAS man, less than two hundred yards out and closing fast.

"Go, Alex!" Bree shouted.

I wrenched back on the throttle. The tracks spun.

But instead of hurling us back up onto the packed trail, the sled bogged down and slid sideways toward even deeper snow.

"Get off!" I shouted and felt her weight leave immediately.

The tracks spun but then gained purchase, and the sled jumped up onto the road; it almost went off the other side before I could stop it.

Malcomb said, "Kill them all, Bean. I'm tired of this."

"Straightaway, M."

Sampson opened fire from behind us, shooting into the trees, then out at Bean, then back at Toomey, both of whom were closing on us as Bree struggled to get up the bank.

Bean swerved off at John's cover fire. So did the janitor.

Bree finally got up onto the packed trail and shot at Bean from a hundred yards away. The former SAS operator ducked and stopped his machine behind some bushes.

Bree jumped on, yelled, "Wait, Alex, we've got to give John cover!"

I looked over my shoulder, saw Sampson running from the scattered trees toward the idling sled and us; he was no more than forty yards away.

Bree twisted and shot at Toomey, who was arcing his sled at us, just out of range.

"Go!" Sampson yelled when he was twenty yards from the other sled.

"Once more at Bean!" Bree said, twisting again to shoot at him.

But the Maestro operator had left his sled and moved to his right. He was on his knees when he pulled the trigger.

Sampson shuddered, spun ninety degrees, fell onto the side of the sled, and crumpled beside it in the snow twenty feet from us.

"Go!" John gasped into the mic, talking over the helmet radio. *"Go!"*

82

LEAVING MY BEST FRIEND who'd been hit hard like that went against every instinct I had. But Bree shouted, "The medical kit, Alex! It's his only chance!"

I twisted the throttle. We lurched forward, gained traction, and began to accelerate. Bree opened fire on Bean, forcing him to take cover once more.

I could not lower the visor because I could barely see through the cracks and bullet holes. I had to leave it pushed up while I got low behind the windshield.

We hit thirty miles an hour in seconds. I blinked back tears at the wind getting around the shield as Toomey's voice crackled on the radio: "Maintaining contact off their eastern flank, M."

I glanced right and saw the janitor there about one hundred

yards out, paralleling us in deeper snow, which forced him to keep both hands on his handlebars. Bree swung on him and fired a quick burst that slowed Toomey down again.

Malcomb said, "Bean? I'm having trouble with your camera. Update."

"I just put lead in Sampson, M. On my sled now, closing ground on their western flank. We've got—"

"Come back?"

"I just realized they took helmets off my men. I think they can hear what you're saying. Or Cross can."

For a moment, Malcomb said nothing.

"Is that true, Dr. Cross?"

He sounded amused. I don't know exactly why that made me want to attack him, throw him off balance, but it did.

"Dr. Cross? Can you hear me?"

I reached up, turned on the mic. "So loud and clear, I can hear the Sean Malcomb Wallace in your voice," I said.

For several moments as we sped toward that snag on the rise in the far trees, all I could hear over the radio was M's tortured breathing. I'd hit a nerve.

"I have told you—I am not my brother."

I purposely laughed and decided to bait him as we got within a quarter mile of the trees and the low ridge at the north end of the meadow.

"Whatever your supposed noble purpose or thinking, you are no different than Sean," I said. "How could you be different? You're twins. And I don't believe your story about your parents' murder. You were twins. I think you both went in naked through the basement window. You're deluding yourself, Malcomb. The two of you evil bastards were born of the same bad seed. Face it. You're as defective in mind as your evil—"

Malcomb thundered over the radio, cutting me off. "You want to see the Sean in me, do you? Fine. Bean? Toomey?"

"M?"

"Here, M."

"I don't care if the good Dr. Cross can hear us. Hunt them down, kill them, then take their bodies to the rookery below my big window. I want to see them fed to the ravens and the wolves."

CHAPTER

83

IT WAS GETTING LATE, less than forty minutes of light left by my estimate, when Bree and I closed on the far end of that long meadow
and the fir trees below that slight rise, the snag tree now silhouetted in the falling snow.

I kept taking glances at the sled's dark control panel, thinking
I was going to need headlights at some point, and touched something that lit the panel.

"Ah, there, see? You can't get out, Cross. You don't have
enough fuel."

"Tell it to the ravens and the wolves, Malcomb," I said, but I
glanced down again, saw the fuel gauge showed half full.

"Told you so."

I realized some kind of camera was mounted in my helmet
that allowed him to see what I was seeing. I also realized that we

did not want to go straight at the snag in the last hundred yards. If we did, we'd have to abandon the sled and wade uphill in deep snow, easy targets for Bean and the janitor. I tried to throw my left sleeve over the front of the helmet to somehow block the camera.

We almost flew off the trail before I grabbed the handle and kept us going uphill into the fir trees.

"Weren't you taught to keep both hands on the steering wheel, Dr. Cross?"

I ignored him. I could see the top of the rise in front of me. As we crested it, I saw the opening in the woods I was looking for, slammed the shattered helmet visor down, hit the brakes, and pulled in.

"That's not playing fair, Cross. I was enjoying the cinema verité quality of that footage."

I drove us forward into the old trail that cut across the ridge, figuring that Malcomb had given me leverage in a way. "I'll raise the visor if you up the stakes."

"I don't know how the stakes could be much higher for you."

"Your stakes," I said, stopping the snowmobile and silencing the engine. "You've got us. You know that's true. You can pour more men into the field. We'll never get to the trailhead. But just to make it interesting, to raise your stakes: What is your endgame in the killings of the potential Supreme Court nominees?"

Bree had jumped off the sled, had her helmet off, was listening for the sounds of our pursuers in the forest. Malcomb did not answer for several beats.

"It was never about the judges we killed. But I can tell you I fully expect the balance of power in the judiciary to change cataclysmically during the inauguration and afterward. Now raise the visor."

Bree waved, pointed at her ear. I took off my helmet, listened, heard multiple snowmobiles in the distance, but nothing close. Maybe Bean and Toomey had stopped and were listening for our position, or maybe they were waiting for reinforcements, or—

I heard the helmet crackle, held it so I could hear him.

"A deal is a deal even among fierce enemies," Malcomb said. "I raised the stakes, now you raise the visor. Show me what you are doing."

"You spoke in riddles, so no deal," I said, climbing off the sled, the pain in my ankle overwhelmed by the adrenaline still pumping through my system. I began to push my way through the brush toward the snag tree.

"Talk to me, Cross. I can hear you are in the woods, no longer on your sled. Are you thinking of your dear fallen friend, Sampson? He must be consuming your thoughts at this point. And what of the danger you've put your wife in?"

I said nothing, glanced over my shoulder, and saw Bree walking backward, covering the snowmobile and the trail beyond it.

"C'mon, Cross. I'm fascinated. Where do you think you're going? What do you think you'll find there in the middle of nowhere?"

We reached the snag. I faced north, found my eleven o'clock, and headed down through the thick Christmas trees there, snow falling from the limbs onto my bare head and making me shiver wildly. At last I reached the clearing I'd been looking for.

Bree had her helmet back on. She put her thumb up as she came out of the Christmas trees. I pointed east fifty yards to the edge of the woods where I'd stashed the two weapons and the pack and started that way in knee-deep snow.

The light had been different, almost gone, when I'd stashed the guns and gear what felt like a lifetime ago. And a good foot of snow had fallen since, much of it still clinging to the trees, which disoriented me as I got to within twenty yards of the woods. Snow coated nearly every fir, side to side and up and down, like some fairy-tale winter scene, cast in a pale blue light that made it all feel terribly sinister.

I struggled ahead and noticed a cluster of young trees with much of the snow gone from their lower limbs. I took a few steps toward them, puzzled; it looked like some kind of animal had plowed along the base of those trees and then gone back north to the edge of the woods.

Bree came close behind me, whispered, "What's going on?"

I turned off the mic.

"Don't know," I said. "Something or someone's been by the trees where I put the stuff."

"Bear?"

I hadn't thought of that. I picked up the helmet and walked to the tracks. The snow was deep. The walls of the tracks had caved in places. And fresh flakes were settling in the bottoms.

There was no doubt that those were human boot prints. But were these the exact trees where I'd left the guns and the pack? I went closer still, peered into the limbs, saw no guns or pack there.

"Is this the spot?" Bree said.

"I think so, but—"

I caught a flash of green through the lower limbs of the trees a split second before the helmet radio crackled again.

"Missing a few things, Dr. Cross?"

CHAPTER

84

I WANTED TO HURL the helmet when Malcomb chuckled.

"You didn't think I'd send a man to look where you said you left your weapons and pack?" he asked. "You didn't think the helmet you're wearing had an internal GPS beacon that has been telling me your exact location since you put it on? Too late, Dr. Cross. Too little imagination, Dr. Cross.

"And you, Chief Stone, throw down your weapon or die right now."

I dropped the helmet. Bree and I both spun around to find Lucas Bean and two other Maestro men in the clearing at our nine o'clock, forty yards away, guns aiming at us. Bean had lost his helmet but wore a radio headset over a black watch cap and was now stalking toward us in our own tracks.

Bree glanced at me. I nodded, and she tossed the machine pistol into a bank of snow; it vanished under the powder.

Bean and his operators converged on us fast, their weapons never leaving their shoulders, their attention never leaving us. Other snowmobiles were coming closer from the south.

"M says pick up the helmet, Dr. Cross," Bean said when he stopped about fifteen yards from us. "Pick it up and put it on."

I hesitated, then picked up the helmet and put it on.

"Better, Dr. Cross, but raise the visor now. And you as well, Sarah. I want to watch this grand finale from your perspective as well."

I raised the visor. The person behind Bean raised the visor, revealing the beautiful and steely features of Sarah, the former Mossad operator.

"What a remarkable alpine setting and stunning light in which to die. Don't you agree, Dr. Cross? Chief Stone?"

Before either of us could answer, Malcomb began to cough. It went on for almost ten seconds. He cleared his throat and cleared it again.

Bree turned on her mic, said, "How long do you have to live, Ryan?"

There was a pause. "A lot longer than you, Chief Stone."

I said, "You should know something before you kill us."

"What's that?"

"You screwed up. Or whoever you sent to search for my weapons did."

Malcomb chuckled. "Highly unlikely. Right, Bean?"

"Impossible," Bean said.

"Can I show you?" I said. "You'll see it in the camera if they'll let me turn."

Another hesitation. "Hands clasped behind you when you do, or Sarah will shoot you in the back. You have no pride, no sense of honor, do you, Sarah?"

"None," the woman said, staring at us with an expression that was colder than the swirling snow.

I put my hands behind my back, turned, took a step, and crouched, trying to aim the front of the helmet at the lower limbs of the tree. Nothing happened for five and then ten seconds.

"You're boring me, Dr. Cross. Bean, Sarah, when he stands up, kill them one by —"

The green light flashed in the low limbs.

"There," I said. "You could not have missed that."

I caught a strain in his voice when he replied, "What is it?"

"A Jiobit. Tells moms and dads where their kids are. Transmits a GPS signal to any satellite on earth."

"And yet I told you we jam all GPS frequencies in the area."

"Except for ten seconds every twelve hours when your generators are switching over."

There was an even longer pause before Malcomb laughed. "Touché, but ultimately, it's unlikely that the signal was broadcast and received during those ten-second gaps. Stand up, Dr. Cross. Turn and face the end of our story together."

I straightened slowly, turned, and stepped over to Bree. I held out my gloved hand and she took it.

"I love you," she said, looking terrified.

"I've always loved you," I said.

"Oh, please. Sarah? Bean? Finish them and then we'll go to extreme measures. And destroy that device. Sarah, you will shoot first."

"Extreme measures?" Sarah said.

Bean said, "That necessary, M?"

"You heard the man. A ten-second signal every twelve hours. We can't take the chance."

"Roger that," Bean said. He stepped toward us.

Sarah did the same.

Bean said, "For my mates you killed, Cross."

"And mine," Sarah said, shifting her aim to Bree and hurling me into a panic.

CHAPTER

85

TWO FLAT REPORTS. TWO flashes to our right.

The shots caught Sarah between the eyes, blew out the back of her head and helmet, and dropped the former Mossad operator in her tracks.

Bean spun with his rifle toward where the flashes had come from. I tackled Bree and we landed in a snowdrift.

I looked up just in time to see Bean open fire; his bullets whizzed and cracked past us and then the SAS man's body was riddled with a volley of return shots. He arched and crumpled into the snow amid the rising chaos.

Two of the four operators who'd come into the clearing to back up Bean and Sarah started firing. The other two spun around and made for the trees as Malcomb started yelling in the helmet radio: "Extreme measures, Maestro! Repeat, extreme measures in place!"

More shots erupted from our right. One of the gunmen dropped. His partner ran for the woods, bullets slashing the snow at his heels, then vanished.

It all went quiet except for the ringing in our ears.

"What the hell just happened, Alex?" Bree asked in a shaking voice.

I looked up and saw several silhouetted figures, all carrying weapons, slipping from the trees and moving toward us single file in the gloaming. Snowmobile engines fired up in the distance.

The first silhouette said, "Dr. Cross? Are you okay?"

My jaw dropped. "Officer Fagan?"

"And me, Alex," Ned Mahoney said, coming out from behind Fagan and turning on a headlamp. "And a lot of Mounties."

Third in line, a big guy with a Viking-like beard caked in ice and snow said, "Captain John Olson, RCMP. Hell of a spot you got yourself into."

I was so shocked by the sudden turn of events that for several moments, I didn't know what to say.

And then I did.

"Sampson was shot thirty minutes ago about a mile from here," I said. "We've got to get to him. Now."

CHAPTER

86

MINUTES LATER, BREE, MAHONEY, and I were up the ridge, moving as fast as we could by the light of the headlamp toward the sled we'd left near the dead snag. Olson, Fagan, and three other Mounties had gone for their snowmobiles.

"How bad is he hit?" Ned said, gasping in the thin air as he trudged through the snow.

"Bad," Bree said.

"There's an EMT with us. And we're supposed to get a break in this storm in the next hour or so. Maybe enough time to get a chopper in here."

"He's going to need it," I said, relieved to see the snowmobiles where we'd left them. "Follow us," I said. "We need to use Malcomb's helmets, so we won't hear your comms. Blink the headlights at us if you need us and we'll pull over."

"Better," Ned said, and handed Bree a two-way radio.

I pulled on the helmet in time to hear Malcomb say, "Cross has returned to his sled, Toomey. Go back to Sampson before returning to base."

"And do what? That sounded like a goddamn army up on that ridge."

"I don't care. Do what you always do, janitor. Clean things up."

"Not today," I said into the microphone. "We're coming for you, Toomey. Officer Fagan is not dead, and she and half the Canadian Mounted Police are coming for you."

That last part was not true. Olson had several other Mounties with him, but I still felt like we were taking the fight to Malcomb and Maestro. I turned off the ridge and gunned the throttle back down the wider route toward the meadow.

It was pitch-black dark by then, and the snowfall had lightened. I knew the headlights gave our positions away, but I kept mine on full power, slashing the night. I had no choice. The life of my oldest, dearest friend, my partner of countless years, was at stake.

To our left and back a good four hundred yards, Olson and his Mounties were entering the meadow. I felt a tugging at my heart as we neared the grove of scattered trees where we'd begun fighting back.

Suddenly, there was the sled. Suddenly, there was John in the snow on the ground behind it, waving at us weakly, pointing to our right, to the west.

I stopped.

He yelled, "Ambush!"

Bree and I dove off the snowmobile just as someone opened fire from the west. We tumbled off the bank of the packed trail, heard bullets smack the sled behind us.

We landed in deep, powdery snow below the grade of the trail, so it took a moment to get upright. Bree shouted into the hand-held radio for Captain Olson to stay back.

My helmet radio crackled with the first Maestro transmission in several minutes: "Got eleven guns on me, M. This might be too much to clean up alone."

"Cavalry's coming, Mr. Toomey. Everyone I can spare."

I turned off the microphone and said to Bree, "I'm going to John."

"I'll come with you."

A soft red light appeared ten feet away, and I started to swing my gun toward it but then saw it was Mahoney wearing a head-lamp. He tossed me a backpack.

"Blood-clotting agents and pain meds," he said. "How many bad guys out there?"

"Not sure. One that I know of," I said, shouldering the medical bag. "But reinforcements are coming from that mine. I'll need the radio, Bree."

CHAPTER

87

BREE LOBBED THE RADIO to Alex and watched him go, then turned her attention to Mahoney.

"Do you have a better idea how many are out there?" he asked.

Bree shook her head. "No, but their numbers are down. I know of ten dead, including members of Malcomb's inner circle."

Mahoney tried to relay that information to Olson's Mounties, who were halted to the north, headlights off. But all he got back was a sharp hiss.

"Jamming us," Bree said. "They can do it in a large radius around the mine."

Somewhere in the darkness, someone—Bree assumed it was the janitor—opened fire again with a short burst; it struck the side of the sled that was giving Sampson cover. Bree swung her attention south, panicking to think that he'd seen Alex trying to get to John.

"Got to give Alex some cover fire," Mahoney said.

"Agreed," Bree said. She started to climb the bank.

"Wait," he said. "Let's make this count. Here's what I want you to do."

Two minutes later, Bree was lying on her belly in the snow just below the edge of the packed trail and right behind their stalled snowmobile.

She eased up and over the lip, crawled to the sled's track system, and took off her helmet. She turned on the headlamp's red filter, put the lamp on the helmet, balanced the helmet on the barrel of her rifle, raised it until the headlamp barely cleared the sled's saddle, then pulled it down. After a thirty count, she did it again but this time she kept the helmet and red lamp there.

The janitor opened fire.

Slugs smacked the sled and sent the helmet flying; Mahoney started shooting from behind his sled, aiming at the muzzle flashes that had given away Toomey's position.

In the stillness that followed, even with the gunfire ringing in her ears, Bree heard the wailing and groaning of someone who'd just been shot.

CHAPTER

88

I WAS FIFTY YARDS to Bree's and Mahoney's south, and the jamming must have temporarily been cut because the janitor's anguish, every whimper and moan, was broadcast loud and clear over my helmet radio.

Over that, I heard Malcomb say, "Toomey?"

"Janitor's a goner, M. Sorry. Bug out. Bug out now."

The broadcast went to static as the jamming resumed. I got up over the lip of the packed road and scrambled to Sampson, who looked at me with glazed eyes. "What took you so long?"

"Another time," I said, switching my headlamp to full power. "Where's the hit?"

"Left side, low. Been pressing snow into it. Can't see what else is going on."

As I searched for the blood-clotting kit, Bree turned on her

340

headlamp and started toward us. Behind her, Mahoney waved his headlamp toward the north.

The headlights of the Mounties' snowmobiles came on and raced toward us.

"Here comes the real cavalry," I said. I pulled out the kit.

Bree and Mahoney reached us as I opened Sampson's parka and lifted his vest, sweaters, and blood-soaked long underwear. Bree and I shone our headlamps on John's abdomen and saw a bullet wound oozing blood. It wasn't gushing, but it smelled sour.

I reached around his back with the blood-clotting cloth, felt for the exit wound, and was surprised to find none. Then I felt a bump.

"You are one lucky son of a bitch," I said, bringing the clotting agent around and pressing it into the entry wound. "Bullet's still in you. I think it caught part of your small intestine, but there's no huge exit wound. You'll live."

"If we get him out of here fast enough," Mahoney said as the Mounties' sleds arrived, their headlights making the scene as bright as a baseball field under sodium lights.

The EMT rushed to John's side. I stood back to let her work on him. Officer Fagan and Captain Olson came over to us, their helmet visors pushed back.

Mahoney said, "We're going to have to send someone out of their jamming range to call for a chopper and reinforcements."

I said, "I heard over my radio that Malcomb was sending more men out here, but I'm questioning that now."

Olson said, "Why?"

Bree said, "We heard someone tell Malcomb to bug out."

"They're a long way from nowhere to be bugging out," Fagan said, smiling at me.

I smiled back at her. "I want to hear how you survived another time, Officer. Captain Olson, I think you should send men to cover the entrances to that mine."

"I don't know the entrances."

Bree described the old mining building with the steel sliding door and pneumatic elevator, and I told him about the switchback road on the other side of the butte that led down to the camouflaged retractable-door system. "I saw at least twenty snowmobiles in the bay there," I said. "And a big Sno-Cat, and a four-seater helicopter that's loaded up on a dolly. My bet is he's not sending in reinforcements. Malcomb and what's left of Maestro will try to run."

"And soon," Bree said.

CHAPTER
89

ONE OF OLSON'S MEN rode north to call in a medevac helicopter from Kimberley.

The EMT assured us that Sampson was stable for the moment and began to gather wood for a fire to warm him, so Bree and I agreed to lead Mahoney, Olson, Fagan, and the rest of the Mounties back up the butte so we could prevent anyone from leaving the mine.

"It's the entry on the far side that we've got to worry about," I said as we went to the sleds. "That's the escape valve."

Bree said, "Someone should still watch the mine building."

Fagan nodded. "When rats abandon a ship, they go out any hole they can find."

Captain Olson said, "We'll surround that big entrance and hold it until dawn. After that, I can fly in as many officers as we need."

We set off with Bree behind me on the sled. She was in constant communication with the Mounties as we found the trail that led through the thick woods that had foiled the tracking drone an hour before.

The snow stopped. The clouds broke. The moon shone down through a vent, again casting that strange blue color across the landscape glistening with fresh powder.

Since our descent on foot, at least seven sleds had come down the switchback trail, packing down the snow in the process.

There was one tricky spot where we had to negotiate what was left of the big drift on the upper switchback before we popped up on top near the northeast corner of the plateau.

Two inches of snow had fallen since we'd crossed the flat. We could clearly see the long, low line of the mining building five hundred yards away.

I stopped my sled, killed the engine, and pulled off my helmet; I wanted to speak directly to Olson. Bree and the Mountie captain and Officer Fagan did the same.

Gesturing at the mining building, I said, "Bree and Officer Fagan will stand watch there while I lead you to the road off the north side."

"How far is that?"

"Less than a mile?"

"A kilometer, then," Olson said.

One of the other officers flipped up his visor. "Captain, they stopped the jamming again," he said. "I can talk to Randolph. He's talking to Kimberley. There's been a definite break in the weather and the medevac chopper is lifting off as we speak."

I grinned and high-fived Bree just as we heard a low thumping noise followed by the roar of a heavy diesel engine.

"They're bugging out!" I jumped back on my sled, Bree right

behind me, and yanked on my helmet. I started the sled and was about to twist the throttle when the radio crackled.

"I hope you're out there listening to my voice, Dr. Cross. I wanted to say goodbye. I have evaded you once again. Maestro's mission goes on."

I triggered my mic. "Malcomb, I—"

The helmet radio went to hissing again.

In that weird blue light thrown by the moon, we saw the silhouette of Malcomb's helicopter rise over the far end of the butte, no running lights, and arc out of sight. Two seconds later, the snow-covered ground beneath our sleds and then the sleds themselves began to tremble.

Over the sound of our engines came a rumbling.

"Earthquake?" Bree yelled.

Before I could reply, the rumble became a full-throated roar.

From five hundred yards away, through the busted-out windows high on the side of the old mining building, we saw a flash of brilliant gold and red light; the flames gathered and blew the entire structure to smithereens.

The energy of the blast smashed into us.

Then a second explosion erupted out of the southwest flank of the butte, out of that huge door—a massive fountain of flame and red-hot debris gathered force, arched, and bent upward, lashing at the winter night like some dragon's last, furious, blast-furnace breath.

CHAPTER

90

Washington, DC
Inauguration Day

CLUTCHING CUPS OF HOT coffee, Bree, Mahoney, and I hurried into a large briefing room adjacent to the FBI director's suite of offices and stood at the back.

It was four o'clock in the morning, but despite the early hour, the scene was intense. You could feel energy pulsing off every top law enforcement official involved in security for the swearing in of Susan "Sue" Winter as president of the United States.

U.S. Secret Service special agent in charge Alan Wilson was responsible for the overall detail and he spent the first fifteen minutes reviewing the sequence of the day's heavily scripted events and describing a few last-minute assignment changes. He stood aside when acting FBI director Marcia Hamilton entered the room, looking very put together and all business.

"Thank you, everyone, for all your efforts so far," Hamilton said. "Let's take this day home flawlessly, show the world how the greatest democracy on earth changes hands peacefully, just like the old days."

A murmur of approval swept around the table.

The acting director went on. "I want to brief you on a credible threat I learned of only four hours ago."

Every commander at the table straightened.

The acting director nodded, then introduced the three of us and asked Mahoney to bring them up to speed.

More than two and a half days had passed since we'd watched Ryan Malcomb's wilderness redoubt go up in flames. John Sampson was airlifted to a hospital; Bree and I arrived there two hours later, and after a doctor splinted my ankle, we spent the night and the next day answering questions from a team of RCMP investigators.

We'd been allowed to leave Canada after the U.S. attorney general intervened, and we'd briefed Hamilton on the situation as we flew east. She had asked us to come straight to the meeting when we landed.

Mahoney condensed our history with Maestro, M, and Ryan Malcomb into a ten-minute briefing that included the murders of the potential U.S. Supreme Court nominees, their links to the informal nominating committee, the words of the assassin caught on tape, and our capture and escape from the vigilante group and its leader.

"Where is Malcomb now?" Wilson, the Secret Service commander, asked.

"In the wind with whoever was with him when he escaped," Mahoney said. "He's the target of a massive manhunt in British Columbia and Alberta."

Bree said, "Malcomb's helicopter was found abandoned one hundred and fifty miles from the mine, and he hasn't been seen or heard from since. Nor have any of his other operators, some of whom escaped by Sno-Cat."

Director Hamilton said, "We're putting Malcomb and his associates at the top of our most-wanted lists effective immediately. Post-inauguration, his capture and the destruction of his vigilante network will be one of our top priorities. But not today, correct, Mahoney?"

"Well, again, we believe that the best thing that can happen today is the seizure and immediate shutdown of Paladin, Malcomb's data-mining company," Mahoney said. "If he has remote access to his supercomputers and real-time NSA data, he might already know everything about the inauguration plans, including security details."

The Secret Service commander shook his head. "But if you shut down Paladin, we won't have access to the data that we need in real time."

Hamilton nodded. "I'm ahead of you, Mr. Wilson. After Winter is sworn in, she will be taken to a room in the Capitol, where she will sign a series of national security documents. Among them will be executive orders for the federal seizure of Paladin and the installation of a digital protection system that will keep everyone except U.S. law enforcement out of Paladin."

Wilson said, "But that doesn't help us before she's sworn in."

"No," Hamilton allowed. "We're roughly seven hours from that."

Chief Barry Thomas with the U.S. Capitol Police said, "But you don't think Malcomb will try to come here himself, do you?"

"No," I said, speaking for the first time. "But we believe that if he has the opportunity and capability, he will go on offense."

Wilson said, "Define *offense*. Assassination?"

"I have no details, but that's in the realm of possibility," I said, and held up my hands at a few grumblings around the table. "Hear me out. During our escape, I asked Malcomb what his endgame was with the murders of the potential Supreme Court nominees.

"He said, and I quote, 'It was never about the judges we killed. But I can tell you I fully expect the balance of power in the judiciary to change cataclysmically during the inauguration and afterward.'"

CHAPTER

91

U.S. SECRET SERVICE SPECIAL agent in charge Wilson sat forward, studying me.

"He definitely said 'balance of power in the judiciary'?"

"One hundred percent," I said.

"Nothing about the executive branch?"

"Not specifically."

Chief Thomas said, "Nothing about an assassination attempt?"

"Nothing directly," I admitted. "But given the nature of my question to Malcomb and given his tacit admission that he'd ordered the killings of potential Supreme Court nominees, an assassination plot has to be considered likely."

Chief Thomas said, "But the assassination of whom, exactly?"

Bree said, "It could be anyone in power in the federal judiciary system, from the incoming attorney general to, frankly, the acting director of the FBI. But it makes sense for the target to be a U.S. Supreme Court justice."

"Or two, or more, from a cataclysmic perspective," I said.

"Two or more?" said Diana Zhang, marshal of the U.S. Supreme Court. She wore combat fatigues and, judging from her expression, believed her worst nightmare had come true.

Nodding soberly, I said, "One successful assassination attempt would upset the balance on the court. But two? It would radically change the court for decades."

Bree said, "And remember that Malcomb has already, in effect, culled the pool of potential nominees so the ones who remain are to his liking. This is very real."

"What do you mean, to his liking?" Zhang said.

I said, "I've been thinking about what M told me, that it had never been about the judges they'd killed, and I believe that he meant that the goal wasn't to murder those judges but to move the ones who remained to the top of the list."

Director Hamilton said, "You think the possible nominees are compromised?"

"From my perspective, I think everyone left on that list should be looked at very closely."

Wilson, the Secret Service agent, held up his hand. "I agree, Dr. Cross. This is all a very real threat. But I cannot let that interfere with my job to protect the inauguration."

"Exactly," the acting FBI director said. "Which is why the Bureau is going to work closely with Marshal Zhang and give her whatever manpower she deems necessary to protect the justices starting ASAP. Does that work, Marshal?"

Zhang, who was in charge of all security at the court,

including the protection of the nine justices, nodded. "It works. And I'd like to point out that two of the justices have been sick, though they are both determined to be at the inauguration."

"You'll provide us with all routes of travel, companions, and the names of the officers on their regular security detail?"

"I'll make that happen right now, Director," Zhang promised.

Hamilton gave her a half smile. "I'm not director yet, Marshal. But thank you. And Mr. Reilly? CIA? We're hoping you can be of help."

Timothy Reilly, a whippet-thin operations chief for the Central Intelligence Agency, sat forward and said, "Unless I have to break laws."

"Not today. We're looking for information on a former Russian national."

I said, "We knew her as Katrina White. Malcomb said she was once a GRU Sparrow."

Reilly lost color. "You think there's a Sparrow involved? Here in DC?"

Mahoney said, "She'd be a likely candidate. We believe she was the shooter of the potential court nominees."

Bree said, "No, we *know* that she was. Malcomb said as much. And we believe Katrina White was not with the other Maestro operators hunting us as we escaped."

Reilly nodded, said, "I'll start searching names and aliases straightaway. But if we do have records on her at Langley, especially biometrics, I'd have to seriously wonder how she'd get into the U.S. without triggering alarms. I mean, we share that information with immigration, border patrol, FBI, and NSA. She should have been picked up trying to come in."

CHAPTER

92

DIRECTOR HAMILTON TOLD REILLY to notify her immediately if anything on Katrina White came up in the CIA files, then asked Ned, Bree, and me to come to her office; Marshal Zhang would follow ten minutes later.

It was 4:55 a.m. when Hamilton closed the door behind her. Her assistant offered us more coffee, which we all accepted gratefully.

"I know I said some pretty nice things about you last night on the flight, but I wanted to commend you all in person again. I will be briefing the president-elect at five and I'll be happy to tell her of the destruction of that fortress and your rescue."

Mahoney said, "Why do I feel like there's a *but* coming?"

Hamilton sobered. "Because there is, Ned. Even with what you have done, I don't know if it's enough to make Winter change my status from acting director to director."

Bree shook her head. "What would be enough?"

I said, "You want us to catch this Sparrow if she's here. Make her the face of the end of Maestro's reign of terror, then lean on her until she gives us Malcomb. Then arrest him too and bring M to justice at last."

The acting director smiled. "Yes, Dr. Cross, I think that would do it nicely. And if you're successful, I haven't thought it all through yet, but I'm considering a special team that would work the Bureau's most pressing and sensitive cases with you three and your Detective Sampson as the core group."

Mahoney gave her an awkward smile. "A discussion for another time."

Hamilton grew serious. "Of course. How can I be of help? What am I missing?"

Ned said, "There should be a team of Boston agents on standby near Paladin's headquarters, ready to seize it immediately when the president signs the order."

"Done."

I said, "You should have Keith Karl Rawlins from cybercrimes at the Quantico lab up there with them. He'll be your best bet at getting control of their supercomputers."

"We'll make it happen," Hamilton said, and looked toward her assistant; he pulled out his cell phone.

There was a knock at the door and Diana Zhang entered, looking harried.

"I've had the security package delivered to each of you, including timetables and location changes for all nine justices during the course of the day," the high court's marshal began. "I've also noted the locations where the justices will transfer vehicles and travel in threes to the Capitol with their spouses following."

That had all of our interest. "Why threes?" Mahoney asked.

"Capitol Hill police asked us to limit the number of vehicles because of the crush to get all dignitaries through the garages and up to the western front of the building. Only the president and the president-elect and their entourages will enter above-ground on the east side."

Zhang called up a map and showed us where the Supreme Court justices lived and the routes they would take to the three rendezvous points outside DC, where they would transfer to armored limousines. She proposed a doubling of the detail assigned to each of the limos, and Director Hamilton readily agreed, giving her one of the Bureau's top counterterrorism teams already on standby for the inauguration.

"Thank you," Zhang said. "Anything more I can do?"

Mahoney said, "Patch us into your comms? We'll be working different angles, but I think we all want to be in close touch."

The marshal agreed, took down our cell phone numbers, and promised to get us the court police frequencies ASAP. Hamilton asked us for an update on the hour and then excused herself to prepare to brief the president-elect.

After she left, Bree said, "I know Zhang has to consider the safety of all nine justices, but we need to narrow our focus. That's how Malcomb thinks. He's a data sifter, a narrower."

I nodded. "He'll target for maximum impact."

CHAPTER

93

THE NIGHT BEFORE THE inauguration, using the alias Katherine Blanco, Katrina White sailed through the U.S. Global Entry preclearance site for U.S. Customs. She left Vancouver on an Air Canada red-eye flight and landed at JFK International at ten minutes past five in the morning.

White had flown business class and slept a solid five hours, more than enough to prepare her to face the day ahead. She was first out of the plane and walked briskly, tugging a roller bag and wearing chic après-ski clothes that fit her cover as a bond trader returning from a four-day trip to Whistler.

She was now a brunette, not a blonde. And contact lenses had turned her eyes from a piercing blue to a soft brown.

As the Sparrow walked through the long halls, she got out a

burner phone and sent a text to a memorized number: Your work at Vancouver was flawless.

She slowed to let a few other passengers pass by. The phone buzzed: I promised you were invisible.

White smiled and picked up her pace.

I don't care how good his brother was with the algorithms, Malcomb's more than a genius, White thought as she smiled and walked up to a U.S. Customs agent. He checked her U.S. passport and took her slip.

When he has his hands on the keyboard, when he's surfing the flow, going anywhere he wants online, he's like a god, all-knowing, able to work miracles—like stopping certain information from emerging from law enforcement and intelligence databases.

That thought gave the Sparrow utter confidence. She went outside and hailed a cab to take her to Penn Station. When she was in the taxi, the burner phone rang.

"Smooth as I promised?" Malcomb asked in a hoarse voice.

"Like I wasn't there," White said.

"Good. Above all, patience today. You have all the time in the world."

"I know. How are you feeling?"

"Glad I have my own doctors." He went into a coughing jag as her cab reached the train station. She paid in cash and entered the soaring reception area, barely noticing the stunning architecture of the Moynihan Train Hall. On the phone, his coughing subsided.

"M?" she said.

"Be careful now," he said, gasping. "And do you remember what we talked about?"

"Low-hanging fruit," the Sparrow said.

"That's right," Malcomb said, sounding relieved. "No need for heroics."

"We'll speak later."

After a pause, he said, "Yes, we will."

White hung up, went to an Amtrak ticket booth. The clerk inside looked like he hadn't seen the sun in years. "Where to?"

"Baltimore," White said.

CHAPTER

94

BREE, MAHONEY, AND I were still debating the likeliest targets twenty minutes before U.S. Supreme Court chief justice Winston Hale was set to be picked up by his normal security detail at his house in Falls Church, Virginia.

The team would take Hale to the White House, where he would join the sitting president and president-elect for coffee. Afterward, he would head to the Capitol for a larger reception and the swearing-in ceremony.

There was no question in our minds that the death of a chief justice would have a cataclysmic effect on the judiciary and would give the new president tremendous leverage and political power on day one of her administration. Because of that, Mahoney and Marshal Zhang had moved in an FBI counterterrorism squad to back up the detail assigned to the chief justice.

They had also beefed up security around the homes of seven other justices and at George Washington University Hospital, where Justice Mayweather was recovering from cancer surgery.

We listened to the radio chatter as the pieces of the security apparatus slid into position. We studied the various pinch points on the travel routes the other justices were set to take on their way to Capitol Hill, especially the locations where they were to transfer vehicles: two at a park in Alexandria, two at a park in McLean, and three in a school parking lot in Chevy Chase.

FBI agents were already in those spots and setting up surveillance and perimeters. A similar group would back up the detail protecting Justice Mayweather, who would travel in a private ambulance from the hospital to Capitol Hill at the last moment and return to the hospital following the formal ceremony.

Bree threw up her hands. "I don't know what else we can do."

"Maybe we shouldn't be thinking about specific locations," I said. "Maybe we should be thinking about specific targets. I mean, who would he most want to kill?"

Mahoney said, "The justices likely to oppose his way of thinking?"

"I think they'd all oppose his way of thinking," I said. "Especially Keller and Damaris."

"Chan too," Bree said.

"But remember what Malcomb said—it's not about the judges they kill."

"It's who they put in the dead judges' place," Mahoney said. "I get it. But that doesn't change the fact that we want zero justices dying today."

Bree said, "Exactly. And Chan and Damaris both change vehicles in McLean."

Mahoney got on his radio, called the leader of the FBI team

moving into position around the state park there. "Stay sharp. This could be focused on Chan and Damaris."

"Roger that, SAC," the team leader came back. "We have a small army surrounding this place at the moment, working dogs, heat-sensing devices. You'd have to be Houdini to get in here without us knowing."

In the minutes that followed, Chief Justice Hale was picked up at his home without incident and driven into Washington with armored black SUVs front, back, and sides. He arrived at the White House at seven thirty a.m. as the other justices were being picked up.

Justice Margaret Blevins was first, driving with her escort from Potomac to Chevy Chase. Several days before, while we were being held by Maestro, Blevins had fainted in her office. She had been taken to the hospital but released not long after, and doctors attributed the episode to low glucose levels. The justice had even been well enough to go for a run earlier that morning.

By eight fifteen, seven justices had been successfully transferred to their various vehicles. Forty-five minutes later, the last of those vehicles entered the garage off Independence Avenue, and eight justices were inside the Capitol Building.

At five minutes to nine, a motorcade bearing the old and new administrations left the White House and headed to Capitol Hill. Fifteen minutes later, an FBI agent called over the secure radio we were monitoring: "Justice Mayweather is en route. Looking strong for a guy who just lost part of his liver."

Bree's brow furrowed.

"What?" I asked.

"Private ambulance. Looks to me like a pretty easy target for a Sparrow."

CHAPTER

95

KATRINA WHITE WALKED WEST on Constitution Avenue as brazenly as she'd walked through DC's Union Station, as brazenly as she'd gone to a security locker and retrieved a runner's pack with an empty water bottle and drinking hose, knowing that the security cameras there and indeed all around Capitol Hill would pick up her image again and again.

But they would never match her up biometrically.

Not a chance. Ryan Malcomb is a god at these kinds of things.

The Sparrow had changed clothes in the bathroom at the Baltimore train station. She'd left her ski togs in a wastebasket and now wore gray wool pants, sturdy insulated shoes, a pink turtleneck, a single strand of pearls, an off-white cashmere vest, a puffy blue parka, a darker blue neck gaiter, and an insulated blue ball cap with earflaps. She'd also bought a lapel button celebrating the inauguration of Sue Winter and one of the small American flags being waved by nearly everyone crowding the sidewalks and crosswalks of the broad avenue that led from Capitol Hill to the Vietnam and Lincoln Memorials.

A few blocks behind her, along Pennsylvania Avenue, a crowd roared. It was nine fifteen. The presidential motorcade must be approaching.

White did not care. She kept walking away from Capitol Hill, against the flow of pedestrian traffic and away from the heart of the inauguration activities.

Once she crossed Twelfth Street, the crowds began to thin. Independence Avenue was virtually empty except for police cars parked sideways, their lights flashing.

The Sparrow could barely hear the U.S. Marine Corps band playing over speakers when she neared Fourteenth Street and the Washington Monument. Her attention jumped to the intermittent wailing of an approaching ambulance's siren.

White stopped by a small knot of tourists staring up at the monument and watched several black Chevy Suburbans with tinted windows lead a private ambulance through the various police blockades, heading toward Capitol Hill.

The Sparrow checked her watch. Half past nine now.

She got out the burn phone again and texted: Half past nine on the dot!

There was a pause, and then: We aim to please.

She smiled, texted, And I will be pleased to aim.

Several moments passed before a reply came: Patience, my little Sparrow. Patience above all.

CHAPTER

96

THE INAUGURATION WENT OFF without a hitch, and at eleven a.m., the nation had a new leader.

Despite my exhaustion, despite my anxiety over Ryan Malcomb wanting to cause cataclysmic damage to the judiciary, and despite the general divisiveness everywhere in the country, I found myself pretty damn proud of America and caught up in President Winter's vision of a nation that "rewarded aspirational adults while addressing first and foremost the pressing educational and health needs of our youngest citizens, our children."

After Winter described how an administration focused on bettering the lives of kids would dramatically benefit the country in fifteen years, Bree said, "She makes a lot of sense."

"She does," I said, yawning. "Makes me want to go home and see our own kids."

Mahoney said, "Stay with me until we get the justices moved again. Mayweather's ambulance is about to pull out." He called up a feed from an FBI drone hovering over the Constitution Avenue exit of the Capitol's underground garage complex. His cell phone rang.

"Mahoney," he said and listened, then put it on speaker. "I have Dr. Cross and Chief Stone here as well, Mr. Reilly."

"Call me Tim," he said. "And I ran our databases on Katrina White and the GRU's Sparrow program and got zilch. I'm sorry. Anything else I can try?"

"Nothing I can think of offhand," I said. "But thank you."

"I'm right here if you need me, though I may take a nap in the next hour."

"We're running on fumes here too," Mahoney said, and hung up.

We turned our attention back to the screen and the drone feed, which showed Justice Mayweather's ambulance exiting the garage and heading out on Constitution Avenue. We listened to the radio traffic from the security detail and from the presidential motorcade making its way down Pennsylvania Avenue.

Twice, the ambulance slowed—at police barricades at Twelfth and Fourteenth Streets—and I thought the opportunity was there for an attack. But it never materialized.

By then it was pushing noon and we'd been up for an ungodly number of hours with only catnaps and high-voltage coffee to keep us going. "We're heading home for some much-needed sleep," I told Ned. "We'll check in when we wake up."

Mahoney nodded and yawned. "I'll bunk here after I contact Rebecca and see how Sampson's doing this morning. I'll text you."

John was recovering from abdominal surgery in Kimberley. Rebecca Cantrell and Willow had flown up to be with him.

Bree and I gathered our things, opened the Lyft app, stared in disbelief at the outrageous surge pricing, then booked the ride. We just didn't care.

A half hour later, we arrived home to find our house empty. Nana Mama had gone out to lunch with one of her friends. Ali was at a friend's house. Jannie was at Howard.

We both took showers and fell into bed. I closed my eyes and started to drift off.

Bree muttered, "Maybe Malcomb or the Sparrow got spooked by the Canadians getting so close to grabbing them and decided not to follow through on the threat."

"Somehow I just don't see that happening," I murmured back, and I fell away into darkness before she could reply.

CHAPTER

97

I AWOKE SLOWLY, GROGGILY, to the muffled sounds of Nana Mama downstairs in the kitchen. I looked at the clock; it was 5:20 p.m.

Groaning, I closed my eyes, wanting to fall back into deep sleep. Instead, I drifted into that buzzing state between fully awake and fully asleep when your subconscious often bubbles up some insight or angle on whatever is simmering deep in your brain.

Images floated behind my closed eyelids: Katrina White, dressed in running wear, killing Judge Franklin and her driver. Killing Judge Pak and Professor Carver and not seeming to care much about the cameras.

The subconscious insight bubbled up then, and I snapped awake. I glanced at Bree, was happy to see her sound asleep, got slowly out of bed, and took my cell phone into the bathroom.

I found the contact and called. The phone rang three times before someone picked up.

"I don't know why I'm answering you, Cross," said Keith Karl Rawlins, the smartest guy I knew when it came to computers.

"You're mad at me?"

"Well, a little anger, a little love."

"Why the anger?"

"You didn't warn me that Director Hamilton was going to have agents pound on my door at five in the morning and deliver me to a Boston suburb."

"I apologize. But what about the love?"

Rawlins lowered his voice and said in a conspiratorial tone, "This place? Paladin? It's extraordinary what they can do. When I'm at the keyboard, it's like I'm driving a Ferrari."

"Have you put fences around the Ferrari like Hamilton asked?"

"It's proving more challenging than I expected. I could just pull the plug on the place, but there are so many federal agencies that have data flowing through here on a constant real-time basis that I'd shut half the government down in the process."

"Okay, so here's why I called. I want to know, given that mega-data flow through Malcomb's computers, could he somehow erase someone? Digitally, I mean."

After a long pause, Rawlins said, "Interesting. I don't think he could erase them from every data bank in the world, but…it's likely that some kind of filter in the Paladin algorithms could exclude certain data from search results."

"Data like biometrics?"

"Maybe."

"While you're up there working, could you look for a filter like that? It would be specific, for a woman named Katrina White. A Russian national. A GRU Sparrow."

"An actual Sparrow?" Rawlins said. "That is interesting. I'll see what I can find."

I hung up and took a shower; Bree came in while I was finishing.

"Good sleep?" I said, shutting the water off. I grabbed a towel.

"Zombie sleep," she said. "I'm hoping a shower will help."

"It will." I saw two texts from Mahoney. The first said Sampson was weak but showing no signs of infection. The second said Ned was back overseeing the protection of the six justices who were attending the seven presidential balls around the city that were about to kick off.

I texted him that we were up and on standby if he needed us. I dressed and went downstairs as Bree was getting out of the shower.

CHAPTER

98

NANA MAMA WAS BROWNING chicken at the stove and Ali was on his iPad when I walked in.

"Dad!" Ali cried and rushed to hug me. "You made it!"

"By the skin of my whatever," I said, laughing and hugging him back. "Thanks for telling Ned that Willow's Jiobit had gone off."

"But why only for a few seconds every twelve hours?"

My grandmother put a lid on the skillet and came toward me. I said, "I'll explain that later. Right now, Nana Mama needs some love."

"I do," she said and slipped into my arms. "When we heard you'd all gone missing in the Arctic, I thought I'd never see you again."

"It wasn't the Arctic," Ali said.

"It was close," I said. "Coldest I've ever been, anyway. Way below zero."

She shivered, then pulled back and looked up at me. "No frostbite?"

"Miraculously, no."

Ali said, "The news reports out of Canada said there was a Mountie with you who crashed a snowmobile into a canyon and survived."

I nodded. "That's true. Officer Fagan went off the edge and fell thirty feet, but she got free of the sled, and she and the machine landed in ten feet of snow on a ledge. We both had serious survival gear in the snowmobiles. She got to her sled, put up the double-wall tent, and stayed in it through the worst of the storms."

Bree walked in, a towel around her hair. "I still don't know how she survived and how she charged her satellite phone with the emergency solar panel even though the sun was hardly ever out."

"She got just enough juice to send an emergency text giving her coordinates."

"And John?" my grandmother asked. "Have you talked to him?"

"Thanks for reminding me," I said. I called Rebecca Cantrell, who answered on the second ring.

"Alex!" she said in the most excited tone I'd ever heard from her. "We were just talking about the Cross family! Let me put the phone on speaker so John and Willow can hear."

"I'll do the same," I said. "Bree, Ali, and Nana are here too."

"John?" my grandmother said. "How are you?"

In a raspy whisper, Sampson said, "Sore, strong as a kitten, and never happier, Nana Mama."

Before any of us could respond, Willow giggled and said, "Daddy and Rebecca are going to get married!"

We all started cheering and clapping. Bree said, "When did he ask?"

"I asked," Rebecca said. "Just a few minutes ago. Willow said I should, so I did!"

"And I said yes!" Sampson laughed a little, then groaned.

Rebecca said, "It hurts when he laughs. Can we call you back? The doctor's here."

"You call when you're up to it, and congratulations again!" I said.

When I hung up, we were all grinning like fools.

Bree said, "I needed that. A little pure joy for once, you know?"

I hugged her and said, "I do know."

Jannie came by for dinner a few minutes later. We called Damon and talked with him before Nana Mama served chicken marengo, which tasted even better than the last time she'd made it.

After dinner, we watched some of the coverage of the presidential balls, and Ali made us check out a Korean reality-television show that put the hundred strongest people in that country through a winner-take-all series of tough physical challenges. It wasn't my grandmother's cup of tea. She went to bed shortly after it started.

Bree fell asleep on my shoulder before the end of the first challenge: who could hold on the longest to a bar suspended above deep water. I made it long enough to say good night to Ali but nodded off during the late news.

CHAPTER

99

MY CELL PHONE WOKE us both from deep sleep. I looked around, confused, then grabbed the phone off the table, thinking it would be Mahoney.

It was Rawlins.

"I found a batch of exclusionary filters here in the Paladin algorithms," he said.

"I'm putting you on speaker. Bree's here. She knows I asked about them. Do any belong to Katrina White?"

"As a matter of fact, yes."

We bumped fists.

Bree said, "What would happen if you removed the filter?"

"I already did, and she popped up," Rawlins said and laughed. "A real GRU Sparrow. Disappeared in Istanbul four years ago."

I said, "Do you have biometrics on her?"

"There's not a lot of pictures of her coming up so far, but I think there's enough if I put together a composite."

I asked him if he could access the biometric immigration data from all the people who had entered the United States from Canada in the past forty-eight hours.

"Does a bear crap in Yellowstone?" Rawlins said. "Gimme a second here…and cross-reference…and search. And son of a bitch, there she is."

"What?" Bree cried. "How is that possible that fast?"

The computer expert said, "Total number of people crossing from Canada into the States in the past forty-eight hours is one hundred forty-seven thousand, six hundred and fifty. Not that many to look at when you've got an AI sifter with the power of Paladin's."

I said, "We get you love their system, KK. Where and when did she come in?"

"JFK." Rawlins sniffed, sounding mildly irritated. "Air Canada overnight from Vancouver. She entered on a U.S. passport under the name Katherine Blanco."

I looked at my watch. It was thirty minutes past midnight.

"Can you run a universal search with her biometrics? I mean, all the data that passed through Paladin in the past forty-eight hours?"

"I can try. I'll get back to you," he said, and hung up.

"You need to tell Ned," Bree said.

I called. He answered in a moan. "I'm just getting into bed, Alex. The night went smooth. Not a single problem."

"Until now," I said. "There's been a breach in our national security courtesy of Ryan Malcomb. His Sparrow is here."

CHAPTER

100

AFTER SPENDING THE AFTERNOON and evening in a luxury room at the Hay-Adams, Katrina White changed into green hospital scrubs, a black zip-collar, a long-sleeved top, the blue puffy jacket, and a knit cap embroidered with the emblem of the University of Texas Longhorns.

At 3:50 a.m., she walked toward the main entrance to the university's medical center near the Foggy Bottom neighborhood in the District of Columbia. White carried the gray pack she'd retrieved at Union Station.

She had the burn phone in the pack along with her cover passport, other supporting cover documents, and what looked for all intents and purposes like a fancy portable boom box, complete with an antenna of braided flexible wire that she'd fed through an insulated sleeve meant to keep a hydration line from freezing.

What looked like a small black microphone was screwed into the end of the braided wire and clipped to the right side of the pack's shoulder harness.

At the bottom of the stairs to the front entrance to the hospital, the Sparrow slowed for several beats, searching in her pockets for an employee badge on a lanyard, courtesy of Maestro. When she found it, she hung the badge around her neck, put on a surgical mask, and went inside.

Acting glad for the sudden warmth, she was aware of the cameras in the high corners of the lobby but did not pay them much attention. She pulled back her hood, crossed to the scanner, and slid the badge through, confident that the guard on duty would see her come up as Cynthia Del Torre, a traveling nurse from Dallas recently hired to work on the oncology ward.

"You're a little early," the woman said.

"First day on the job," White said to the guard and hurried off to the elevators, thinking that it really was amazing what M could do when he had access to a computer system, even one with as many security bells and HIPAA whistles as GW's.

The burner phone in her pack rang twice but stopped before she got in the elevator. As the car rose, she looked at the camera in the upper right corner, tugged her mask down below her lips, and smiled, knowing no one would notice, not really.

After all, she was invisible.

CHAPTER

101

MY CELL PHONE STARTED vibrating at 3:45 a.m.

Feeling punchy at all the interrupted sleep, I looked at the phone, saw it was Rawlins. I did not want to wake Bree, so I slid out of bed, hurried to the bathroom, shut the door, and answered.

"I said the Paladin systems were like driving a Ferrari, but I was wrong," Rawlins said. "They're more like driving a rocket ship."

"Okay?" I said and yawned.

"You sound bored."

"I haven't really slept in days, Keith. What have you got?"

"Everything," he said. "Get your laptop, call Mahoney, and get into the secure chat room I'm about to send you the info for."

"Bree want to hear this?"

"Everyone does."

Ten minutes later, Bree and I were grumpy but dressed and downstairs in the kitchen with both of our laptops open and drinking coffee. Ned's face appeared in the secure meeting room Rawlins had arranged for.

"This better be good," Ned said and suppressed a yawn.

The cybercrimes expert's face appeared; he looked perturbed. "I heard that, and it is good, Mr. Mahoney. Very good. I'll share my screen now."

Our laptops' screens switched to a series of feeds showing Katrina White at JFK, New York's Penn Station, Baltimore's central train station, and then DC's Union Station, where she retrieved a small gray knapsack and left with it and a roller bag.

Mahoney said, "It's like she knows the cameras are there and doesn't care."

Rawlins said, "Because she thinks the filter's still in place."

Bree said, "Where did she go after Union Station?"

More images of the Sparrow appeared. He said, "She crosses Pennsylvania Avenue, walks down Constitution all the way to the Vietnam Memorial around noon, and I lose her in the crowd. But not to worry, I've got new filters scanning all active security cameras in a forty-mile radius."

I was kind of shocked. "You can do that?"

Rawlins said, "Malcomb's machines and software can, and... hey, now, we just had a partial hit on your Sparrow."

Mahoney said, "What does that mean?"

"She was wearing a surgical mask, but the AI thinks it's a better than fifty-fifty chance she's...nope, a hundred percent now."

The screen jumped, showed White in an elevator in hospital

scrubs. She pulled down a surgical mask and looked right at the camera with a smile.

"Where the hell is that?" Ned demanded.

Rawlins said, "GW Hospital. She just got off on the oncology floor."

"Oncology!" I said. "She's going for Justice Mayweather!"

CHAPTER

102

IN THE WAITING AREA of the oncology ward, Katrina White took off her parka and hat and opened the pack. She turned on the boom box, got out a stethoscope, closed the pack, and put it back on.

White reached into the pocket of her scrubs, found two chunks of malleable silicon, and mashed them into her ears. Next, she released the little microphone-like device from the clip on the harness. It dangled from the insulated hydration sleeve as she pushed her way through double doors and walked confidently down the hall.

The Sparrow was immediately aware of a smell she knew intimately, the odor that people give off when they're at the end of their lives, dying after a long illness or facing whatever weapon White had decided to use that day.

Sourness, she thought as she saw the two Supreme Court Police

THE HOUSE OF CROSS

officers sitting outside the hospital room where Justice Mayweather lay recovering from the rigors of the inauguration and
his latest surgery.

*It's always that sour smell. I think it has to be some primitive physiolog-
ical response, the body trying one last time not to be eaten by the wolves of
time and chance.*

Then, as she'd been trained to do, White made her mind go
blank so she could fully mirror her situation and surroundings.
She walked past the nurses' station and saw an aide in her periph-
eral vision, her back turned.

One of the police officers sitting outside Justice Mayweather's
room looked up at her approach. The Sparrow smiled, adjusted
her stethoscope a little as a distraction as her other hand found
the little microphone device and her thumb settled over a button
on it.

"I'm Cynthia, his new nurse," she whispered in a genial,
slightly conspiratorial tone. "I promise I won't disturb him unless
it's absolutely necessary."

She had the attention of both guards as she closed to within
ten feet. Both their phones began to ring. They reached for their
phones as she smiled her way to six feet and mashed the button
with her thumb.

The little device bucked in her hand. The sound of the super-
focused sonic wave bringing its invisible violence came through
the silicon earplugs as a low soft thud, like distant thunder heard
through a closed window.

But the effect on the man and woman guarding the Supreme
Court justice was instant. When the energy wave hit them, their
heads jerked back as if they'd been coldcocked by a prizefighter
and they slid back in their chairs, their cell phones falling to the
floor, their brain waves scrambled into unconsciousness.

The Sparrow checked her six: nothing. She pushed her way into Justice Mayweather's room and in the glow of the monitor lights, she saw not a giant of the legal system but an old, withered rooster of a man at the end of his time on earth.

She could smell the sourness in the air. She aimed the microphone at Mayweather from the foot of his bed and mashed her thumb down a second time.

At near point-blank range, the vibration hit Justice Mayweather like a sledgehammer, and the monitors all around him went dark.

Strangely, no alarm sounded. As she left the room and strode past the still unconscious guards toward the nurses' station, White decided that the pulse had to have completely fried the electronics that surrounded the justice.

Oddly, the guards' phones were ringing again. The nurse at the station came into the hall, blocking her way to the elevators.

"You're early," the nurse said.

White held her belly as if fighting a stomach cramp and hurried around the woman. "I am. But right now, I am in desperate need of a bathroom. I'll be right back. I just checked on Mayweather and he's sleeping soundly. So are his guards."

The Sparrow went through the double doors, snatched up the parka, took the stairs to the lobby, and went to the first exit she saw. Halfway out the door, she heard a code blue called.

White put her hood up and hurried away, telling herself she'd change in an alley and then figure out the best way to reach her final target.

She was three blocks away from the medical center when the burn phone began to ring. She ducked into dark woods at the edge of Rock Creek Park and answered with the words "It's done."

She heard Malcomb exhale with relief. "Good. Because they

found the filters that made you invisible. They can see you. End your mission now."

"No," the Sparrow said without hesitation. "I don't care if they can see me. I'm going to finish what we set out to do. For you, M, and for Maestro. And no matter what happens afterward, we will have changed the world for the better."

Sirens began to wail in the distance. For several moments, all she heard over the phone was Malcomb's rattling breaths. "M?"

"It worked, the new device?"

"It's far superior to the one we bought in Havana and used on Blevins. Well worth the money you spent."

There was another long silence, and M started to cough and hack. When the coughing subsided, White said, "You're sick again."

"It's nothing. Are you sure you want to go on?"

"Yes."

"You need to know, then," Malcomb said with sudden, surprising emotion, "that you were special to me, to our cause, Katrina."

"Ryan Malcomb getting sobby," she said. "You're either drinking scotch for the first time in a long time or you are sick. I will call you when it's done."

The Sparrow hung up, divorcing herself from the genuine affection she had for the mastermind behind Maestro and focusing on actions to be taken, just as she'd been taught as a young recruit in the Russian GRU. She needed to get far away from the sirens approaching the hospital and figure out a way north before dawn.

103

BREE AND I ARRIVED at GW Hospital within seconds of Mahoney. We all ran up the stairs to the main entrance as Ned told us he'd spent the drive over trying unsuccessfully to reach the Supreme Court Police officers guarding Justice Mayweather, then calling for a dragnet to be set up in a six-block radius around the hospital with the image of Katrina White in the elevator going out to all patrol cars.

Sirens were wailing toward us when we entered the lobby and presented our credentials to the security guard. It was two minutes past four.

"Did you see her?" Mahoney asked.

The guard nodded. "Just checked in. New nurse. From Dallas."

"Shut every entrance to the medical center," Mahoney said. "Chain them closed if you have to."

That rattled the guard. "I don't have that authority."

"I do," Mahoney said. "What room is Justice Mayweather in?"

She lost color. "Four-oh-two. But they just called a code blue on four-oh-two."

We took the elevator to the justice's floor and found a chaotic scene with multiple nurses and doctors and techs running between two adjoining rooms. Ned, who always had a cool head under fire, managed to stay out of their way while learning that the power had gone out in Mayweather's room before he was discovered without a heartbeat.

Dr. Beatrice Foley, the head of the code team, came out to tell us they'd been unable to resuscitate the Supreme Court justice but were still working on the police officers who'd been guarding Mayweather.

Foley said, "Both officers are alive and conscious but exhibiting symptoms of severe concussion—slurred speech, headache, confusion—as well as abnormal heart rhythms. It's not clear what caused it."

"Your best guess?" Bree asked.

Her eyebrows went up. "I served in Iraq. It's like they were hit by the shock wave of an IED but avoided the shrapnel. We're going to sedate and intubate them until we can determine the full extent of their injuries."

"We need two minutes with the one who's most with it," Mahoney said. "And all footage from security cameras on this hall."

"Can't help you with the footage, Mr. Mahoney," the doctor said. "But I'll give you two minutes with Officer Kenerson."

A nurse named Elena Walters came up to us. "I saw who did this."

Bree looked at me and Mahoney. "I'll talk to her."

Ned and I followed Dr. Foley into the room next to the late Supreme Court justice's.

A doctor was sedating Officer Denton Hodgson. A nurse was taking the vitals of Officer Natasha Kenerson, whose eyes were closed.

"Natasha?" Dr. Foley said.

Officer Kenerson, a brunette in her thirties, groaned softly as her eyelids fluttered open. She looked at Foley, Mahoney, and me.

Mahoney identified himself and said, "Did you see who did this to you?"

Kenerson swallowed. "Nurse. Some hose thing. She…fired it?"

"This it?" Mahoney said, showing her the picture of White in the elevator wearing a knapsack with an insulated hose clipped to one side.

Kenerson nodded. "Hose."

I said, "There has to be something on the other end of that hose that created whatever hit them."

The officer did not respond, closed her eyes.

"I have to intubate her now," Foley said, and we left the room.

CHAPTER

104

BREE SAW US AND waved us over to the nurses' station where Elena Walters had pulled up footage of the hall from less than fifteen minutes before.

"It's her," Bree said. "She comes from the waiting room, and you get a better look at her face. But this is what you want to see."

Walters hit Play. Katrina White, knapsack on, back to the camera, walked to Officers Kenerson and Hodgson, leaned toward them, then reached out, extending the hose from the pack. The camera shook, then steadied; the two guards slumped in their chairs and the Sparrow went into Justice Mayweather's room.

The hospital room went totally dark a moment later. The Sparrow left the room, mask still on, walking back toward the nurses' station, the hose and the strange little device at the end of it dangling from the pack harness. She swung around Nurse Walters and headed toward the waiting room and the elevators.

Then the security guard from the front desk came up to us with an iPad and showed us a video of White leaving the hospital and heading west on foot at almost the same time we'd arrived, which put her a good twenty minutes ahead of us.

Mahoney got a call, listened, then said, "Form a second perimeter at fifteen blocks and again at eighteen blocks, including the bridges out of the District. If she's on foot, she's probably still carrying the knapsack. If she's in a vehicle, it's probably with her. Consider whatever the hell is in it to be lethal. I repeat, lethal. But I want her captured, not killed. Do you understand me? Captured." He hung up and looked at us. "Now we have to get lucky and spot her before she gets away."

I said, "Unless she's not looking to get away."

"How's that?" Mahoney said.

"I'm trying to think like M. As long as she's at large, you have to figure he'll want to keep her going. How was it he put it back in the mine, Bree?"

"Maximum impact," Bree said, nodding.

"So, you think she has another target?" Ned said.

"That's my bet," I said.

"Mine too," Bree said. "It's like you said, Alex, one opening on the court gives Winter power but two openings allows her to change the course of history."

Mahoney checked his watch. "Twenty-three past four now, and—"

"Mr. Mahoney?"

Dr. Foley had come up behind us.

"I'm sorry to interrupt," she said. "But there is something about the symptoms the officers exhibited. It makes me think of

388

Havana syndrome—you know, where all our diplomats there got sick all of a sudden? Dizzy. Slurred speech and blurred vision. Nausea. Fainting spells. And that reminded me I recently saw a patient exhibiting very similar symptoms. I hadn't put it all together before."

I said, "Who was the patient?"

She looked anxious and upset. "Justice Blevins. I was the first doctor to see her after she collapsed in her office."

CHAPTER

105

MARGARET BLEVINS WOKE UP to her husband's raspy snoring at ten minutes to five; she reached over and turned off the alarm on her cell phone before it could sound. She didn't want to wake Phillip, who had stayed late at one of the inauguration balls and, judging by his snoring, had drunk a little too much wine.

Well, Blevins thought as she went to her walk-in closet, closed the door, and began to put on her running clothes. *He rarely drinks, doesn't fool around, and he is the best of men. Let him snore to his heart's content.*

Besides, beyond a little muscle stiffness from yesterday's run, she felt better than she had in weeks, certainly since before Christmas.

The Supreme Court justice put on her sports bra and paused, looking at the shorts she usually wore in the basement gym and at the cold-weather leggings she wore to run outside. Usually, she alternated weight days and running days to give her security detail a break every other day, and she'd run yesterday, so she wasn't planning on running today.

But the morning before had been so spectacular, clear and cold, and there'd been something about the dawn and the brilliance of the winter sun in the woods and the frosted birch trees near the end of her usual loop. The justice had carried that sense of wonder into the day, watching as the new president took the oath of office, forty feet from history.

The memory made Blevins's skin tingle and she shivered as she found herself wanting to regain that sense of wonder. Besides, until yesterday morning she'd been cooped up in the hospital and at home.

It would do her good to get more fresh air, and her doctor had told her it was important to be outside early in the day, no sunglasses, especially in winter to help keep her vitamin D levels up. And there really was no need to call and wait for someone from her security team to join her. That could take forty minutes. Maybe more.

The justice was soon downstairs, dressed for the chill weather. She wore her winter trail runners, a Christmas gift from Phillip, with tiny sharp studs in the soles that prevented her from slipping. She fitted her AirPods into her ears and linked them to her phone. Blevins put on music by a woman named Deva Premal that she always found calming, stuck her phone in the pocket of her reflective vest, and pulled on a wool cap, a headlamp, and thin wool gloves.

She checked her watch. Ten past five.

The house phone began to ring, which was odd. No one used it anymore.

The justice went out the door thinking that if she timed her run right, she'd be entering that beautiful birch grove at dawn.

106

"DAMN IT!" MAHONEY CURSED and pounded on the dash. "No one's picking up!"

"We're almost there," I said. I was driving Mahoney's vehicle while he tried to raise anyone at the Blevins household in northwest Potomac.

"What about her security detail?" Bree asked from the back seat.

"They're on their way. They weren't supposed to come on until six because of all the parties last night and because Blevins was set to work out in her basement gym," Mahoney said, the tension rising in his voice. "I'm calling in locals until we get there."

"We'll be there before them," I said, speeding up as we passed the Falls Road Golf Course heading north.

"I'm calling anyway," Mahoney said, punching 911 into his cell.

THE HOUSE OF CROSS

I turned left onto Glen Road as he explained the threat to a Montgomery County dispatcher. She promised to send multiple sheriff's patrol cars to seal off the area around Blevins's house as we took a right onto Gregerscroft Road, an upscale suburban street just east of Wayside Elementary School.

The justice lived at the end of a cul-de-sac abutting Watts Branch Park in a large Colonial home shielded from the road by a hedge and big pines. I pulled into their long drive.

Mahoney ran to the front door and began pounding on it and ringing the doorbell. Lights began to go on upstairs and we could hear voices.

A minute later, as sirens were approaching, a bleary-eyed Phillip Blevins answered the door in a maroon Georgetown hoodie and matching pants. His teenage children were in their pajamas on the staircase behind him.

"What is this?"

"FBI, Mr. Blevins," Mahoney said, breathless. "We believe your wife is in danger."

The justice's husband's demeanor changed in an instant. "What danger? From whom?"

I said, "From the same woman who killed three potential Supreme Court nominees."

"And Justice Mayweather just an hour ago," Bree said. "Is your wife here?"

"Mayweather?" he said, panic in his voice now. "I think Maggie's in the basement working out."

"No, Dad," one of his teenage daughters said from the stairs behind him. "I heard her go out."

Her brother said, "She must have broken the rules again and gone out for a run."

I said, "In the dark like this?"

Blevins's other daughter said, "She wears a headlamp and runs the same route all the time."

Her brother said, "Through the park and the woods, mostly, so no one sees her."

"Show us the route," Mahoney said to their father as Montgomery County patrol cars started up the drive, sirens wailing, lights flashing. "Now!"

107

KATRINA WHITE AVOIDED LAW enforcement efforts to hem her in near the medical center by going through the woods, crossing Rock Creek Parkway, and calling an Uber to pick her up near Rose Park in Georgetown. The driver, a woman, took her up Wisconsin Avenue and dropped her at an all-night Whole Foods Market off Fortieth Street before the second and third series of checkpoints were erected in the city.

The Sparrow had walked out of the Whole Foods and immediately hailed a second Uber. It brought her out the River Road to Potomac and then northwest to a memorized address off the heavily wooded Lloyd Road.

She had the driver, a male, drop her at the mailbox. She waited for him to leave, then started up the darkened driveway, thinking how a routine was a weakness to be exploited. At least it was in her profession. Routine allowed a predator to learn the patterns of its prey and wait in ambush if it knew just the right spot.

White knew just the right spot. She'd known it for well over eight weeks, almost as long as she and other Maestro operatives had been studying U.S. Supreme Court justice Margaret Blevins's day-to-day habits.

The justice, they'd discovered, wasn't exactly an athlete, but she worked out on a daily basis, often with a three-and-a-half-mile run through her neighborhood and the surrounding area. She ran three or four days a week, rain or shine, cold or hot, darkness or daylight.

With or without a member of her security detail, Blevins always turned off St. James Road, ran northwest on Betteker Lane to a trailhead beyond Bevern Lane, then went down into the matrix of pathways that crisscrossed Watts Branch Park.

The creek that bisected the park and separated Lloyd Road from Gregerscroft Road was shallow enough to wade through in most places. But the paths Blevins liked to run all converged on the footbridge not far from the cul-de-sac where the justice lived. A thicket of dense fir trees grew on the near side of the bridge. But she loved the birches that grew on the far side near the bench where she often stretched before continuing the rest of the way home.

The Sparrow heard sirens begin to wail in the distance.

The Sparrow stayed well outside the yard of the house on Lloyd Road, paused, and dropped into the west side of Watts Branch Park. She studied the sky, which was turning a pale gray as the stars began to fade.

Dawn was coming. And the sirens were getting closer.

White pulled up a GPS app on the burner phone to take her to the path and the bridge. She plunged into the woods and headed downhill at a gentle slant. At the bottom, she quickly found the trail, turned on her flashlight app, and began to run.

When the Sparrow was almost to the footbridge, she stopped and listened, hearing the creek and little else save the sirens, which were whooping in the near distance toward Blevins's house.

They're coming for her, White thought, moving out of the pines and seeing the birches near the creek just ahead of her in the growing light. *But I'm here first. If she went out for her run this morning, I'm here first.*

With those positive thoughts coursing through her head, the Sparrow slipped in among four bushy hemlock trees on the creek bank by the footbridge. They were no more than six feet tall and the only conifers growing there.

Amid the hemlocks, there was a low spot that she'd hid in when she used the first sonic weapon M had bought in Havana, the one she'd trained on Blevins several times in the prior weeks as the justice crossed the bridge on her run.

But the sonic device in her pack now was different, far more powerful. It would do much more than make her sick. And if that didn't work, she had a gun she'd stashed in that low spot in the hemlocks a month before.

The sirens died as White dug up the pistol from under the ground, removed it from its plastic case, and set it aside. Then she shrugged off the knapsack and turned on the device.

Malcomb had paid a fortune to one of her old corrupt bosses at the GRU for this weapon, the latest tool Mother Russia was developing to neutralize enemies of the state in public settings.

Feeling the hum of the device booting up, the Sparrow heard a squirrel chatter at the dawn and the faint sound of a distant car passing.

Then she heard the definite clicking of something metal against rocks and then footfalls amid the clicking. She peered through the hemlocks toward her back trail and the noise and saw the headlamp bobbing and coming closer.

White lifted the triggering device and aimed it toward the bridge, roughly twelve feet away, close enough to hit Justice Blevins hard, killing her outright or stunning her so badly the Sparrow could easily move in and follow up. She lowered it again and waited.

The clicking was louder, and the headlamp was closer, no more than fifty yards back, where the trail to the bridge left the pines. Suddenly the headlamp went off, but she could see the outline of her prey still running, still coming right at the footbridge.

The Sparrow took her attention off Blevins, raised the trigger again, aimed it at the west side of the little bridge. She quickly glanced to her right, saw the justice coming around the close bend in the trail.

Her thumb found the button.

CHAPTER

108

BREE WAS LESS THAN two hundred yards from Alex and Mahoney when she spotted Justice Blevins's headlamp coming through the woods. At the same time, she spotted a gray smudge she thought could be a person crouched amid hemlock trees on the opposite creek bank.

She slipped down the bank into the running water, ignoring the wet and the cold, using the sounds of the creek to mask her movement, closing the gap in the low light, wanting to be sure she wasn't seeing things.

Then she saw the headlamp go off and the form on the far bank shift as Justice Blevins came closer to a footbridge that spanned the creek. At ten yards away, Bree brought up her pistol, popped up, aimed it over the bank at the figure in the hemlocks, and shouted, "Put the weapon down, Katrina! Down!"

What happened next unfolded in a matter of seconds.

Justice Blevins heard the shout, startled, and skidded to a stop on the path, blocked from White's view by the hemlock trees but mere feet from her waiting assassin. The Sparrow shifted toward her target.

"I'll put one through the back of your head, Katrina!" Bree shouted. "It's over!"

Alex and Mahoney came charging onto the scene, drawn by the shouting.

"FBI!" Ned yelled. "Justice Blevins, stay where you are!"

"Drop the weapon!" Bree shouted again.

"Drop it!" Alex said, coming near the bridge and aiming at Malcomb's assassin from another angle. "We don't want to kill you, Katrina!"

White hesitated and then did something none of them had expected.

The Sparrow put the triggering device in her mouth, raised her hands, turned to face them, and bit down.

CHAPTER

109

THREE WEEKS LATER, ON Valentine's Day, I got out of my car and started toward the house with a dozen red roses for Bree and a dozen yellow roses for Nana Mama.

The uproar over the killing of Justice Mayweather, the shock at the attempt on Justice Blevins's life, and the greater story of Maestro continued.

Paladin had been seized and nationalized by the new administration. The intellectual property, the algorithms, and the supercomputers would be shared by the NSA, FBI, CIA, and other U.S. law enforcement agencies. Every employee of the company was being investigated, as was Theresa May Alcott, who'd been thrown off the judicial nominating committee by an enraged President Susan Winter.

Congress was set to hold hearings on Malcomb, Paladin,

Maestro, and the plot to shift the balance of power inside the highest court in the land. And the media was speculating wildly over who Winter would nominate to take the late Justice Mayweather's seat.

At the same time, secretly and with great intensity, according to Ned Mahoney, FBI and Pentagon scientists and engineers were studying the device that had killed Mayweather, concussed the justice's guards, and liquefied the brain of Katrina White.

Despite all the scrutiny and media attention, despite a global manhunt, and despite his own computers and algorithms being used against him, Ryan Malcomb had not been found.

As I climbed up our front steps with the roses, I heard playing inside. I could hear people chattering with excitement as I crossed the porch. It was a Saturday, late afternoon, and we'd decided Valentine's Day was the perfect occasion to have a proper engagement party for Rebecca Cantrell and John Sampson, who'd been home from British Columbia for two weeks.

Bree had organized the whole celebration, from the caterer to the DJ to the bartender. All I had to do was show up and show love to all the important people in my life.

What could be better? I asked myself as I set Bree's roses on the porch swing and reached for the front doorknob.

My cell phone buzzed with a text and then began to ring. I didn't recognize the number, checked the text.

Answer, Cross.—M

I answered and said, "Give yourself up. We're coming for you, Malcomb."

He said, his voice hoarse, weak, "You'll never find me."

"We will if it takes a lifetime."

Malcomb began to laugh, which turned into racking coughs.

"That's the rub, Cross. I'm dying. Days to live now, my doctors tell me."

"You're lying."

"Not this time. I'm over. Maestro's over. Enough, Cross. Enough. You win. Go to your party and enjoy yourself and forgive me and forget about me."

The call ended.

I stood there for a long moment looking at my phone until I heard my family and friends explode with laughter. I opened the door, picked up the flowers, and went inside to them, knowing that even if Maestro was over and even if Ryan Malcomb was terminally ill, he would never be forgotten or forgiven.

Not a chance.

CHAPTER

110

INSIDE, I LEFT MALCOMB behind, embraced Bree and Nana Mama, and greeted all the family and friends who'd gathered to celebrate the engagement of John Sampson and Rebecca Cantrell.

I gave each of them a hug and offered my formal congratulations.

Rebecca said, "Thank you, Alex. You've made me feel like I'm part of a big, loving family."

"You don't know how good that makes me feel," I said.

"I don't have to give a speech, do I?" Sampson said.

"You can bet Nana Mama's expecting one."

"You should say something, John," Rebecca said.

"Here," I said, taking an envelope out of my pocket. "I found this in your pack in Idaho. I haven't opened it."

Sampson grinned and snatched it from my hands. "That'll do."

A few minutes later, we all picked up drinks and toasted the couple: "To John and Rebecca!"

"And me!" Willow said, holding both their hands.

"Of course and you," Rebecca said.

"Speech, John Sampson," Nana Mama yelled.

"No way out of it," he said, holding the envelope. "I guess this says it all."

He tore it open, took out a piece of paper, and cleared his throat.

"'Dear Rebecca,'" he read. "'I'm on a plane with Bree, who informs me that I have to be more romantic if I'm to keep our relationship alive for the long haul. So here's my first attempt. When I met you, within a day I was thinking that you are one of the smartest, strongest, and most beautiful women I'd ever met.'"

A soft "Ahhh" rippled through the room. Rebecca put one hand on Willow's shoulder and the other on her own heart.

John cleared his throat again. "'Then I learned you were a widow, and I felt you understood loss. Within a week of knowing you, I felt for the first time since Billie's passing that I really wanted to live again. I knew I was in love with you inside a month, which was not in my plans. Not at all.

"'But you have a way of taking over someone's heart without even trying, Rebecca Cantrell, and I guess—no, I know—it's time you were in my plans for good. No matter what happens in this investigation I intend to come home and ask you to marry me and take my heart forever.

"'Love, John.'"

There were actual tears rolling down Sampson's cheeks when Rebecca jumped into his arms, and they kissed, and we all cheered for the new life they'd both been given.

ABOUT THE AUTHOR

James Patterson is the most popular storyteller of our time. He is the creator of unforgettable characters and series, including Alex Cross, the Women's Murder Club, Jane Smith, and Maximum Ride, and of breathtaking true stories about the Kennedys, John Lennon, and Tiger Woods, as well as our military heroes, police officers, and ER nurses. Patterson has coauthored #1 bestselling novels with Bill Clinton and Dolly Parton, and collaborated most recently with Michael Crichton on the blockbuster *Eruption*. He has told the story of his own life in *James Patterson by James Patterson* and received an Edgar Award, ten Emmy Awards, the Literarian Award from the National Book Foundation, and the National Humanities Medal.

Season 1 premieres November 2024
on Prime Video

For a complete list of books by

JAMES PATTERSON

VISIT
JamesPatterson.com

 Follow James Patterson on Facebook
@JamesPatterson

 Follow James Patterson on X
𝕏 **@JP_Books**

 Follow James Patterson on Instagram
@jamespattersonbooks